# N E W
## WORLDS

# The Coming
# of the Queen

An Erimem novel by
Iain McLaughlin & Claire Bartlett

Published by
Big Finish Productions Ltd
POBox 1127
Maidenhead SL6 3LN

www.bigfinish.com

Range Editor: Ian Farrington
Managing Editor: Jason Haigh-Ellery

ISBN 1-84435-156-4

Cover art and design by Stuart Manning 2005

First published September 2005

The Coming of the Queen © Iain McLaughlin & Claire Bartlett

With thanks to
Xanna Eve Chown, Gary Russell and Steve Tribe

The moral rights of the authors have been asserted.

Printed and bound in Great Britain by Biddles Ltd
www.biddles.co.uk

# Prologue

*Today*

arra Wilton wiped the sweat from her face and pulled her hat down so that the brim shaded her eyes from the sun's oppressive glare. The handkerchief she had used to mop herself was now coated with an unpleasant mixture of sweat and sand. Par for the course with Egypt, she thought.

Still two years shy of thirty, Carra was the youngest professor of Egyptology in England. She also had a reputation as one of the toughest, a reputation she had earned and embellished in equal measure. She was of average height but that was the only average thing about her. A bright mane of long red hair was currently trying to free itself from under the comfortable straw hat – a man's straw hat – that was jammed onto her head and intelligent green eyes surveyed every action taking place on her dig. Her full lips pursed unhappily as she saw the dig foreman approaching her yet again. She rearranged her worn old denim shirt so that her chest was less obvious and cursed both nature for endowing her so heavily and the foreman for not even having the decency to make a pretence of not staring at her cleavage. On the last day of the dig, she had vowed to make him squirm. She would look down at her bosom and say, 'Talk to the man. Go on. He's been talking to you since the dig started and you haven't said a word back. Come on, say something.' She'd say it in front of the entire crew, and on the last day, she knew the crew would have their families present for the celebration her university planned. That would show the sleazy beggar.

1

The foreman duly arrived, accompanied by two of his lackeys.

Carra pushed her favourite shades over her eyes. 'No,' she said before he could speak.

'What?' the foreman said, flustered.

Carra strode off for the dig's main excavation and the foreman had to run to catch up. 'Whatever it is,' she called over her shoulder. 'The answer is no. No to longer lunch breaks, no to extra money and especially no to your brother-in-law getting his job back.'

'No, no, you do not understand,' the foreman jabbered, grabbing Carra's arm. She shook herself free.

'What is it then?'

The foreman was almost hopping from foot to foot with excitement.

'Spit it out,' Carra demanded. 'I don't have all day.' And then she realised that it could only be one thing. 'You've found something?' The foreman nodded breathlessly. 'Well, why didn't you say so?' Carra demanded and then she turned and ran to the main excavation, shouldering past the student who had got one word into his question. She leaped into the pit and slid down the steep slope, not bothering with the wooden ladder and ignoring the stabbing pain from the loose stones tearing at her legs through her canvas trousers. Her feet hit solid rock at the base of the slope and she bumped to a halt, the jolt dislodging her hat and setting her wild red hair free. Maura, her Irish student, the best in her class, was crouched over a broad indentation cut into the face of the rock formation. From a distance it looked like the product of natural erosion but as Carra moved closer she could see that the cut was precise and the indentation was regular. And carved onto the face she could see hieroglyphs.

Maura turned to her. 'You were right,' she squeaked excitedly. 'You said there was an uncovered tomb here.'

'Let me see.' Carra had been through enough disappointments to know better than to claim this was the unopened tomb she had been tracking for nearly eight years, but as she inspected the hieroglyphs and traced the line of the doorway – the indentation could be nothing else – it was clear that this was indeed a tomb and one that had never been opened. As she trowelled sand away from the bottom of the pit to unearth more of the doorway, it was obvious that the door was intact. 'Sand must have covered the doorway not long after the tomb was sealed,' she thought aloud. 'Given the position of the tomb, a good wind from the west would blow sand and dust along the valley piling everything up here.' She looked upwards at the sandy outcropping of rocks overhead. 'And anything that fell from up there would have finished the job. The tomb might have been hidden within days.' She held a hand out impatiently to Maura. 'Brush,' she demanded. Using Maura's brush, she gently cleared the sand from the ancient carved hieroglyphs, letting the soft bristles coax the sand free so that the pictograms became easy to read. Her heart thundered as she read the inscription aloud, oblivious to the muttering crowd of students and workmen gathered around the rim of the pit. 'Herein lies the great one,' she read. 'Son of Horus, beloved of the gods, slayer of thousands, king of the two lands of Egypt.' Carra's breath caught in her throat. Oh, Christ,' she breathed. 'It's a bloody Pharaoh.'

'Are you sure?' Maura asked. And then wished she hadn't. 'Of course you are. Carry on.'

'Lying in the peace of eternal rest,' Carra picked up the inscription. 'In the tomb ordered built by the mighty Erimemushintep... I can't see the rest.' Carra stopped suddenly, a puzzled frown on her dusty face. 'Erimem?' she muttered softly. 'Who the hell was Erimem?'

# Chapter One
## Return of the King

*During the 18th Dynasty in the Second Kingdom...*
*... in the reign of Amenhotep II*

he army could be seen long before it actually came into view. The dust
kicked up by hundreds of horses and thousands of soldiers' feet
climbed into the air, announcing the return of Pharaoh's troops while
the soldiers themselves were still half a morning's march away. Only from
the highest vantage point in Thebes, one of the giant towers within
Pharaoh's palace, could any of the soldiers actually be seen, although they
appeared barely larger than ants.

General Antranak, commander of Pharaoh's palace guard, was slightly out
of breath by the time he reached the top of the tower. Each time he climbed
those stairs he felt it weary him just a little more than the last time but he
took a great pride in knowing that he still had the stamina to climb the stairs
which so many of the younger members of the palace household avoided.
Now well past his fortieth summer, Antranak was a bull of a man. He was
just a little taller than average but his great shoulders and barrel chest stood
him apart from most men. Pharaoh had once commented to his court that
Antranak had been blessed by Ra with the strength of ten men and the heart
and loyalty to match. That praise had cemented Antranak's position in the
palace and Antranak had rewarded his king with unflinching loyalty and
friendship.

Antranak wiped the sweat from his forehead and replaced his helmet
before walking out onto the balcony. As he had expected, a small, slim figure

had beaten him to the balcony. She wore a simple white, pleated linen dress with a blue belt tied at the waist and her shaved head was uncovered. A pair of sandals lay carelessly discarded nearby.

'Hello, Antranak,' she said without turning.

'Erimem, I should have you guard one of the gates,' Antranak chuckled. 'Your hearing is sharper than a lion's.'

'But I'm not nearly so fierce.' The girl turned and beamed a huge smile at her friend. She was sixteen and a startlingly pretty girl with intelligent and warm brown eyes that sparkled when she smiled, a slim, delicate nose and a wide, expressive mouth that was more at ease laughing than when holding a serious expression. Though she was slim, her muscles were clearly well honed beneath her soft brown skin.

Antranak chuckled indulgently. 'I'm not so sure of that,' he said. 'I hear you cut one of my guards today when you were practising with the swords.'

'He had been laughing with his friends that a girl shouldn't carry swords,' Erimem said sourly.

'Most men in Egypt would agree with him,' Antranak commented sternly, then a smile softened his face. 'I imagine he's not laughing now?'

'I don't think so, but I didn't cut him on purpose,' Erimem sniffed. 'Anyway, I think the blame belongs with my teacher. He's the one who taught me how to fight.'

Antranak sighed. 'I suppose it is my fault for teaching you how to use the sword and spear. Your father would not approve, little one.'

Erimem stiffened a little at the mention of her father. She had no doubts that he would disapprove of her learning to fight. It seemed that he disapproved of most of the things she chose to do. 'I don't suppose he would. I wish...' she cut herself off. 'It doesn't matter what I wish, does it?' she said far more harshly than she had intended. She saw Antranak stiffen with discomfort as he always did when she spoke of her father as being anything less than perfect. She wouldn't have expected anything less of Antranak. Her father was Pharaoh, Divine Ruler of the Two Kingdoms of Egypt and an infallible living god. Had she been anyone else, Antranak would probably have thrown her in jail for even thinking the Pharaoh wasn't perfect. In truth, she knew that if she had been anyone else, Antranak would have long since sent her to the House of Pain to have those thoughts burned from her. To ease her friend's discomfort, she changed the subject, looking out into the desert where the army's dust cloud was steadily growing larger. 'Don't you miss it, Antranak?' she asked. 'The war? The campaigns?'

'I don't miss the fighting,' Antranak answered with an honesty that surprised even himself. 'But I do wish I was there when he goes into battle.'

Erimem couldn't help but be touched by the devotion and love in Antranak's voice. 'To protect him.'

'Pharaoh doesn't need protection by a mortal like me.'

Erimem said nothing. Her expression said enough.

'Oh, all right,' Antranak conceded unhappily. 'I would rest easier if I knew I was there to protect my Pharaoh.'

Erimem squeezed her friend's arm warmly. 'You protect him when he is in the Palace.'

Antranak harrumphed. 'Which counts for precious little when he is thirty days' march away waging war with the Mitanni.'

'Then you protect me.'

'Hah!' Antranak exclaimed. 'And who protects my soldiers from you and your sword?' He tried to sound stern but Erimem knew him too well to fall for it. He nodded out at the approaching column. 'The army will be here before long.'

Erimem looked at the plain dress she was wearing. 'I should prepare to meet the parade,' she said. 'This isn't really suitable, is it?'

Antranak grunted. He never commented on women and their clothes. 'And my palace guard should meet Pharaoh at the city gates.'

Erimem's eyes twinkled mischievously. 'I'll be downstairs before you,' she laughed, running for the stairs.

Antranak shook his head in resignation. She was sixteen but, at heart, Erimem was still the girl who had ridden on his back all those years before. 'Erimem,' he called and pointed to her abandoned footwear. 'Your sandals,' he said. 'It wouldn't do for a princess of Egypt to greet her father, the Pharaoh, in her bare feet.'

Erimem stopped in her tracks and turned back for her shoes. 'You're right,' she sighed.

'I know,' Antranak nodded. And then he bolted for the stairs. 'And I'll be at the foot of the stairs before you,' he called, the top of his head disappearing from view as he sprinted down the steps.

Erimem's jaw dropped open. 'You cheat!' As she ran after Antranak, Erimem was sure he heard him guffawing like a small boy.

The sun had reached its zenith when Pharaoh's army reached the gates of Thebes. The soldiers looked filthy, sweaty and exhausted from their long march but they marched with straight backs, accepting the adulation of the city. At their head, Pharaoh Amenhotep rode in an ornately decorated chariot trimmed with gold and precious lapis lazuli and drawn by two magnificent white stallions. Slaves ran ahead of the horses scattering perfumed blossom across the road, making the way fit for the living god. Clad in a white kilt, gold-plated armour and pectoral, Amenhotep wore the blue battle crown of Egypt as a symbol that he had been triumphant. He was taller than average and while he carried a little more weight than he had in his earlier years, he had by no means run to fat and was still clearly a vibrant, virile man even though he was now heading towards his fiftieth year. Normally he would have had a driver for his chariot, usually the best driver in the elite Isis chariot squadron but, on occasions like this, Amenhotep shared the honour of leading the army with no one. It was his right and duty to be at the head of the procession. Egypt had to see that he was strong, and just as importantly, so did the spies of her enemies who would doubtless be among the crowd who lined the broad streets, singing praises to Pharaoh and prostrating themselves in the sand as his chariot passed. Most had seen this procession a dozen times before – Amenhotep had won many victories in countless campaigns over the years of his reign – but there was something slightly different in this parade. A second chariot, almost as ornately crafted as Pharaoh's own, followed Amenhotep only a dozen paces behind the tail of his chariot – far closer than any man who valued his life should dare. But this man knew he had nothing to fear. Thutmose was Amenhotep's eldest son and his similarity to his father was seen by many in the city as a sign of his divinity. He shared a similar build to Amenhotep and had inherited Pharaoh's hooded eyes and slightly hawk-like nose. Even his expression was the same as his father's – proud and indomitable. When the procession passed a line of small slim brown objects which looked at first like twigs, but then became clear as human fingers – the little fingers cut from the left hands of one thousand of the defeated enemy – both Amenhotep and Thutmose looked at them with disdain before turning their heads away and looking towards the palace. The crowd roared their approval then, as Pharaoh and his beloved son passed through the gates of the palace and moved out of sight, the crowd's attention turned to the weary but victorious soldiers. Musicians played while, despite the heat from the noon sun, prostitutes and dancing girls writhed sensually, reminding the soldiers of the delights they had missed during the campaign. They knew they were going to be busy. Thebes, home of Pharaoh and capital of the Two Kingdoms of Egypt, was going to spend the next few days celebrating.

Once inside the palace gates, Amenhotep's chariot turned onto a broad path that led past a wall covered with carvings depicting the great military deeds of previous Pharaohs. His own name was already prominent among the carvings and soon craftsmen would be hard at work, preserving word of this great victory for future generations. As the chariot passed along the path, soldiers high on the wall prostrated themselves until he had passed and then resumed their duties. The path was part of a perfect square forming the edge of a broad courtyard, running for several hundred paces before turning sharply towards the palace, then sharply again to run the breadth of the palace entrance, and then again, heading back to the main gates. Pharaoh had chosen the most theatrical route to take in heading towards the party waiting to greet him, making them wait while he paraded along the sides of the courtyard.

Erimem slipped into place beside Antranak, just as her father's chariot made the final turn towards the soldiers and priests gathered in front of the palace.

'I thought you weren't going to make it, little one,' Antranak said quietly. 'One of these days you will cut things a little too fine.'

'It wasn't my fault,' Erimem protested quietly. 'My handmaidens were too excited about the army coming back to get me ready properly. I'd have been far quicker tending to myself.'

Antranak tutted. 'Which would hardly be fitting for a royal princess of Egypt.' He allowed a quick smile. 'Your handmaidens may not have had their minds on their work, but they performed their tasks well. You are as beautiful as your mother was at your age.'

Even though the temperature was already baking hot, Erimem's cheeks blushed a little hotter. 'Thank you, Antranak.'

Her friend sniffed. 'Though she knew how to be on time for such occasions.' His voice was stern but there was a smile in his eyes as he cast her a quick, sideways glance. She wrinkled her nose in return.

'Get ready,' Antranak said softly. 'He's almost here.'

Amenhotep's chariot was now only fifty paces away and priests began scattering more scented petals anointed with holy oils and perfumes across the path in front of Pharaoh's horses while the choir continued to sing a hymn to Pharaoh's greatness in a high, sweet-sounding harmony.

The chariot passed the end of a small pool, which was the sign for Pharaoh's subjects to kneel. They dropped to their knees and lowered their heads. They could hear the chariot pull to a stop and the sandy thump of Amenhotep leaping to the ground, but kept their eyes fixed on the sand until Pharaoh chose to give them leave to do otherwise.

Amenhotep strode to the waiting assembly and surveyed them for a moment before telling them to rise. First to his feet was a tall, slim man, dressed in the robes of the Temple of Horus. His head was covered with a sharply beaked hawk mask showing that he was the High Priest of the Temple and, as such, leader of the Council of Priests. When he spoke his voice managed to be strident while staying dutifully obsequious. Antranak suppressed a sneer. He knew the priest, Horemshep by name, all too well. A scheming politician, and Antranak had little use for politicians. Thankfully, neither did Pharaoh.

Horemshep bowed from the waist to Amenhotep. 'Mighty Pharaoh, all Egypt sings praises to the gods for your safe return and for your mighty victory. Our enemies tremble at the sound of your name and quake at the thought of your anger. Your deeds will pass into legend and stand as a barrier protecting this land from her foes.'

Amenhotep raised a hand to halt Horemshep's speech – the priest looked as though his welcome could last the entire afternoon. 'I'm sure they will,' Amenhotep said without a hint of irony. He knew that his actions in the recent war with the Mitanni, their neighbours to the north, would keep other nearby nations in check. The war had been swift and brutal and the remnants of the Mitanni army were scattered. After the final battle, Amenhotep had ordered the small fingers to be cut from the hands of 500 Mitanni captives and another 500 were taken as slaves. He had ensured that the captives were paraded past every Mitanni settlement on the route back to Thebes. Word of the devastation he had caused to the Mitanni army would spread across every nation in the known world. No one would dare threaten Egypt while Amenhotep sat on the throne. He found it curiously disappointing.

Once he had passed the Council of Priests and accepted blessings from them all, Amenhotep found himself looking at a welcome face. 'Antranak!' he said warmly, grasping his friend by the arms.

'My Pharaoh,' Antranak bowed.

'My good friend, I have so many stories to tell you.' Excitement was bubbling through the Pharaoh's voice and he sounded like a small boy eager to share his adventures with a friend.

Antranak couldn't help but smile in return. 'Pharaoh always has stories of great victories to tell.'

Amenhotep barked a laugh. 'I had feared they would not be so great this time, old friend, without you by my side.' Antranak bowed at the compliment and felt a degree of satisfaction knowing that this praise from Pharaoh would leave Horemshep seething with envious rage. 'But the stories I will tell most will not be of myself,' Amenhotep continued.' He waved a hand, bidding Thutmose to join them. Thutmose dutifully leaped from his chariot and moved to stand by his father, taking care to ignore the priests. His antipathy towards the priests – Horemshep in particular – was well known at court. Amenhotep continued, 'I will tell stories of my son, Thutmose.' Amenhotep spoke loudly enough for the entire gathering to hear. 'I will tell of his courage in battle, I will tell of how he led his chariot squadron's attack on the Mitanni army, I will tell of the hundreds I saw him slay with his bare hands.' He slapped a hand on Thutmose's shoulder. 'Only my son could have replaced Antranak by my side in battle.' It was a high compliment to both men and they both bowed in appreciation to Pharaoh. 'So,' Amenhotep went on. 'Tell me news, Antranak. What happened in the city while I was absent? Is my palace safe?'

'One misguided – and ill-informed – Mitanni tried to enter the palace to assassinate you,' Antranak said nonchalantly. 'He was captured halfway over the outermost wall. The expression on his face when he was told that you were leading the army into battle yourself...' Antranak chuckled. 'I almost let him go out of pity.'

'I assume you didn't?' the demand came from Thutmose. His voice was brusque and less amiable than his father's. It was often commented around the palace – in hushed tones – that Thutmose had all of his mighty father's virtues except for the warmth. No one could imagine Thutmose in a conversation as genial as those Amenhotep often had with the men he called his friends. Indeed, it was also commented that Thutmose had no friends.

Antranak forced a smile in answer to the blunt question. 'No, my lord,' he answered. 'The Mitanni is in the House of Pain having the truth burned from him. I believe he knows more than he has said but little that will be of consequence. I will show him some of the Mitanni taken as slaves to prove that the war is over and we are victorious. Perhaps that will loosen his tongue. If not, I shall hand the captive to Pharaoh's judge and let him deal with the matter.'

Thutmose grunted. 'That is acceptable,' he said grudgingly.

Antranak gave a half bow as though accepting high praise.

'Now, Antranak,' Amenhotep clasped his friend's arm. 'I am dusty and in need of a bath, then we will celebrate long through the night.'

'Indeed, Majesty,' Antranak laughed. 'I have often said your celebrations last longer than your battles.'

'Long may it be so,' Amenhotep said sincerely. 'I much prefer the taste of wine to that of war, and song is a sweeter sound than that of battle.'

Antranak nodded his agreement. He had long thought that only those who had fought in war, and who accepted that they might have to do so again truly understood the tragedy that went alongside the glory. Anyone who hadn't felt the thrill of combat and the fear of death that comes in battle couldn't understand the mixture of sorrow and elation that came when the battle was over. The smell of blood that put fire into Antranak's soul during combat had made him vomit afterwards. 'My Pharaoh is wise as always,' he said. 'I will settle for a lifetime engaged in celebration rather than war.'

'Come now,' Amenhotep gripped his friend's arm and led him up the path towards the palace, ignoring the rest of the gathered dignitaries. 'Let me tell you of my son's victories before we decide we are old men who should sit close to the fire to see out our days. We must prepare for a celebration and I will tell you of Thutmose.'

Antranak allowed himself to be led away by the Pharaoh. As he went, he cast a quick glance back to Erimem, who simply shrugged and joined the crowd in bowing her head at the departing Amenhotep.

'What did you expect?'

The soft voice in her ear made Erimem jump and she stifled a yelp. She turned and saw a familiar grinning face. 'Mentu,' she scolded. 'Must you creep up on me like that?'

Mentu only smiled more and Erimem could see why so many of the girls at court talked behind their fans and giggled about her brother. He was shorter than Thutmose by half a head but he had a broad smile that came from his eyes as much as his mouth. He was as warm and friendly as their brother was cold and distant. Sometimes, Erimem knew, Mentu could be more than friendly. He was nineteen and still unmarried but his liking for spending time with an attractive girl was already well known throughout the city. 'How could I creep up on you, little monkey?' Mentu laughed. 'I hear you are the mightiest warrior in the palace.'

'Not now that the glorious Thutmose is home.' Erimem ignored the joke and glowered at Mentu.

Mentu knew his sister well enough to know that when she was in this sort of mood, teasing her was slightly more dangerous than taunting the Nile crocodiles. 'What did you expect?' he repeated. His voice had changed, the playful tone giving way to a more reasonable manner. 'Thutmose is his heir. One day, he will be Pharaoh. Our father has never forgotten that.'

'Though he seems to have forgotten us,' Erimem grumbled.

'Quietly, monkey.' There was a note of warning in Mentu's soft voice. 'This court is full of vipers who would be happy to use outbursts like that to their own ends. Not even Pharaoh's only daughter is allowed to criticise him.'

Erimem looked around quickly. The crowd was dispersing, dignitaries returning to their business, priests going back to their temples and an armed guard waited to escort Pharaoh's wives back to their home in the Palace of Concubines. A small group of Nubian eunuchs was herding the gaggle of women towards the guards. Erimem looked at the women but couldn't find Rhaoubak in the crowd. No matter. She would visit the Palace later to pay respects to her mother. Erimem was also relieved that no one seemed to have heard her fit of temper. 'I know,' she conceded. 'And I do not mean any disrespect. I love our father dearly.'

'But sometimes you wish he would actually remember that we exist?' Mentu offered a wry smile. 'I know that feeling very well, sister,' he sighed. 'But we must remember that our father is not a mortal man. He is a living god and how can we know what a god thinks or feels?'

'I know all that,' Erimem said, watching her father disappear from view, obscured by a huge, carved column. 'But I just wish...' her voice tailed off and she looked helplessly at her brother.

'I know,' he nodded. 'I do know.' His eyes glanced to the doorway Amenhotep had passed through and an unusually solemn expression crept onto his face, a wistful, sad expression completely at odds with the Mentu everyone was used to seeing laughing and joking around the palace. For the first time Erimem realised how much Mentu must feel that same confusion about their father that she did. And then the smile was back on Mentu's lips as though he had pulled on a mask, but he couldn't hide that this smile didn't reach his eyes. 'but we have a celebration to prepare for, little monkey,' he said, just a little too brightly.

Erimem knew better than to confront Mentu about his sudden change of subject and slipped into the familiar easy banter. 'Will your gaggle of admirers allow you to attend the celebration?' she teased. 'I hear you have a girl in every street.'

'Every house,' Mentu corrected. The relief at being back on familiar ground was evident in his eyes. 'And more than one in some. If you believe the rumours,' he added.

'I don't listen to rumours,' Erimem said earnestly and then a smirk broke onto her face. 'I start most of them.'

Mentu sniffed. 'I've never liked you. I just wanted you to know that.'

Erimem stuck her tongue out at him. 'And I like Thutmose better than you.' She opened a parasol and sheltered from the sun beneath it. 'But since you are here, you may walk with me to the Palace of Concubines.'

'Wouldn't you prefer Thutmose?' Mentu asked with mock indignation in his voice.

'He's not here so I'll make do with you,' Erimem said haughtily.

'I've still never liked you.'

Erimem wrinkled her nose. 'You smell.'

They walked away along the path leading to the gardens and then to the Palace of Concubines, happily bickering as they went.

# Chapter Two
## The Master of the World

*Our king is mighty,*
*He has coloured the sand red with the blood of our enemies.*
*He has returned to us, his head high and proud.*
*He is adored by the gods and the Sun respects his commands.*
*None may stand against him and see another sunrise.*
*He is life and death. Our king is mighty.*

he choir of hesets sang in the corner of the grand banqueting hall in the palace, their sweet harmonies singing one hymn of praise for Pharaoh after another. They would sing the glories of their Pharaoh as long as the banquet lasted, even though their song was regularly lost under the rumble of conversation in the hall. The hall itself was as full as anyone could ever remember. Even old Shemek, the ancient palace astrologer, had never seen a celebration so grand. The great and good from all walks of Thebes society sat on cushions at long, low tables covered with the finest food and drink in the kingdom. The meats were tender and glistened with their own juices, the fruits were ripe and fresh and the wines and beers were of the highest quality.

In response to the grandeur of Pharaoh's banquet, the guests had dressed in their finest. The men mainly wore variations of long white kilts with white sleeveless tunics that crossed over at the front. Those with sashes or medals denoting a position of power in the city wore them proudly and vied to be closer to the Pharaoh. The women, meanwhile, wore straight ankle-length, form-fitting dresses held up by thin straps. The dresses were mainly in either white, blue or green and were worn with a belt of complementary colour that tied at the waist and the end of which hung almost to the floor. The women wore a dazzling range of jewellery in gold and precious stones to accompany their dresses and many even had gold and precious stones woven into their elaborate wigs. Cakes of perfumed wax rested in the wigs, melting as the evening wore on releasing a scented oil which was both pleasing to the nose and refreshingly cooling. An evening like this was a chance for social point-scoring that came only rarely. Careers and fortunes could be made on nights like these.

As befitting the daughter of Pharaoh, Erimem wore a more intricately styled dress than the other women. The skirt fell in tight pleats to the ankle and another pleated band swung under her arm and across her chest, the pleats fanning out as they stretched from right to left and somehow managed to emphasise a bust that had not yet truly appeared. Each pleat was trimmed with a line of gold and had small, twinkling gemstones stitched into folds so that the dress glittered as she moved. Her sandals were made of a gold material which complemented her dress perfectly. Erimem wore less jewellery than most of the other women but the rings, bracelet and necklace she wore were of the highest quality, created by the finest craftsmen in the Two Kingdoms. The golden asp which curled around her arm from the elbow to the bicep had alone taken half a year to complete. Gold and jewels also decorated the black wig which hung to her shoulders. Her make-up was also immaculate, her handmaidens having spent a considerable time carefully applying kohl around her eyes, henna to dye her fingernails a golden orange and a red ochre to her lips. As they had worked, Erimem had listened to the girls chatter excitedly about the banquet and heard Hanek, the eldest of her handmaidens, say that they wished that they could have been invited. She had joined in the joking but had found herself wishing she could have swapped places with one of them.

'Thank you,' Erimem accepted a compliment on her appearance from the hatchet-faced wife of a minor priest and moved into the shadow of a giant pillar, which was covered with scenes of a long-past Pharaoh slaying his enemies and being praised by all the gods. From her position, Erimem could watch the movements of the various guests, and could see the politics and social climbing in action. High-ranking officials were being feted by those of a lower level, while the wives of those in junior positions moved in on the more prominent wives and started work on them. It was all a game and Erimem found it both amusing and depressing.

An imposing figure passing by her hiding place caught Erimem's eye. 'Thutmose.'

Her brother stopped and turned, looking slightly confused until he picked Erimem out in the darkness. 'Oh, it's you, Erimem,' he said. As usual, he didn't sound pleased to see her. In fact, he didn't sound anything but a little uncomfortable and eager to be way from her.

Erimem was tempted to let Thutmose go on his way but she felt duty-bound to say something to him. 'You must have shown great courage in battle for our father to be so proud of you.' She nodded towards the raised dais on which Pharaoh and his most honoured guests sat at a table. Antranak was among them, laughing and listening intently to her father.

'I did my duty,' Thutmose answered and Erimem waited for him to add something more. Instead his impatience at being held up just showed more clearly on his face.

Erimem gave up. It was the same every time she tried talking to Thutmose. 'I give praises that you are both returned safely,' she said, bowing slightly.

Thutmose took his cue. 'Thank you,' he said and with obvious relief made his way past an array of bowing guests.

Erimem sighed deeply and turned away from the sight of her brother to find herself looking at another brother approaching.

Mentu smiled broadly as he joined Erimem. 'How is our brother?' he asked.

Erimem wrinkled her nose.

'As charming as ever,' Mentu interpreted. 'Forget him,' he suggested firmly. 'Forget him and enjoy the celebration.'

Mentu led Erimem to a low table where he had spotted Shemek sitting in conversation with Fayum, one of the youngest priests present and also one of their closest friends. Fayum had played with Mentu and Erimem when they were all children and the friendships had stayed strong. Fayum looked pleased to see them approach, as did Shemek, though the old man had squinted for a time before his failing eyes had worked out who they were.

'Do not stand,' Erimem waved a hand, indicating for Shemek to stay seated.

'As generous as you are beautiful,' Shemek wheezed. 'Thank you. At my age by the time my knees let me stand up it's time to sit down again and even that takes so long, by the time I'm settled everyone else is getting up to go home.' His old face wrinkled into a broad, toothless smile. 'We are honoured that you choose to spend time with two as lowly as us on a grand night like this.'

'You old charlatan,' Erimem scolded Shemek fondly. 'You know you're one of the most respected men in the palace.' Shemek beamed and didn't argue. 'Besides,' Erimem continued. 'It is only fitting that I should spend time with my friends.'

Erimem sat on a cushion beside Shemek and Fayum and the three slipped into the continuation of a conversation they had apparently been having some time before. Mentu waited until he was sure Erimem was comfortable with her friends before slipping away into the crowd in search of the girl he had spotted earlier. A few moments later, Erimem noted her brother's absence and suppressed a smirk. She was surprised – and touched – that he had stayed for so long. She sat with Shemek and Fayum a little longer before excusing herself then, as inconspicuously as she possible, she stole away from the hall and returned to her own chambers.

*　*　*

For the next few days after the celebration banquet, Erimem waited to be summoned by her father and reprimanded for leaving so early. As a member of the royal family she would have been expected to stay late and be seen to be enjoying herself. But the summons didn't come. In fact, for the next dozen days or so, Erimem didn't see her father at all. He was, she knew, still in the Palace – there was always a more active atmosphere when Pharaoh was at home – but the palace consisted of dozens of buildings and covered such a huge area that it was easy to live within its walls and not see someone from one moon to the next.

And so, Erimem's life slipped back into the same comfortable, if slightly repetitive routine, that she had enjoyed for the past few years. She spent time studying with Shemek, who had become an unofficial tutor to her some years earlier. Though it was unusual for a female to be as educated as Erimem, Shemek was simply pleased to have someone eager to make use of him and was happy to teach her the arts of reading and writing in more than one language. He taught her mathematics, astrology and told her stories of the philosophies of far-off lands, and commented that no matter how much Erimem learned she always wanted to hear more.

Although her father had returned and Antranak had less time free, Erimem cajoled and nagged her friend into ensuring that she was able to continue her training with the sword and the battlespear. Each morning, Antranak oversaw her training personally at a quiet courtyard in the shadow of a sycamore grove. They were far enough away from the busier sections of the palace for them to be able to work uninterrupted, and ensured that Erimem only worked with two of his most loyal and discreet soldiers. They had been lucky to keep quiet the injury Erimem had inflicted on the soldier who had laughed at her before Pharaoh had returned. Antranak did not want to risk word of a similar incident reaching Pharaoh's ears. Erimem, in turn, surprised both Antranak and the soldiers he had assigned to tutor her by being a quick student who had grasped the basics of the sword and spear quickly. Although she was lacking the power of the men she faced, Erimem was sharper on her feet and moved with grace during the sparring. She was also tenacious, unwilling to yield when her more experienced opponents clearly had her beaten and always demanding that they work just a little longer. In time the soldiers began to forget first that she was a princess and then that she was a mere girl. When Antranak saw the glimmer of respect in their eyes for Erimem's hard work, he assigned the two, Terak and Bezel, as Erimem's personal bodyguard.

The rest of Erimem's time was spent in the company of her handmaidens listening to their often ribald stories of life outside the palace, of the boys they met, of which dignitary was visiting which brothel, of the priest's wife who was having an affair with a guard captain... somehow the handmaidens knew every piece of gossip in the city.

'It's very easy,' Liram had said one afternoon as Erimem and her handmaidens sat in the shade of a palm tree. 'The handmaidens and servants from all sections of the palace are quartered in one area. Nothing in the palace stays secret for long.' That had produced a stream of giggles – obviously a joke Erimem wasn't privy to.

'That isn't true.' Linsis, the darkest skinned of Erimem's servants held a finger aloft. 'There is one secret we have yet to find the answer to.' She turned her gaze to Hanek. 'And that is the name of Hanek's secret love.'

Hanek blushed furiously and concentrated on the goblet of wine she held.

'Hanek?' Erimem asked. 'Is this true?

The girl shifted uncomfortably under the scrutiny of half a dozen pairs of eyes, eyes studying her as a jackal studies its prey, though her tormentors were more interested in gossip they could trade in the palace than in food.

'It's true,' Linsis assured Erimem. 'Who is it, Hanek? We won't tell.'

'Who is it?' The girls all seemed to chorus the question.

Hanek ignored the giggling and the slightly taunting tone of the question and cast a pleading look to Erimem.

'All right.' Erimem took pity on the girl. 'Whoever Hanek's love is – if she has one – is her affair alone. She will tell us when she is ready.'

For a moment Linsis showed annoyance at having her fun brought to a premature end but she hid her anger quickly. She never forgot that her mistress was the daughter of Pharaoh. 'As you wish, princess,' she said meekly.

'Good,' Erimem flashed a glance at Hanek that said she expected to hear every single detail in due course before turning her attention back to Linsis. 'Tell me, Linsis. Do you have a boy?'

'Oh she has many,' giggled Valu, the youngest of the girls and the rest of the group chorused tales of Linsis's many admirers. This time it was Linsis who squirmed under the scrutiny.

Hanek caught Erimem's eye and nodded her thanks.

Later that evening, after a small meal of a roast duck and sweet bread followed by what the farmer who produced them called 'the only dates in the Two Kingdoms sweet enough for a great and mighty Pharaoh's house', Erimem had retreated to her suite of rooms, discarded her wig and settled back into a set of enormous cushions. The sun had set but the heat of the day lingered. Without a breath of wind to shift it, the heat would probably last through the night. The handmaidens were also clearly feeling the effects of the heat. As soon as the gossamer-sheer drapes had been drawn across the windows and doors to keep insects at bay, the handmaidens had let the tops of their dresses slide and went about their duties topless. Taking a goblet of wine from Hanek, Erimem unconsciously made sure that the straps of her dress were keeping it securely in place. It was common enough for girls to be seen topless when the dry heat was as intense and unrelenting as this, and Erimem felt no embarrassment in seeing her handmaidenens almost naked. She saw them fully undressed most days when they bathed her, but she did feel a little uncomfortable when she compared their womanly figures to her own more girlish build. Even Valu, a full year younger than Erimem had a proud chest compared to her princess.

'Do not worry, little one,' her mother had said, the last time Erimem had visited Rhaoubak in the Palace of Concubines, a grand building set in its own grounds within the palace and home to Pharaoh's wives. 'You will be a fine woman soon enough. And a beautiful one.' But Erimem didn't feel particularly beautiful or like a woman. Her body clung to a girlish figure and she knew she was still treated as a girl even though most girls of her age outside of the palace would long since have been married. She recognised the mood she was falling into and she dismissed her handmaidens, who jabbered their thanks, bowed and hurried for the door as fast as etiquette would allow. Erimem watched them leave and then noticed that Hanek was still seated in a large cushion by her side.

'What of you, Hanek?' she asked. 'Are you not going with them?'

Hanek shook her head. 'I will stay with my princess,' she said, a quiet resignation in her voice.

'They are not going to their beds, are they?' Erimem asked. There was no condemnation in her voice, only a little amusement and perhaps a touch of wistful jealousy.

Hanek laughed dryly. 'Linsis may well be going to bed, but I doubt that she will be rested in the morning.'

Erimem smiled but was glad that the low light cast about her chamber by the oil lamps would hide her blushes. 'What of you?' she probed. 'Would you not rather see this boy of yours than sit here with me?'

For a time it seemed that Hanek wasn't going to answer but she eventually did speak, again with a wary kind of weariness. 'I cannot see him often,' she said. Her eyes flashed at Erimem. 'Please do not tell Linsis and the others that I have admitted to seeing this man,' she pleaded. 'They will only make sport of it.'

Erimem nodded her assent. 'It's unfair,' she said after a long moment.

Hanek's face screwed up on confusion. 'What is, princess?'

'That all my other handmaidens have gone to have fun while we are stuck here on our own.' Erimem stood sharply and pulled Hanek up with her. 'If they can have fun,' Erimem stated firmly, 'So can we.'

Evading Erimem's bodyguards, who stood on either side of the main doors to her chamber, proved disappointingly easy. Hanek left Erimem's chambers and returned a few minutes later with a yawning serving girl in tow. The girl was small and slim, and had a shawl placed over her head. Shortly after, Hanek and the serving girl left Erimem's rooms, the serving girl slouching, her head bowed wearily. They trudged their way to the end of the corridor and it was only when they were sure that Erimem straightened up and moved the serving girl's shawl from her face.

Hanek led the way through the palace and across the grounds to a small gate on the west wall guarded by a single bored soldier who let them through the gate without bothering to ask their names. They followed a well-worn path into Thebes and through dusty streets that were barely lit by occasional oil lamps. Hanek led the way to a bright, well-lit tavern where she said the other handmaidens would be and, despite the raucous noise from inside, Erimem had been delighted to be out of the darkness. By the end she had been sure that murderers and robbers were lurking in every shadow. They didn't join the handmaidens but instead took a small room on the first floor – little more than a balcony really – that looked down into the tavern's main room where they could observe the drunks, the gamblers and the prostitutes.

The beer was rough but by her fourth mug Erimem was becoming used to it. She wasn't drunk but she was pleasantly relaxed. 'Now tell me of this mysterious boy of yours,' she said.

'I cannot meet him often. His father...' Hanek shook her head sadly and took a deep breath. 'His father would not approve of us.'

'Why not?' Erimem protested. 'You come from a good and respected family and you are a handmaiden to Pharaoh's daughter. If you are good enough to serve Erimemushinteperem, daughter of Pharaoh – and, I hope, be her friend – then you are good enough for any boy in the Two Kingdoms.

'It's not that easy,' Hanek began, but Erimem cut across her.

'Tell me the name of this man,' she demanded. 'And I shall talk with him. I shall summon him to the palace to explain this insult to my handmaiden and through her, to me.'

For a moment hope shone in Hanek's eyes before she locked it away. 'No,' she said with resignation. 'I know it cannot be and I have accepted that. Some things cannot be forced.'

'But...'

'Please.' There was a desperate unhappiness in Hanek's voice. 'Please,' she repeated more softly. 'Let it pass.'

'All right,' Erimem conceded. She would return to the subject later but now wasn't the time to push Hanek. 'So,' she forced brightness into her voice. 'Should we watch a fisherman cheat at Senet?' She waved a finger at a table set in a corner of the room, well clear of the prostitute and her client. Four men were squatting on thin, underfilled cushions around a low table on which a game's board was set out with pieces in the shape of cones and reels.

'How can you cheat?' Hanek protested. 'Senet is a game of chance.'

Erimem again pointed to the table but this time to one of the two men not playing the game. 'Watch him. The one with the eyes of the snake.' As they watched, Snake-eyes as they dubbed him, surreptitiously nudged and pushed the game, distracting his friends so that he could alter the casting sticks as they fell. His movements were subtle and practised, and his friends who were becoming steadily more drunk and more interested in the girls of pleasure than in the game failed to notice his cheating or that he was drinking considerably less than his comrades.

One of the bar-women moved out of the shadows and walked slowly towards the table. At most, she was twenty and she walked with a grace that seemed out of place in such murky surroundings. Her long, pleated dress was tailored to cling to a narrow waist and round, voluptuous hips. The top consisted of broad pleated straps which covered the nipples but gave a clear view of the side of her large, rounded breasts and of her cleavage. When she reached the table, she leaned over and inspected the game. She showed no discomfort at all four men staring at her barely covered chest, moving with grace to avoid pawing hands. She looked at the table, nodded once and then straightened up. She flicked a small signal with her fingers and two men lumbered from the shadows. Snake-eyes scrambled to his feet and tried to run but the men caught him quickly. The woman explained to the other three men at the table what had been happening and they turned angry, drunken eyes on their friend. At a nod from the woman, her two men hauled Snake-eyes out with his friends lurching after them.

'What will happen to him?' Erimem asked. She wasn't certain she wanted to hear the answer.

'Oh, they won't kill him,' Hanek answered reassuringly. 'They'll probably beat him and then throw him into animal dung. And by morning everyone will know he is a cheat.'

Erimem's eyes were drawn again to the young woman who had returned to her place in the shadows. 'Who is she?'

'Ebrok,' Hanek answered. 'This is her tavern. She took it when her husband died. They say she was one of the girls who worked here before he took her as a wife.' Hanek leaned forward conspiratorially. 'They also say he died because he took her as a wife.' Hanek shrugged and relaxed back into her cushion. 'But they also say that she is a sorceress, that she is the vizier's mistress and that she can charm snakes. I think she likes the rumours. They're good for business.'

Erimem sat back and sipped her beer. She and Hanek spent a good part of the night laughing at the drunken antics of the bar's customers as they came and went. They judged the prowess of men on how long they had taken with the bar's girls and gave them nicknames depending on how they had performed. Later in the night, when the drunks had lost their interest, Erimem listened as Hanek talked about her family. All Erimem had known was that Hanek's father was a merchant and that she was the eldest daughter in the family. She hadn't known that Hanek had four sisters and three brothers, or that she now had two nieces she thought were the most precious things the gods had given her family, or that Hanek's father had taken a second wife two summers after Hanek's mother had died from a poisoned tooth. Listening to Hanek's stories of her and her sisters playing with other children in her father's garden, or getting involved in mischief in her father's store-rooms, or simply of the time the family spent together, warmed Erimem, but also made her feel curiously empty, as if her pampered upbringing had missed something vital. Her eyelids were just beginning to feel heavy when there was a commotion from one of the rooms on the far side of the corridor behind them, the shriek of a young woman and the crash of a door being thrown open. Suddenly there were a dozen voices shouting and yelling and shouting loudest was one familiar voice.

'Linsis,' Hanek said quickly.

Instinctively, Erimem hurried to the doorway and pushed the curtain aside. Framed in the doorway across the corridor, a young man in the uniform of Pharaoh's chariot squadron was holding Linsis's wrists. He was drunk and angry and vivid scratch marks ran down his cheek. He pushed Linsis back, stopping her nails from doing further damage.

'Savage,' he spat.

'You tried to force yourself on me,' Linsis screamed, pulling a torn strip of her dress back into place.

'You knew why I was meeting you,' the soldier sneered.

'I'm not a whore to be treated like this!'

The soldier snorted. 'Every woman is a whore for the right man.'

If he saw Erimem's hand flashing towards him, the soldier didn't have time to react. The heel of her hand slammed into his nose, breaking it with a satisfying crack. He looked at her, shocked, as blood poured from his broken nose. He tried to back away but Erimem caught his ponytail and heaved it down across his shoulder, yanking his head back.

'I am the princess Erimem,' she said coldly. 'And if you have abused any of the girls in my service you will answer to my family.'

She yanked the ponytail again and the soldier lurched forward, his face thudding against the cold stone wall.

Linsis stared from Erimem to the charioteer and then at Erimem again. She opened her mouth but couldn't find anything to say. The other handmaidens had gathered in the door, some with young men of their own, others holding goblets or mugs of beer.

'Are you all right, Linsis?' Erimem asked.

The girl nodded dumbly.

'It is all right,' Erimem promised. 'I swear by Horus that I am not angry with you and I will not tell anyone of this.' She nodded towards the charioteer, who lay clutching his broken face. 'Has he hurt you?'

'He tried,' the girl answered.

The charioteer made a move to pick himself up. He collapsed backwards as Erimem kicked him hard in the stomach. 'You should be buried alive in the red lands for this. Or perhaps I will send you to the House of Pain. Castration would stop you doing this again.' She had pulled her foot back to deliver another kick when a sharp voice came from the bottom of the stairs.

'What's going on up there?'

Ebrok, the tavern's owner – the young woman with the revealing dress – was striding up the stairs. 'Well?' she demanded. 'What happened to him?'

'He dishonoured my servant,' Erimem stated briskly.

'Did he?' Ebrok sniffed with disinterest. 'What did he do?'

'That is none of your concern,' Erimem answered, a dismissive tone in her voice. 'And I would suggest that you have more care over the customers you allow into your tavern.'

And why should I care what you suggest?

'Because she is our mistress,' Hanek hissed.

'Your mistress?' It took a moment for the meaning of Hanek's words to sink in. 'What would your mistress be doing here?'

'Leaving,' Erimem said haughtily. She turned and walked regally down the stairs and out of the door into the dark courtyard beyond, her handmaidens scuttling after her, boyfriends and lovers abandoned with a hasty kiss or squeeze of the hand. Ebrok looked around at the bewildered young men and at the charioteer who was still on the floor by her feet, moaning and clutching at his bloodied face.

'Oh, for Seth's sake, shut up,' she snapped and kicked him in the groin.

Erimem managed to stride elegantly around the corner out of the square and into a darker side street before she began giggling. Within moments, she was surrounded by a gaggle of excited handmaidens, all filled with wonder and questions. What had she been doing at the tavern? How long had she been there? When had she learned to fight like Horus himself? It was only when she saw the lost, befuddled Linsis trailing at the back of the group that Erimem remembered why she had been forced to act as she had and she held up her hands to quieten the chatter.

'Later,' she said. 'I will explain everything later. First, we must return to the palace and hope none of us have been missed.'

The girls agreed and the little party set off for the palace at a brisk walk, huddling into their cloaks and shawls to keep the cold desert night at bay. Despite their haste, the sun was beginning to burn the horizon a golden copper when they reached the western gate and they only just reached the palace before the sun crested the horizon. Again, Erimem was disappointed at how easily she slipped past her bodyguards, this time as part of a group of handmaidens and, after they had helped her undress then washed and anointed her with scented oils, Erimem flopped onto her bed and was asleep by the time the handmaidens reached the door to leave.

# Chapter Three
## The Olive Branch

rincess!'

It took one word for Erimem to know that her trip outside the palace had been discovered. She was walking in a grove of fig trees having left a small group of her handmaidens in the shade of a palm tree a hundred paces behind and, as Antranak dropped into step beside her, she knew that she had been found out – he only ever called her by her title when he was annoyed with her.

She flashed the most cheerful smile she could muster. 'Hello, Antranak. Are you well, this afternoon?'

Antranak sniffed and kept his eyes firmly rooted ahead of them. 'Better than you, I think. You look tired.'

'I didn't sleep well,' Erimem answered quickly.

'But you did sleep late,' Antranak countered. Before Erimem could answer, he carried on. 'I heard a most puzzling thing this morning.'

'Did you?' Erimem's heart sank. 'What was that?'

Antranak's leather kilt swished as he kicked a stone off the path. 'That a fight was started in a tavern last night – the early hours of the morning to be more accurate – by a young woman claiming to be the Princess Erimem.' He stopped and turned to her. His expression was neutral but his eyebrows were raised in the way Erimem knew meant disapproval.

'That's silly,' she answered as steadily as she could.

'That's what I thought.' Antranak started walking again and Erimem skipped a few steps to catch up. 'Because I'm sure you would have been in bed last night when all of this happened.'

Erimem nodded. 'I was.'

'And a handmaiden stayed all night?' Antranak left the question in the air, and Erimem understood his meaning instantly.

'Hanek,' she said automatically. 'She stayed until the morning.'

'I thought as much,' Antranak said briskly. 'It's not uncommon for a handmaiden to stay through the night, in case you should need something.'

'No,' Erimem agreed. 'It is quite common for her to stay.'

'I will have to hear this from the girl herself,' Antranak said thoughtfully. 'I will ask her... three days from now?'

Erimem could have hugged her old friend. He was giving her time to prepare Hanek's answers and they both knew it. 'That will be acceptable,' she smiled. 'I will tell the girl to expect you.'

A firm expression slid onto Antranak's face. 'I hope this impostor doesn't try this trick again,' he said sternly. 'I'm not sure I could keep the news from Pharaoh's ears twice.' He held Erimem's gaze. 'I doubt if he would approve.'

'No,' Erimem agreed slowly. 'I'm sure he would not.'

'Then we need not speak of this again?'

'No,' Erimem shook her head making the gold charms stitched into her wig tinkle gently. 'We need not.'

'Good.' Antranak's expression softened. 'You know, this girl who started the fight, she broke a soldier's nose – among other things.'

'I am sure he deserved it,' Erimem answered. 'Perhaps for trying to force himself on an unwilling girl.'

'Really?' Antranak stiffened a little. 'Perhaps I should have this charioteer posted to a garrison well away from any women.'

'I am sure that would be wise,' Erimem replied. 'It would be a kindness to him to take him clear of temptation.'

Antranak nodded. 'I shall do so this afternoon.' He paused thoughtfully. 'Of course, I can't say this officially, but she must be a remarkable girl to do this to a trained soldier, even a drunk one.' He had tried, but Antranak hadn't been able to completely take the pride from his voice.

'I'm sure she had a good teacher,' Erimem replied, and Antranak beamed.

'I'm sure she did, though he won't be pleased if she misses any more lessons.'

Erimem bowed slightly. 'She won't. I'm sure of it.'

'Good.' Antranak hefted his helmet and reluctantly set it back on his head. 'And now I have a great deal to do before tonight.'

'Tonight?' Erimem was puzzled. 'What's happening tonight?'

'Of course, you won't know.' Antranak swatted at a fly. 'The Mitanni are sending an ambassador to discuss a permanent peace between their people and Egypt'

Erimem snorted. 'My father won't meet with a Mitanni ambassador. He hates the Mitanni.'

A concerned frown shadowed Antranak's weathered face. 'That is what I thought too, little one, but Horemshep has persuaded him to meet this ambassador. And to hold a banquet in his honour, no less.'

'And my father agreed to this?'

Antranak nodded. He looked set to say something but he bit off any reply. 'My Pharaoh knows what he is doing,' he said finally. 'Pharaoh is never wrong. Our duty is to obey.' There was a tight resignation in Antranak's voice and it occurred to Erimem that this was the closest she had heard Antranak come to ever openly disagreeing with her father.

After the soldier had excused himself and returned to his duties, Erimem turned on the path and started back towards her handmaidens. She was halfway back to the group of girls when, on an impulse, she turned from the path and cut across a broad stone square towards Mentu's rooms. She hadn't seen her brother in a number of days and always felt a slight pang of concern when he was out of sight for too long. Despite his relaxed, carefree appearance, Mentu could be impetuous and had a habit of finding his way into trouble. Wondering what her brother would make of his supposedly sensible sister's adventure the previous night put a spring in Erimem's step. Would he be shocked? Would he demand to join her on another trip outside the palace? Or did he know the tavern already? There were times Erimem wondered if her brother knew every girl younger than twenty in all of Thebes. Interestingly, though, he had not been so vocal in bragging of his conquests. In fact, he had talked more than once of a particular girl who had taken his eye.

The broad, open doorway of Mentu's apartments was unguarded as usual, and Erimem wandered easily into the rooms. Mentu's quarters were richly decorated with the same painted murals and frescos as her own rooms, and similar embroidered tapestries adorned a wall, telling the story of a Pharaoh's life. Mentu had mentioned which of their ancestors it had been but Erimem had been too young to pay attention at the time. The only significant difference between their apartments was that Mentu was expected to have swords, shields, spears and the assorted weapons of war on show, as befitting a son of a mighty warrior king, even though Mentu himself had little interest in weapons or the army. Despite years of rigorous training, war held little fascination for him.

'We should swap places, sister,' he had once said. 'You spend all day with the soldiers and I will spend my time being pampered by temple girls.'

Erimem's reply had been quick. 'You spend your time with the temple girls anyway.'

'Perhaps you are right,' Mentu had mused. 'I need my soldier's training to keep the girls at bay. And,' he had added with a smile, 'to fight off all the undeserving men who will seek to marry my beautiful sister.'

But there had been no undeserving men and Mentu had never drawn a sword in anger. The weapons in his apartments were purely for show, and Erimem was glad of that. While she could imagine Thutmose, and even Teti, the third of her brothers, charging into battle, she could never imagine Mentu deliberately harming anyone. It would simply be too much effort for him to be bothered with.

At first the rooms appeared to be abandoned, but then Erimem heard the soft scuffing sound of sandals on the hard stone floors, and she followed the sound through into Mentu's bedchamber.

'Mentu?' The small figure that emerged from Mentu's bedchamber wasn't her brother, but she was equally familiar. 'Hanek? What are you doing here?' Erimem realised just how stupid a question it was even before she had finished asking it.

'I was… looking for you?' The girl sounded hopeful rather than convincing.

'And you expected to find me in my brother's rooms?' She looked over Hanek's shoulder at the rumpled bed and then at the girl's own half-fastened clothing. 'And you had to undress to look in his bed?'

'Please, sister, do not be angry with her.' Mentu had emerged from an antechamber and was fastening his kilt. Like Hanek, he was flushed and wore a slightly guilty expression. He squeezed Hanek's hand swiftly as he passed her to confront Erimem. 'Don't be angry with her,' he repeated. 'If anyone is responsible for this deception, it is me. Be angry with me.' His grim expression eased into a wry smile. 'Or be pleased that I have found someone who has fascinated and captivated me.' He reached a hand back to Hanek, who grasped it and let herself be drawn forward. She was unwilling to meet Erimem's gaze directly and appeared to be concentrating on her mistress's shoulder.

'Why didn't you tell me?' Erimem's question could have been for either of them.

'Why do you think?' Mentu answered, more harshly than he had intended. He softened his tone as he continued. 'I am the subject of gossip, rumour and lies inside of the city.'

'Much of which you have brought on yourself,' Erimem reminded him.

Mentu nodded. 'That is true, but should Hanek suffer for my past?' His eyes lingered on Hanek a moment and both seemed to glow with happiness. 

'Very well,' Erimem finally agreed. 'I understand why you kept this matter a secret.' Her lips pursed petulantly. 'But you still should have told me.'

'You will tell no one?' Mentu pushed. 'Please, sister.'

Erimem studied them for a long moment. They seemed well suited. Hanek's family were wealthy and influential though not a particularly old family as Thebes measured such things. Hanek herself was intelligent and kind, and someone Erimem had found herself warming to as a friend. And Hanek also knew the palace, its politics and the way things worked at court. But the source of that experience could work against Hanek. 'Very well,' Erimem sighed. 'I will tell no one. But,' – she turned seriously to Hanek– 'you were right last night. My father will never accept his son marrying a servant.' Her eyes flashed to Mentu. 'You *do* plan to marry her?'

'Yes.' Mentu's reply was instant and left Erimem in no doubt that he was sincere. 'Perhaps our father will simply be pleased that I have taken his advice at last and chosen to take a wife – and perhaps to provide him with the grandchildren he craves.'

'You cannot marry a girl who dresses your sister, Mentu. Hanek, you are dismissed from my service immediately.' Erimem held a pause for a long moment before relenting. 'However, you are invited to stay as my guest. Our divine father is Pharaoh. Who will ask us to explain ourselves except him?' She turned to Mentu. 'Your face was quite the picture, brother. And you,' she smiled at Hanek. 'You must learn how easy my brother is to tease. It will be a useful thing to know when you are his wife.'

Mentu swept Erimem into a bearhug. 'Thank you.'

'Put me down!' Erimem squawked, her toes stretching to stay in contact with the floor, but when Mentu set her down, he saw that his sister was grinning.

'Thank you,' he repeated.

'You are lucky that you are my favourite brother,' Erimem tried to sound stern. 'I would not help Thutmose or Teti in this way.'

'Tch,' Mentu snorted dismissively. 'Thutmose has no interest beyond the army and Teti...' he let the name hang for a while. 'The gods alone know what thoughts pass through his head.'

'Mentu!' Erimem's voice was disapproving. 'Teti is...'

'Yes?' Mentu interrupted. 'What is Teti?' His eyebrows arched with interest.

'Different,' Erimem answered primly.

A hearty laugh erupted from Mentu. 'He's certainly different.'

'Stop it,' Erimem scolded. She hated it when people made fun of Teti and switched the subject quickly. 'You won't have been told of the banquet tonight? The Mitanni have sent an ambassador to negotiate peace.'

'Pah!' Mentu snorted. 'That means they know they can't defeat our armies and have come to beg for their futures.'

'I am pleased you are not Pharaoh,' Erimem said puckishly. 'Your words would start a war every month.'

'I assume I must attend,' Mentu sighed.

'Naturally,' Erimem agreed. 'And as my guest, so must Hanek.' She grasped the other girl's hand and led her towards the terrace. 'You,' she called to her brother, 'will see us later.'

For the reception of the Mitanni ambassador, Amenhotep had chosen the grandest and most imposing of the chambers in his palace. Every wall was adorned with images of Pharaohs smiting their various enemies to the ground and prayers of exultation to the divine power of Pharaoh surrounded the images of the god-kings standing over their defeated adversaries. It was intimidation on a grand scale – centuries of Egypt's proud military history surrounding anyone brought before the current King. Dozens of the palace guard, dressed in their finest, most colourful uniforms stood to attention in daunting rows at the edge of the central square of the chamber marked by enormous, inscribed pillars. A little behind the throne, a choir of girls sang a series of songs glorifying Pharaoh and his deeds to reinforce the message of Pharaoh's absolute might.

*The princes are prostrate, saying: 'Mercy!'*
*Not one raises his head among the Nine Bows.*
*Desolation is for Tehenu; Hatti is pacified;*
*Plundered is the Canaan with every evil;*
*Carried off is Ashkelon; seized upon is Gezer;*
*Yanoam is made as that which does not exist;*
*Isiral is laid waste, his seed is not;*
*Hurru is become a widow for Egypt!*
*All lands together, they are pacified…*

Intrigued by their Pharaoh's decision to meet the Mitanni ambassador, and curious to see the scene unfold, the court of the Palace had attended in full force and the crowd was moving fluidly as people moved from group to group, gathering the latest gossip and rumours, passing the latest titbits of news and, in some cases, dropping useful snatches of misinformation that would come in useful in the various rounds of politicking which were such a large part of life at court.

Antranak had been the first man inside the great chamber for the proceedings and had every intention of being the last man to leave. He moved through the crowd with a grace belying his size, playing the social game, nodding to those who required polite greetings, answering such questions as he had to before moving on. All the time he circulated, he was glancing from entrance to entrance, giving and receiving in return small, almost invisible signals from the men he had stationed around the room. Everyone entering the room would be scrutinised and anyone who raised even the slightest suspicion would be removed for interrogation. Besides the men inside the palace building, he had trebled the guard at every station and on patrol. He had also ensured that the army was on alert and ready for battle should this peace overture prove to be a ruse of some sort.

His good spirits disappeared as Horemship slid into view. The priest had his shrewish wife, Peshal, in tow and Antranak veered off to the side, joining briefly in a dull conversation until Horemshep had moved on and then Antranak continued on his way. The only person at court he despised more than Horemshep was the priest's wife. She was, if anything, more devious and ambitious than her husband. Every word said to her was memorised and returned later, twisted to suit her purposes. Antranak avoided the woman as if she were a leper. He was sure she was involved in unpleasant and illegal dealings in Thebes though he had never been able to find any solid evidence. He had often imagined the pleasure he would feel if, one glorious day, he was able to bring Horemshep and Peshal to their knees in front of the judge at the House of Justice. When found guilty – and in Antranak's dreams they were *always* found guilty, screaming their innocence and pleading for their lives – they would be executed. Horemshep's position would merit him a very special death. Perhaps buried up to his neck in the red lands for the jackals to feast on his eyes while he was alive, or perhaps buried alive in a casket of snakes. Peshal would die in agony. Her gut would be sliced open and her belly filled with insects and rats before being stitched shut. The creatures would eat her alive as they tried to free themselves. It would be a brutal and agonising death but, if even half of the stories Antranak had heard of Peshel and her cruel perversions were true, it was more lenient than she deserved.

The thought of putting Horemshep and his miserable harpy wife to the sword quite restored Antranak's good spirits and a broad grin had appeared on his weathered face as he passed Fayum and Shemek, heading for a large archway behind the gold throne.

'He looks happy,' Fayum murmured.

'That's not like him,' Shemek sniffed. 'He's usually a miserable jackal. He must have had some good news – or a pleasant thought. I wonder what…'

Fayum watched Antranak diappear from view. 'It's too late to ask him now,' he told Shemek.

The old man shrugged. 'We'll find out soon enough. I assume you'll be meeting us later?'

'Of course,' Fayum nodded eagerly. The three men met several times a month in one of the small courtyards near Antranak's quarters. On the surface it was simply three friends meeting to spend an evening in pleasant company but in truth there was far more to it than that. Each man spent his days in a different part of the palace's social circle. Antranak was a soldier and so knew the latest developments concerning the armies while Fayum, as a priest, albeit a lowly one, sat in a minor position on the Council of Priests and knew the latest political intrigues and rivalries among the various priests and temples. And Shemek? Somehow Shemek seemed to know absolutely everything else. Romantic entanglements, family feuds, business dealings… Shemek knew them all. Both Antranak and Fayum had long since given up asking how the old man came to know so much.

'Good lad.' Shemek patted his young friends shoulder. 'These days I'm too old to carry Antranak indoors by myself if he gets drunk.'

Fayum laughed indulgently. Though the three never drank heavily at these meetings, Shemek usually drifted off to sleep as the night wore on. Antranak would carry him indoors and put Shemek in his own bed before continuing his discussions with Fayum. It was an unspoken rule that Shemek's age and frailty were never mentioned.

Seeing a movement in the area behind the throne, Fayum nudged Shemek.

'Well spotted,' Shemek wheezed. 'You have eyes like a hawk. Just as well you don't have a nose like one or we'd never find a girl for you. Come on.' Clutching Fayum's arm for support, Shemek jostled and shoved his way through the crowd, making for his designated space. Everyone had an allocated area set by rank, age and seniority at court. To take a place was considered an unacceptable breach of protocol and was, on occasion, seen as an insult to Pharaoh. Some summers before, a merchant had stood among the elder priests to get a better view of Pharaoh. His punishment for this lapse had been to have his eyes plucked from his head so that he might not be tempted to look so closely at a living god again.

The movement Fayum had noticed was two lines of trumpeters, clad only in short white kilts moving into position just inside the arch Antranak had gone through. Ten stood in a row on each side of the doorway, an arm's length from his neighbour, and separated from the man opposite by around eight cubits, a distance roughly equal to the combined height of three average men. At a signal from the other side of the arch, the musicians raised their trumpets and blew a fanfare. The music was strident and imposing, demanding nothing less than absolute attention from the gathered crowd. When the trumpets brought their fanfare to an end, the sound was replaced immediately by the light trill of flutes and the soft, sweet voices of the choir singing the glories of Pharaoh. As their song reached a high crescendo a cymbal crashed and the music stopped. Amenhotep strode through the arch, followed by Thutmose with Antranak a further footstep behind. On either side of Antranak came Erimem and Mentu. Six of Antranak's most trusted soldiers marched in single file on either side of the group. Nesmut, Pharaoh's vizier had positioned himself by the throne and bowed low. The rest of the crowd dropped to their knees and bowed till their heads touched the floor.

Nesmut spoke in a loud, clear voice: 'Divine Pharaoh, living god and brother of Horus. Slayer of thousands, conqueror of Egypt's enemies. His arrows fly like lightning from the skies to vanquish his foes and his wisdom is without end. All-powerful god among us, Amenhotep, Pharaoh of the Two Kingdoms of Egypt.' Nesmut bowed low from the waist.

Amenhotep strode to his throne and stood looking out over the bowed heads in front of him. He left them bowing for a long moment as his father had taught him and turned to Thutmose who was, as ever, at his shoulder. 'Let them bow for a good time,' he said quietly. 'Always remind them of who is Pharaoh.'

Thutmose nodded expressionlessly. His eyes flicked to the side as a movement caught his attention. Six slaves were moving a heavy chair, ornately carved in a similar style to Amenhotep's throne into position alongside the Pharaoh's seat.

'You will sit by me,' Amenhotep nodded as the chair was set in place.

Thutmose eyed his throne a little nervously. 'My father does me a great honour.'

'No,' Amenhotep countered. 'Your father is proud to call you his son and heir, and if you are to take my place when I have joined my own father and the gods in the West, you will need to watch me and learn.'

Thutmose bowed. 'As my father wishes. But,' he added, straightening, 'if my father will permit it, I will continue to feel honoured.'

'I would not disagree with my son,' Amenhotep nodded. 'Now, have they bowed long enough or should they wait a little longer?'

'I would let them rise now. I am eager to see this emissary from the Mitanni.'

'Not just yet,' Amenhotep said gently, lowering himself into his throne and nodding for Thutmose to sit also. 'Never let them see you sit. When they look up they must see you seated and watching over them. And as for the Mitanni?' He snorted dismissively. 'Let them wait. They are here to beg. Let them beg when Egypt sees fit to hear them.' He surveyed the room for a moment longer, satisfying himself that no one had dared to look up before speaking. 'Rise,' he commanded.

Obediently, the assembled mass rose to their feet with Fayum helping Shemek haul himself upright. Slightly to the side of the raised level, Erimem and Mentu were seated on seats far plainer than those their father and brother occupied. Behind the two thrones, Antranak stood looking suspiciously out into the hall, his hand resting on the hilt of his sword. Amenhotep leaned back and spoke quietly to Antranak, who nodded quickly. Pharaoh looked as if he had expected no other answer and gave a slight gesture to Nesmut.

'Pharaoh will now accept the Mitanni,' the vizier announced. On his words, four Nubian eunuchs heaved at the giant marble doors at the far end of the hall. Slowly, the doors swung open revealing the Mitanni delegation. Six huge Mitanni soldiers stood in a row, each of them looking uncomfortable at being in the heart of their enemy's home and even more uncomfortable at being there completely unarmed. The two figures in front of them looked less on edge. One was a man so thin that even through his cloak it was obvious that he was little more than a skeleton. His grey skin tone and sunken eyes told of the disease that was eating at him. Despite his ailment, he stood proud and upright. Beside him was a smaller figure, also wearing a cloak with a hood pulled over the head concealing the face. At a signal from the vizier, the small party entered the hall and walked towards the throne at a respectfully slow pace. The soldiers' eyes flashed all around the hall, taking in the overwhelming numbers surrounding them but the two leaders kept their heads still and the man's eyes never wavered from the throne. Ten paces from the foot of the steps leading up to the throne the Mitanni soldiers stopped in a line. Their leaders continued five more paces before halting and bowing low in front of Pharaoh.

'Mighty Pharaoh does us great honour by agreeing to grant an audience.' The old man's voice wavered a little and there was a rattle deep in his throat when he breathed.

Amenhotep bowed graciously and signalled for the old man to continue.

'For many generations our nations have repeatedly gone to war...'

'Which we of Egypt have won,' Amenhotep interrupted smoothly.

The old man's head tilted slightly, deferring to Pharaoh. 'We are tired of these wars,' he said. 'My king would rather see peace between our lands than these constant battles.'

'I am not surprised,' Amenhotep roared with laughter. 'I, too, would weary of constant defeat.'

Again, the old man offered only a deferential nod.

'Do you have a name, old fellow?' Amenhotep asked.

'I am known as Terek, Majesty, and I am a humble servant of my king, Gadamare.'

'You must be humble indeed to serve a beaten king.'

A slight twitch at the corner of Terek's mouth was the only sign that the insult had caused offence. He ignored the comment. 'My king has sent me to broker peace with mighty Pharaoh. We have fought too often and too many wives of both nations have no husbands because of it. Too many children have no father.'

Amenhotep sat back in his throne thoughtfully. 'There may be some wisdom in what you say, old father. I will think on it and give you an answer in due course.'

Sitting to the side, and only peripherally involved in the proceedings as decoration, Erimem's attention had begun to wander from the exchange between Terek and her father and she let her eyes wander around the hall, picking out familiar faces when Amenhotep's use of the phrase 'old father' yanked her attention back to the throne. The term was usually reserved only for those wise men held in the highest regard. It was almost unheard of for Pharaoh to use the term, particularly to an outsider. She looked quickly to Mentu to see if he had also noted their father's unusual generosity but her brother's eyes were on Hanek, who was positioned near Fayum and Shemek. Obviously Mentu had wanted the girl close to people she would know – people who would take care of her in the scorpion pit of the court. For her part, Hanek gazed back at Mentu, an unmistakable gleam in her eye. Taking everything into consideration, Erimem was sure she had never seen two people fail so completely to keep a secret. A man with no eyes could have seen the fire passing between them. It was only on Erimem's third nudge that Mentu tore his eyes from Hanek and looked quizzically at his sister. She gave a slight nod towards the throne where Amenhotep was still talking with Terek. Despite the crowd and his obvious failing health, the old man refused to be cowed by the occasion.

'I am an old man,' he said. 'And I am not long for this world. I would like to see the young men here grow to be as old as I am and to see their children grow to adulthood – and then to watch those children raise a family of their own.'

Pharaoh sat for a moment. 'I see the wisdom in your words,' he said finally. 'And I feel that you believe them to be true. As a father, nothing is more important to me as seeing my son grow to manhood.' He looked proudly at Thutmose for a moment before returning his attention to Terek. 'But we have been to war too many times for me to be swayed by words alone.'

Terek nodded. 'My own king also knew this to be true. And so he has sent a gift to you – a symbol of his wish to forge an alliance between his kingdom and yours.' He held out an arm, inviting the other cloaked figure to step forward. 'He sends you the most prized possession from his palace.'

The figure reached up and pulled the hood back, letting long, thick dark hair fall loose. The slim shoulders flexed and the cloak slipped to the marble floor. A girl of no more than seventeen or eighteen stood facing the throne. The girl's skin had the olive tone of those who lived further to the north than the Mitanni. Her father had clearly brought a wife from beyond his own borders. Her figure also spoke of the islands to the north with rounded hips, a slim waist and large firm breasts. Beneath the mass of black hair the girl's face was probably the most beautiful Erimem had seen, even at court where only the most attractive girls were considered acceptable. She had high cheekbones, a delicate nose and startling green eyes that stared defiantly at the throne. She pushed her chin forward proudly. Only the continual nervous movement of her hand showed that the confidence was a mask. Her hand was clenched tightly into a fist and she was rubbing her thumb and forefinger together constantly.

Terek bowed. 'My king gives the mighty Pharaoh his only daughter, Miral.'

On cue, Miral prostrated herself at the foot of the step in front of Pharaoh's throne. 'I am your property, given to you by my father.' The girl's voice was strong but wavered a little as she forced the words out. 'Do with me as you see fit.'

Amenhotep looked at Terek in bemusement. 'What does your king expect me to do with her?'

The old man blushed slightly, the first time anything approaching healthy colour had appeared on his grey skin. 'Whatever you wish, Majesty,' he said. 'The girl is yours, given as a sign of good faith.'

For a moment, Amenhotep stared at the girl, who still lay face down in front of him. 'Stand up,' he ordered.

Miral did as she was told, the front of her dress falling open to reveal an expanse of cleavage as she leaned forward to steady herself.

'Your king had something more specific in his mind when he sent his daughter,' Amenhotep stated flatly to Terek. 'What was it? He did not send his daughter to clean the palace or work in my kitchens.'

Before Terek could reply, Miral spoke up. 'If that is what Pharaoh wishes me to do then I will do it.'

'But Pharaoh is, as always, correct,' Terek interrupted quickly. 'My king wishes to form an alliance not only of nations but also of families.'

'He is offering me the girl as a wife?'

Terek's head bobbed in agreement. 'Indeed, your Majesty.'

'I have more than enough wives already and I have said that I won't take another.' Amenhotep scrutinised Miral for a moment. 'Though perhaps she would make a fitting wife for my son.' He glanced at Thutmose. 'She's spirited and attractive enough.'

Thutmose leaned forward sharply and spoke quickly into his father's ear. For a moment, Amenhotep seemed surprised by his son's words but his face relaxed into an accepting expression. They exchanged a few more short words before Amenhotep nodded and turned back to Miral, who stood waiting, impassive except for the nervous rubbing of her fingers.

'Pharaoh has considered your father's suggestion.' Amenhotep said. 'He is correct in thinking that a joining of our families will act to stop hostilities between our nations, and a wise king knows that strength need not always come through war.' Terek's head bobbed in acknowledgement. 'Miral will join my house,' Pharaoh continued. 'She will be married to my son.'

Miral bowed to Amenhotep and then to Thutmose. 'I am honoured to...'

'You misunderstand,' Amenhotep interrupted sharply. 'You will not marry this son. Thutmose has already chosen his brides and selected a queen among them.' He waved a hand towards Mentu. 'You will be married to my second son, Mentuhotep.

Instictively, Mentu snapped to his feet, his mouth opening to protest. 'Father!'

'My son has something to say?' Amenhotep's voice was hard and cold, a tone showing the anger at being interrupted simmering beneath his calm expression. Mentu could only meet his father's unyielding gaze for a moment before wilting. Not even Pharaoh's own son would dare to challenge the king in public and expect to live.

'No, my father,' he said meekly and sank back into his chair. He cast a look of bewilderment at his sister then looked, very briefly, at Hanek's shocked face before turning his eyes to the floor, unable to look at the girl's dismayed expression any longer.

Miral and Terek's audience with Amenhotep lasted only a few more moments. Pharaoh acknowledged Terek's praises and compliments on his wisdom in accepting the offer of peace while Amenhotep graciously sent good wishes and blessings to King Gadamare of the Mitanni, along with a gift of fifty camels and 200 slaves. The precise details and contract for the marriage would be drawn up after negotiations between the two nations but both parties knew that the Egyptians were in the stronger position and the contract would follow whatever rules Amenhotep's advisers demanded. Amenhotep ordered that the union would take place during the festival of the Five Extra Days. Until then, Miral would remain within the palace where she could come to know her future husband. There was also an unspoken inference that she would be instructed in Egyptian life and in the ways an Egyptian wife would be expected to behave. If either Miral or Terek took offence at the suggestion that the Mitanni were less civilised than their Egyptian hosts, neither let it show and both bowed low to Pharaoh before leaving the hall. Terek would return to his king with the news and Pharaoh's gifts while Miral and the three Mitanni bodyguards she had been permitted to retain would be escorted to her new quarters inside the palace.

Mentu fidgeted unhappily as the reception stretched on interminably. He prayed to Ma'at the Goddess of Justice that it would be over quickly but the audience dragged on. He would never have insulted his father by daring to show his impatience but Erimem had spotted his restlessness more than once. Her face was calm but the message in her eyes was clear. He should control his anxiety until the audience drew to its natural end. He had already been too close to causing offence once. A second insult certainly would not be tolerated.

Finally the vizier brought a last wave of compliments and adulation to an end. The gathering fell to their knees and Amenhotep rose from his chair. With Thutmose following and the trumpeters playing a majestic fanfare, he swept from the hall. After a respectful delay, Erimem and Mentu followed. By the time they reached the door, Mentu was almost running.

Amenhotep was sitting at one of his favourite spots in a vine-covered pagoda on a small rise. Through the open sides he could see his gardens and orchards as well as anyone approaching from a hundred paces away. The expression on Amenhotep's face, and the fact that his personal guard had been banished to a respectable – and for them, uncomfortable – distance told Mentu that his father had been expecting him.

He bowed. 'I would crave a moment with my Pharaoh.' He gnawed nervously on his lip. 'No, I would like to speak with my father.'

Amenhotep nodded and indicated for Mentu to join him in the pagoda. 'Have you come to apologise for your outburst?'

The question was posed in a far gentler tone than Mentu had expected but he knew he could only give one answer. 'Yes, my father. I spoke out rashly. It was not my intention to embarrass you.'

Amenhotep waved the apology away. 'Then we need say no more on the matter,' he said, his voice relaxed and easy. He gestured for Mentu to take the padded seat opposite. 'I realise that the announcement will have been a shock for you.'

That brought a half smile to Mentu's face. 'My father has been honoured with many gifts by his brothers, the gods, but I didn't know that understatement was one of them.'

A laugh rumbled from Amenhotep. 'It's not one I use often, is it?'

'Why would a Pharaoh who has conquered as much of the world as is known ever need understatement?' The admiration in Mentu's voice was genuine and Amenhotep's tone softened further.

'I should have given you some warning,' he said wryly. 'Taken time to discuss the matter with you before making the announcement.'

'That would have been...' Mentu paused, searching for the right words. Private moments with his father such as this were rare and he didn't want to break the closeness he felt with Amenhotep. 'A most generous act, which I have no right to expect of Pharaoh.'

'But a father should have spoken to his son first,' Amenhotep countered. 'The choice of wife is an important matter. I should have called you to me first.'

'And I should have spoken with my father on the subject of my wife before now.'

'True,' Amenhotep agreed. 'You are of an age when you should have sons running around the palace.' He paused reflectively. 'In fact, all of my children are past an age when they should have been married.'

'I had found a particular girl. One who made me feel different to how the rest did.'

'Ah.' Understanding filled Amenhotep's face. 'And you love this girl? Then you should have told me.'

'I have made a promise to the girl,' Mentu continued. 'I have told her that I would take her as my wife.'

'And I have made a promise to the Mitanni that you will take their princess as your wife.' A long, heavy breath escaped from Amenhotep. 'Had I known of this other girl I would not have made that promise but I can't break my word now without offending the Mitanni.' He changed tack. 'This girl of yours. She is Egyptian?'

'Yes,' Mentu affirmed. 'Her father is a wealthy merchant in Thebes. I met her in the palace,' he said. 'She and Erimem know one another.'

Amenhotep pursed his lips. 'You cannot marry this girl,' he said finally. 'If she is a loyal subject of Pharaoh, she will understand when she hears.'

'She knows. She was at the reception.' The words were out before Mentu had time to think. He expected to be chastised for having brought the girl to court but there was only sympathy in his father's face.

'You must make the girl understand that this is no indication on her or on her family. We shall have to ensure that the family is shown favour in court and in business.'

So there was sympathy but no hint that Pharaoh would change his decision. 'I love her,' Mentu said simply.

'But you are also a prince of the Two Kingdoms and you have duties and responsibilities to Egypt.' Amenhotep laid a hand on his son's arm. 'You will marry the Mitanni girl,' he said, not unkindly. 'But in time, once you have sired a son by her to cement our alliance with her father you can take this merchant's daughter to your bed. But you must be discreet when you do. The Mitanni are a barbaric lot but the girl showed courage in coming to court, all but alone.' Amenhotep rose and stretched, arching his back to ease the stiffness that set in when he sat for too long. 'Treat her well, give her a son to tend and she will pay no heed when you disappear to see your mistress.'

'And until then?'

'Until then you will not see this girl.' Amenhotep's words cut into Mentu as surely as if Pharaoh had thrust a dagger into his son's heart but Mentu said nothing. 'The girl will know this was not your doing,' Amenhotep carried on. 'And if her love for you is genuine, she will wait a year or so until your wife is occupied with your son.'

A year. How could he be expected to tell Hanek that they could not see each other for a full year? A year in which he would be married to this Mitanni girl and sharing his bed with her. But his father's mind was made up and Mentu knew that nothing he could say or do would change it. Instead, he nodded his head in defeat and his shoulders sank.

'It won't be so bad,' his father promised. 'She's a fine-looking girl for a Mitanni. She'll be a pleasant enough duty for you and an agreeable distraction until you see your merchant's daughter again.'

Mentu forced a short laugh. He stayed with his father a short while longer before bowing and taking his leave. As Amenhotep watched his son leave, he felt pleased with what he had accomplished that day. The marriage would keep the Mitanni in check and a wife would be good for Mentu. The boy had even taken news of not seeing his sweetheart for a year with more dignity than Amenhotep had expected. Of course, he knew that in a year, Mentu would have forgotten this merchant's daughter. His beautiful young wife would make sure of that. But still, he was pleased with his son's reaction. The thought that Mentu might simply disobey his commands never once entered Pharaoh's mind.

And as Mentu walked away from his father, heading back towards his suite, a terrible, burning rage began to eat at him. In the time they had talked, Amenhotep had ignored Hanek's feelings completely. He had thought to buy her compliance with money and influence for her father while leaving Hanek alone for a year before she had the honour of being little better than a prince's whore. But more than anything, what angered Mentu most was that all through their talk, Amenhotep had never once even asked what Hanek's name was. But in spite of his anger, Mentu wore a resigned smile when he passed Antranak and Erimem.

'My father's word is law,' was all he said.

'That is a relief,' Antranak sighed. 'I had expected their meeting to go badly.'

Erimem watched her brother walk behind a column that stood as tall as twenty men. She shared Antranak's relief that Mentu had ultimately accepted their father's decision so stoically, but her heart broke for her brother, and also for poor Hanek. The girl's dreams and future had been ripped away in the cruellest way Erimem could imagine. She thought briefly of talking to her father, of trying to persuade him to reconsider, but she dismissed the thought as quickly as it had come. If Amenhotep wouldn't listen to Mentu, what chance did she, a mere daughter, have? Of his children, Amenhotep only truly listened to Thutmose, and it seemed to Erimem that marrying the Mitanni princess to Mentu had been Thutmose's idea. And that raised another question.

'Antranak, my good friend,' Erimem began in her most appealing voice.

'You want something,' Antranak interrupted. 'You only call me your good friend and use that tone of voice when you want something.'

'You're very suspicious,' Erimem scolded.

'And I'm right,' Antranak sniffed dryly. 'You want to know who Thutmose has picked as his first wife.' Erimem's jaw dropped slightly but she said nothing. 'Very well.'

'Who?' Erimem bubbled with excitement. 'I didn't think he bothered with women.'

'Only with this one,' Antranak assured her. He let his young friend stew for a few moments before relenting. 'The Lady Techvis will be a most agreeable queen, don't you think?'

'Techvis?' Erimem squeaked in surprise. Amongst the girls at court, Techvis was considered plain, dowdy even. She never wore as many jewels as the other girls and her clothes tended to sit uncomfortably on her, and yet Erimem found herself warming to the idea. Techvis had a good heart. She was kind and always gave food to the poor and the injured. Techvis would bring a warmth and generosity that would counter her brother's rather brusque nature. 'She is a good choice,' Erimem responded cheerfully, glad of some good news to raise her spirits. 'I approve.'

'As do I. Though I doubt if your brother was waiting for our approval,' Antranak added wryly.

'Naturally,' Erimem smirked. 'How did you find out? Did my father tell you?'

'Ah, now I must keep my secrets,' Antranak said, chuckling. 'And so must you. The lady's name hasn't been made public, so you must promise me that you will say nothing.'

'The gods themselves could not draw this from me,' Erimem promised.

Antranak eyed the sun with interest. 'You know, little one,' he said mischievously. 'The day is barely half over and two of Pharaoh's children are preparing to be married. Perhaps Pharaoh has something similar in mind for his daughter.'

Erimem hit him.

Mentu strode through the palace grounds, cutting past the guest quarters, heading for the square which would lead to his own apartments. Hanek would be there, waiting for him. Where else would she go at this time? His anger still burned but the object of his rage had shifted from his father to Mentu himself. He was a coward. He should have confronted his father. He should have refused this arrangement of a marriage and stood by the promise he had made to Hanek. He should have stood as a man and taken the consequences of following his conscience. But how could he disobey his father? How could he stand against a living god? He would have been sent to the House of Pain or executed or struck by a bolt of lightning from the heavens. His thoughts were in such a turmoil that he barely registered the presence of the young woman standing in the broad doorway of one of the guest apartments until he was only a dozen paces away and she bowed low in front of him.

'My lord,' Miral said, keeping her eyes respectfully to the ground.

Mentu looked straight at Miral for a moment, shocked by her sudden presence, and then swept by without saying a word or looking back at her.

Miral stayed low in her bow until Mentu had disappeared from sight and then she returned to her apartments and wept miserably.

# Chapter Four
## A Stranger in the Palace

ews of Mentu's impending marriage was greeted as a cause for celebration. The gods were to be praised and Pharaoh's wisdom was exalted in every temple, where extra prayers and sacrificial offerings were made to ensure a happy marriage for the prince. The feeling around Thebes was as much one of relief as of joy for the marriage. Most families in the city had a son or father or family friend who served in Pharaoh's armies and while they all knew it was a noble death to die for Pharaoh and would certainly send their loved one to an exalted place of honour in the afterlife, there was a feeling that this was a time for peace. An alliance that would secure the safety of their border to the north without a drop of blood being shed was something to celebrate. The city, always a noisy, bustling place, went about its business with extra vigour in the footsteps and slightly broader smiles on the faces.

Only inside Pharaoh's palace was there any sign of unhappiness about the marriage, and that was kept well hidden from the eyes of Pharaoh or his acolytes. Erimem had been surprised to find that Hanek had asked to continue in her duties as her handmaiden. In truth, Erimem was far from convinced that it was wise for Hanek to stay in the palace. Everything in the palace was centred on the marriage and would stay that way until Mentu and Miral were joined. Erimem had suggested that Hanek might wish to return to her family home until after the marriage. She had even offered to arrange for the girl to spend some months at one of Pharaoh's residences in Memphis, but Hanek had declined the offers. The other handmaidens had rallied around Hanek, protecting and supporting her. They had used the new bond that had developed with Erimem since the incident in the tavern to persuade their mistress and eventually, despite her reservations, Erimem agreed to let Hanek stay and the girl attacked her duties with a ferocious vigour and a false smile permanently on her lips. Her forced cheerfulness was heartbreaking.

If Hanek was working hard to convince the world that she was fine and that nothing was distressing her, then Mentu was following precisely the opposite tack. In the days following the announcement of his marriage, Mentu spent his time either alone in his rooms, brooding or stomping around the grounds of the palace in a foul temper, snapping orders at anyone he passed. It was only when he was in the presence of Amenhotep or Thutmose that Mentu forced himself to show any kind of cheer. Amenhotep dismissed any signs of unease in his son's behaviour as a result of sadness at giving up the merchant's daughter and nerves at the approaching marriage. He was sure that Mentu would come to terms with his lot given time. He would have been less sure if he had known that Mentu had steadfastly refused to meet with Miral even once in the days since she had been brought to the palace. The Mitanni princess was assigned handmaidens, dressmakers, sandal-makers and an army of all the people she would need to become part of court life, and she charmed them all with her humbleness, good humour and quick smile. The women at court spoke of her as a delightful and enchanting new princess while the men spoke quietly of her extraordinary beauty and of how lucky Prince Mentu was to have such a bride. Even the wig-maker had spoken warmly of Miral despite her refusal to have her head shaved before the marriage.

'If my husband asks me to do this, then I shall do it,' she had said. 'Until then, I will wear my own hair in the style favoured by your most gifted craftsmen.'

Only Mentu was unimpressed.

On a particularly hot and dry afternoon, Erimem found Mentu alone in one of the gardens, brooding. He was standing by a large pond, staring as the surface. Erimem dismissed her gaggle of handmaidens, relieved that the slight fever which was spreading through the palace meant that Hanek wasn't among them. She joined her brother by the pool.

'Oh, dear,' she said sadly. 'I believe the fish have all died.' She looked up at Mentu blandly. 'They saw the expression on your face and it frightened them to death.'

Mentu glowered back sourly. 'What reason have I to be happy?'

Erimem laid a hand on his arm but he retreated, pulling away from any kind of contact. 'Sit down,' she said.

'What?'

'Sit,' Erimem repeated. She slipped her sandals from her feet and kicked them away from the edge of the pond, then pulled her dress up to her knees and sat on the side of the pool, letting her feet dangle into the cool water. 'Like we did when we were young.'

'We're not children any more, Erimem,' Mentu said dismissively.

'Then stop sulking like a child and sit down,' Erimem snapped with a good deal more anger than she'd expected.

Mentu was as surprised by Erimem's outburst as she was and he did as he was told. They sat quietly for a moment, letting the water lap around their ankles. A little fish with scales of every colour in the rainbow swam up to Erimem's foot and took a tentative nibble at a brightly painted toenail. Disappointed that the nail wasn't a juicy morsel, the fish swam away lazily.

'I haven't seen you in days,' Erimem said, watching the fish disappear into the shade thrown by the far edge of the pond. 'Have you been sitting in your rooms, sulking?'

'I have not been sulking,' Mentu answered sharply. He stopped, realising how alarmingly his voice had risen. He had almost squeaked his answer – and sounded as if he *had* been sulking. 'I haven't been sulking,' he repeated in a calmer tone. 'I just feel...'

'Lost?' Erimem interrupted. 'Confused? Unhappy? Lonely because you miss Hanek? You don't know what to do but you think you should be doing something?'

'Yes,' Mentu agreed miserably. 'All of those.' He gave her a sidelong glance. 'When did my young sister become so wise?'

Erimem sighed. 'When she saw Hanek acting in a very similar way – as she has done since your marriage was announced.'

'How is she?' Mentu almost fell over his words in his rush to hear of Hanek. 'Where is she? I noticed she wasn't in your pack of simpering hyenas. Ow!' He yelped as Erimem thumped his leg.

'Do not talk of my friends in that way,' she rebuked him, then her face became serious again. 'Hanek is in her quarters. She and two of my other girls have had the fever for three or four days.' Seeing the worry in Mentu's face, she continued quickly. 'The girls say it is nothing serious. She'll recover in a few days.'

'But she must eat,' Mentu blurted. 'Tell her... tell her that I said she must take better care of herself.'

'Very well, I will pass your message to her.' Erimem didn't sound hopeful. 'And what of you? You should eat as well, and not just drink beer through the night.'

Mentu's eyebrow raised slightly. 'Have you been spying on me, monkey?'

Erimem leaned forward conspiratorially. 'Yes.' Mentu's eyebrow rose a little further. 'Well, actually, no,' Erimem admitted. 'But my handmaidens hear many things and...'

'And they report back to you,' Mentu interrupted. 'Antranak should put you and your girls in charge of his spies,' he said sourly. 'No one would dare make a move against Egypt with you and them on guard. We could all sleep safe in our beds. Except that you'd have such a close eye on us you'd probably want to know what was going on in our beds as well.'

'Most people know what's gone on in your bed,' Erimem riposted quickly.

Mentu looked set to retort angrily but the annoyance in his face disappeared, replaced by a sad resignation. 'Sadly for us both, as little happens now in my bed as happens in my dear sister's.'

'Good,' Erimem answered primly. 'As it should be.'

Mentu snorted. 'And that proves it is long past time you had a husband.'

Erimem was just beginning what she thought was a splendidly witty retort when a movement over Mentu's shoulder caught her eye and the words died in her throat. Mentu waited for the barb to come and it took him a moment to notice that Erimem was distracted. He turned to see what had caught her eye. He stiffened as he saw Miral walking towards them.

Mentu sprang to his feet and reached for his sandals. Without bothering to pull them on, he strode off in the opposite direction from Miral.

'Mentu?' Erimem yelped. 'Mentu, where are you going?' There was no reply. By the time Miral had joined Erimem at the side of the pond, Mentu was long gone.

'I...' Erimem faltered, trying desperately to find something to say to the girl. 'I don't...'

'It's all right,' Miral interrupted, holding up a conciliatory hand. 'The same thing has happened each time I have tried to speak with him.'

Erimem choked. 'He has treated you this way before?'

'Several times. I fear I have offended your brother in some way.' Miral paused, her green eyes questioning. 'You *are* Erimem?'

'Yes,' Erimem nodded.

Miral relaxed a little, clearly relieved that she hadn't interrupted Mentu in some romantic tryst. 'I thought I recognised you from that day I arrived, but there were so many faces.' A slight crack appeared in the girl's calm veneer. 'It was a little daunting. It will take me time to remember everyone's name.'

'I hear you are popular here in the palace already.'

'With the servants and slaves,' Miral said bitterly, and then words began to pour out. 'The man who will be my husband won't look at me and I have yet to meet anyone who isn't a slave or a servant or who hasn't been paid to make me clothes or...' the words caught in her throat and Miral drew a deep breath to calm herself. 'I have travelled to a foreign country, learned to speak a foreign language and been sold into a marriage to spare my people from future wars and the only people I have to speak with are servants and slaves.'

The girl was close to tears. *'Is this what is in store for me?'* Erimem thought. *Sent to a foreign king as a trophy wife to keep a peace between nations but without any hope of ever being happy there? Used as a breeding cow to produce children for a husband she might despise or who might treat her as badly as Mentu was treating Miral now?* She felt a rush of understanding and sympathy for Miral and grasped the other girl's hand.

'I will talk with Mentu,' she said firmly. 'I will make him see you.'

'No!' Miral recoiled as if she'd been slapped. 'I have little enough left to me. At least leave me some shred of pride.'

'All right,' Erimem backed away from the subject. She would still talk with

Mentu but she would be discreet about it – and she wouldn't tell Miral. As a rule, Erimem followed her first impressions of people and her immediate reaction was that she liked this girl. She liked her fire and she admired the courage Miral had shown in facing Amenhotep in his own court. And she also liked Miral's pride. 'All right,' she repeated. 'I won't talk to Mentu.' *For now*, she added to herself.

'Why does he hate me?' Miral asked. 'Does he despise all of my people or is it only me?'

Erimem reached for a sandal and slipped it on. 'It isn't really about you at all. There was a girl. Mentu was very taken with her.'

'Go on,' Miral prompted. 'Please.'

'Well,' Erimem hesitated, unwilling to disclose too much of her brother's life to a stranger. But perhaps if Miral knew some of the reasons for Mentu's actions, she would understand why he was so upset... 'All right,' Erimem picked up her thread. 'There was a girl from the palace. Mentu had decided he wanted to marry her.'

'Ah.' A look of understanding appeared on Miral's face. 'And then he was told that he would marry me'

Erimem nodded. 'Yes.'

'And the girl?' Miral asked. 'Was she in favour of the match?' She hurried on, answering her own question. 'Of course she was. Why would she refuse a prince? Especially one as handsome as Mentu.'

'I don't think it's because he's a prince.' Erimem automatically sprang to Hanek's defence. 'I do believe that she loves him.' She stopped short. Had she seen a hint of jealousy in Miral's eyes? 'Did you say that you think my brother is handsome? I promise I won't tell him.'

A blush crept up Miral's face and coloured her cheeks. She stared coyly at the ground. 'I think I could not have chosen a finer husband for myself. He is young and strong. I am told that he is usually kind and funny.' A shy little smile tugged at the corners of her mouth. 'And I think he as handsome as any man I have ever seen. And now I know that when he loves, he loves with all his heart.' She paused, her voice trailing sadly.

The inference was obvious. Mentu would have been the ideal husband for Miral. Except that he loved someone else.

'My brother can be stubborn,' Erimem offered. 'But he won't stand against my father's wishes. You will be married.'

'But what kind of marriage will it be?' Miral asked. 'I will have a husband that everyone knows would rather be with another woman.'

'But he will be with you,' Erimem countered. For the moment, she thought it best not to mention that the girl in question was one of her own handmaidens.

'Perhaps,' Miral sighed. 'But I must accept that I am in no position to let my pride stand between me and my duty.'

'Give him time,' Erimem urged. 'Once he gets to know you he will happily accept you as his wife. I know him. He is just stubborn.'

'When I was young, I has a horse who was stubborn. No matter how hard I worked with the horse or how much care and affection I gave him, he wouldn't do what I wanted.'

'What did you do?'

'I kicked it and ran crying to my father. I don't think I can do that now.'

'But you can come to me,' Erimem promised. 'And if Mentu insults you again we will both kick him together.'

Miral laughed. It was the first time Erimem had seen any genuine happiness on the other girl's face and the effect was spectacular. For a moment she was vibrant and alive, the natural beauty of her features made friendlier and more appealing by the warmth in her expression. She really was remarkably beautiful. Neither girl spoke for a moment, happy to hold on to the friendly moment. They both knew they would be dragged back to their duties soon enough.

'The gardens are beautiful,' Miral said finally. Her eyes ran from the pond to the thick, lush grass beneath her feet. 'I had no idea that grass could be so green.'

'It usually isn't,' Erimem confessed. 'But my father saw this on one of his marches to the north. He liked it so much he demanded that he have some in his own palace.'

'What else does he have in the palace? I have hardly had time to set foot outside my apartments.'

'It' s past time you saw the palace properly.' Erimem grasped Miral's arm and led her away.

'But I should go back,' Miral protested. 'People will be waiting for me.'

'Let them wait,' Erimem said airily. 'I am Pharaoh's daughter. If anyone has a complaint remind them of that.'

As Erimem led Miral towards her father's favourite orchard, a lonely figure watched their backs slide into the shade of an avenue of sycamore trees. Hanek dropped the tray of wine and figs she had been bringing to Erimem and she fled back to the palace.

# Chapter Five
## Walking with the Dead

Pharaoh was not often troubled. From the moment he was born, the heir to the throne was taught that when he was Pharaoh, he would be infallible; that he would be a god. And when he took the throne, every decision Pharaoh made was unquestioned and every order was followed implicitly. At no time was there any reservation over whether he was right or not – it was a given fact that Pharaoh was always right.

One person, however, was entitled to question Pharaoh – and that was Pharaoh himself. Sitting alone in one of his chambers, Pharaoh was taking in the view the room gave of the wonderful sight that was the flickering lights of Thebes at night. This view of his capital always cheered Amenhotep. People – his people – would be living their lives by eating, drinking, singing or talking. Some would be tending their children, others would be making love, but whatever they did, they did in the knowledge that their Pharaoh would protect them and keep them safe. And at that moment, safety and protection were high on their Pharaoh's list of thoughts.

As he always did in those few moments when he felt the need of advice, Amenhotep had summoned the three men whose opinions he needed. Thutmose had arrived first, followed quickly by Antranak. Horemshep was last to arrive, having had furthest to travel from the Temple of Horus where he had been leading offerings of prayers. He arrived sweating and slightly out of breath but still managed to offer praise and apologies to Pharaoh. Amenhotep waved the obeisance aside. Protocol dictated that he should have invited Nesmut, the vizier, but he had long since given up any hope of hearing Nesmut say anything worth listening to. The man was well suited to ceremonies where his rich voice and respectful choice of phrase were exactly what was demanded by the situation, but in a meeting such as this where an honest opinion was needed, Nesmut was worse than useless. He would listen to everyone's opinion and agree with every one of them, no matter how wildly different they were. The man had no ideas of his own. Or if he did, he hid them behind a fatuous, simpering exterior. Amenhotep had quickly learned not to invite Nesmut to these occasions.

Amenhotep sucked in a deep breath, relishing the slight hint of his favourite jasmine brought by the night's cool breeze. It relaxed him a little. 'As you know, my son, Mentu, is to be married to the Mitanni girl within months.'

No one was surprised that Horemshep spoke first. When he had Pharaoh's ear, he always spoke first. 'And all of Egypt and her people give thanks for it.'

'Not all of Egypt, priest.' Amenhotep disagreed brusquely. 'Mentu himself is still far from pleased.'

'He will come round,' Antranak said with certainty. 'His Pharaoh has spoken. No, his father has spoken,' he corrected himself. 'He will do his duty by you and by Egypt.'

'I don't doubt that for a moment,' Amenhotep said lazily. 'But it's not Mentu that concerns me.' He waved a hand towards the open window and the flickering lights of Thebes. 'It's the people. If we are to have a lasting peace with the Mitanni, there should be a delegation of their people here for that marriage.'

'Mitanni? In the palace?' Antranak choked. 'Pharaoh, I…'

'Think it's a terrible idea,' Amenhotep interrupted, though his tone wasn't unkind. 'You think it's a risk we should not consider taking. Am I correct?'

'My Pharaoh is always correct,' Antranak nodded slightly. 'I have fought the Mitanni too often to ever want to see one stand in this palace, much less an entire party of them.'

'Who will all be unarmed,' Horemshep offered smoothly. He adopted his most persuasive tone, the one normally reserved for wealthy merchants when he was persuading them that a large offering to his temple would make their afterlife more comfortable. 'Majesty, if we are to have a lasting peace with the Mitanni, which we all want…' he paused, waiting hopefully for Antranak to disagree but the soldier stayed quiet. 'Then it is only right that a small party of the Mitanni should attend the celebrations. To snub them would insult their nation and destroy any good feeling between our peoples that the marriage would bring. And,' he cast a sly sideways glance at Antranak. 'I am sure that Antranak's guards can protect us from a handful of unarmed men. At least I would hope so.'

'You would do better to hope that my men are never called on to save your miserable life,' Antranak snapped. 'Should that arise they may prove to be as incompetent as you claim.'

'Enough bickering.' Amenhotep's voice cracked sharply. The exchange ended instantly, though no one in the room had any dobt that the ill-feeling between Antranak and Horemshep would surface again before long. Amenhotep turned to his son. 'Thutmose?' he asked. 'What do you say?'

'My heart is with Antranak on this matter,' Thutmose replied instantly. Unlike Antranak or Horemshep, he had no need to gauge each word carefully and spoke with the confidence his father had drilled into him. 'Like Antranak I have fought the Mitanni. I have tasted their blood. I have seen them kill good men – men I was proud to fight alongside. My heart tells me that we have fought too long to keep them away from our gates to simply invite them in.'

Antranak grunted his agreement.

'However,' Thutmose continued. 'I also see the sense in Horemshep's words.' He ignored the priest's obsequious bow, barely keeping his dislike of the man out of sight. 'We would be wise to invite a party of Mitanni to the marriage – a small party. I would suggest that it be as small a group as protocol will allow and that they be permitted no weapons inside the city boundaries.' He glanced at Antranak, who nodded reluctantly. 'Guests at a marriage celebration in Pharaoh's palace will have no need of weapons.'

Amenhotep thought for a moment before nodding his agreement. 'Like my son and you, my good friend Antranak, I am torn between the messages from my heart and my head.' He pulled a deep breath. Somehow, the jasmine's scent seemed sour to him now, as if its beauty had begun to fade as it did every autumn. 'Very well,' he sighed. 'Bid them come. But keep their number small and have them leave their arms with our sentries at the city's edge.' He slapped a hand onto Antranak's shoulders. 'They will have no need for weapons with you and your soldiers on guard, Antranak. And,' Amenhotep continued, beckoning for a servant to bring wine, 'everyone including the Mitanni will know that that you are watching them as well as guarding us.'

In the days that followed their initial meeting by the pond, Erimem made a point of seeing Miral every day. Even if she could stay only a few moments, Erimem didn't let a day pass without the other girl seeing someone she recognised and, hopefully, trusted. As it turned out, she usually found she had spare time in the afternoon. She spent every morning with her bodyguards, practising with the spear, dagger and sword, and had just started learning the use of the khepesh, a sword with a curved, scimitar-like blade. The daggers felt light and comfortable in her hands but she had struggled with the khepesh. The long curve of the blade meant that the balance of the weapon was different from a sword and it felt unwieldy to her, so she concentrated on working with the daggers and on improving the archery skills she had been learning since she was a child, desperate to join her father on a lion hunt.

When the sun rose too high for the practice to continue, Erimem would return to her rooms and be bathed by her handmaidens, who had long since given up complaining about the risks she was taking. Then she would eat and sleep a while letting Ra, the sun, slip towards the horizon and cast merciful shadows which cooled the palace grounds. It was usually then that Erimem chose to visit Miral. By then the Mitanni princess was normally desperate to escape the clutches of the dressmakers and wig-makers desperate to transform her into the perfect Egyptian bride.

Most days Erimem and Miral would walk in the gardens. They quickly discovered that they were both fascinated by the various plants and flowers that Pharaoh had brought to his palace from the furthest reaches of the world. An army of gardeners fought against the sun to keep the plants alive for Pharaoh and they both wondered what kind of lands were home to these plants. They found that they both shared the desire to travel to these far-off places and to see the world. But they both knew that they were destined to spend their days living inside of the palace, pampered and bored.

As the days passed, a friendship between the girls began to form and Miral began to talk openly of her home and of her family. Her mother had been a Greek woman his father had fallen desperately in love with while he was a young prince, eager for conquest. He had returned from his travels with almost no captured treasure but happy with his new wife.

'My grandfather was not so happy,' Miral said, a wistful, far-off expression ghosting onto her face. 'He had sent my father to bring back treasures he could use to pay for an army. He was uncontrollable with rage until he heard that my mother was pregnant. When he knew he was to be a grandfather, my father's failings were forgiven. More so when she presented him with a grandson. She died six summers ago. And my brother was killed in the last battle between us.' Miral held a hand up quickly to calm any apologies Erimem might offer. 'He was a soldier and the war was caused by my people not yours. You have nothing to apologise for.'

'But it must be painful for you to be here,' Erimem protested.

Miral shrugged. 'It would be more painful for our armies to go to war again. And I think I have a friend here.' She looked to Erimem. 'Do I?'

'Of course you do.' Erimem beamed. 'Now tell me, has my brother spoken to you?'

Miral's lips pursed uncomfortably as she contemplated her answer.

'No.' Erimem answered for her. 'I shouldn't have wasted my breath asking.'

'I am sure he is just very busy,' Miral offered.

'He's very stubborn,' Erimem disagreed in disgust. 'When his mind is made up it is easier to move the great Sphinx.'

'I suppose he must be finding this as difficult as I am,' Miral mused. Seeing Erimem about to question her, Miral carried on. 'I had a good idea that my life would always lead to something like this. He can't have expected this.' She pulled a deep breath and Erimem was surprised to see the lack of condemnation in the other girl's face. 'In fact, I hold less anger towards him now that you have told me of the girl he had planned to take as his wife.' She forced a wry smile. 'I shall have to wait for him and trust your gods that they will have him find a place in his heart for me.'

In her own heart, Erimem had doubts that her brother would ever truly accept Miral as his wife, but she stayed quiet and the afternoon had passed, like most others they spent together in a comfortable friendship.

Later in the day she had spoken with Miral about Mentu, Erimem found that Mentu wasn't the only person caught between Miral and Hanek.

'Have the gods marked me with some plague?' Erimem demanded of Hanek. 'Have I grown an extra head?' she continued. 'Or has the nose on my face turned upside down?' Now she did wait for an answer. 'Well?' she demanded impatiently.

'N-no,' Hanek stuttered.

'Then why have you been looking at me as if I had?' Erimem asked. 'Why are you looking at me as if I were a leper. Why?' Her voice softened. 'Why, Hanek? I thought we were friends?'

'So did I,' Hanek answered miserably.

'What happened?'

'She did. The Mitannite,' Hanek spat the name bitterly. 'She's taken everything from me. She took my husband.'

'She didn't take him,' Erimem countered. 'They were put together by Pharaoh. Neither of them had a choice.'

'And then she took my friend,' Hanek continued. 'Every day you see her. How can you spend your days with her when you know how much she has hurt people here?'

'Because she is as hurt as anyone!' Erimem snapped. 'She is alone here, without a friend and about to marry a man who has made it clear to her that he would rather marry another. She is as lonely and hurt as you are, Hanek.'

'I hate her.'

'No. I will not allow that. You may hate what is happening but Miral is not responsible for that any more than you are. I know you have been struggling against the fever, Hanek,' Erimem said gently. 'And I know that your heart must sicken too. Have you thought again about leaving Thebes for a time? The physicians say that the air to the north can cure the fever.'

'I think I will,' Hanek mumbled. 'Perhaps just before they are married. I couldn't bear the thought of being here while he took her into his bed. I have family to the north. My father's sister. Perhaps I will go there. It will take a little time to arrange.'

'I will deal with that,' Erimem promised. 'I will have Antranak assign you an escort so that you are safe in the red lands.'

'You are very kind.'

'Is it kindness to help a friend?' Erimem wondered which of her friends she had helped by persuading Hanek to leave Thebes – Miral or Hanek herself? *Hopefully both*, she thought.

The night was unusually cold for Thebes and was made even more bitter by the chill wind that blew in a choking drizzle of fine sand and chased the clouds across the sky, occasionally blotting out the crescent moon. Khofrek huddled deeper into his cloak and cursed his luck for drawing night duty again. He should have been at home, lying warm and comfortable in bed beside his wife instead of standing outside freezing half to death. By now, he estimated, just about everyone in the city – even those who did their shady business after dark – would be safely nestled under a blanket near a healthy fire. Another gust of wind blew in more sand. Khofrek choked and spat out the sand but he could still feel it rough inside of his mouth. He thought he had seen the last of breathing in dust and sand when Antranak had offered him the move from the Pharaoh's regular army to the palace guard. There had been a number of reasons for Khofrek to accept. Seeing his children grow up and spending more time with Silliba, to his eyes still the most beautiful woman in Egypt even after bearing him two children, were reason enough but almost as important to him was the idea of not marching through endless deserts breathing in mouthful after mouthful of dry, life-draining sand. He had always hated that. There were times he had felt as if his throat were being stripped of flesh by the rough texture of the sand.

Khofrek was so wrapped up in his thoughts of a warm supper and a warmer bed when he was finally able to go home after his guard was over that he didn't see the slight movement in the darkness behind him. Any sound the figure in the black cloak made was blotted out by the wind. The first inkling Khofrek had that there was anyone near him was when he caught the moonlight glinting on the blade of a long, thin dagger as it flashed upwards but by then, it was too late. He felt deep, sharp pain as the blade slid into his side. He felt the dagger scraping along his ribs and the hot blood begin to pour down his chest. In the few moments before darkness engulfed him, he knew that he was going to die. He tried to say Silliba's name but couldn't find any breath. His last thought was a prayer to Horus to protect his family and then he let himself slip from this world and set out on his journey to the afterlife.

Khofrek's murderer slipped the dagger back into the folds of the cloak and pulled the thick material forward to keep their face hidden. The figure kicked Khofrek's corpse and waited for a reaction. When none came, satisfied that the guard was dead, the killer pulled back the bolt on the door and slipped out into the darkness beyond.

In the morning, as she had been bathed and dressed by her handmaidens, Erimem had watched Hanek carefully. There was a little more life about the girl this morning and she made a point of letting Erimem see her eating some bread and figs. She was still far from the Hanek Erimem had come to think of as a friend but at least there was some improvement and Erimem knew she could hope for little more than that. Hanek's heart had been broken and there was nothing she or anyone else could do about it. She had been wrong to let Hanek stay.

By trying to give the girl the small comfort of staying close to Mentu, she had only extended the pain of the separation. It was for the best that she would be leaving. She would miss Hanek but it would be better for the girl –

and better for Mentu and Miral as well – if the girl did leave to get on with her life elsewhere. She was a pretty girl and from a good, well-connected family. She would find a husband soon enough.

It was only after she had been bathed, anointed and dressed that Erimem noticed a slight change in her bodyguards. They were standing just a little closer than they normally did and their eyes were constantly looking at every door and window and, whenever they saw anyone enter, their hands automatically reached for the handles of their swords. It was as if they were expecting something to happen. Something dangerous.

Erimem waited until the handmaidens were distracted by their tasks before raising the subject with her bodyguards. They refused to comment but passed a message from Antranak that Erimem's training would be cancelled for the next few days. Soon enough, one of the handmaidens scampered in with news that one of the palace guard had been horribly murdered inside the palace grounds near the east gate the night before. A strange mix of dread and excitement ran through Erimem. She was genuinely sorry that one of the honoured guards who protected the palace had been slain but she also felt a slight hint of excitement at something so terrible happening so close to her. Ignoring the protests of her bodyguards, who had no option but to run after her, Erimem set off for the west gate.

The change in the atmosphere inside the palace grounds she noticed en route was startling. Everyone from handmaidens to gardeners to palace guards moved in pairs. No one seemed willing to be alone, and each of the pairs talked in hushed conversations, worry etched on their faces. Even the guards, all of whom she had guessed had seen battle in their time, seemed shaken by the murder. No one seemed able to believe that a murder had taken place inside the palace of mighty Pharaoh.

At the west gate, she found Antranak surrounded by a small group of his troops, priests and their acolytes inspected and tended the body of the guard, anointing the remains with holy oils and saying prayers over the corpse.

'Erimem, what are you doing here?' he demanded. 'This is no place for you.' He turned his rage to her bodyguards. 'And you two were told to keep her away from here. You'll both be punished for this.'

'It wasn't their fault,' Erimem protested. 'Their job is to protect me and I wanted to come here. It's my fault not theirs.'

Antranak grunted. 'What do you want here, Erimem? This isn't an entertainment. It's not something to be gawped at.'

'I know that,' Erimem snapped back, instantly regretting the sharpness of her tone. Antranak took the well-being of his troops seriously. He had been a soldier all of his life and viewed his service in the army as a sacred commitment, an honour granted by the gods. To Antranak, this murder would be an insult to those gods, to Pharaoh and to his own ability as a commander. She also knew that he would feel as though a member of his family had been taken from him. The tortures he would inflict on the killer would be truly awful. 'Do you know what happened?'

'Of course I do,' Antranak snapped. 'I...' His voice trailed off, and he sighed heavily. 'I know less than I should,' he admitted. 'The body makes no sense.'

'In what way?' Erimem slipped past Antranak and peered through the small army of attendants and priests at the body. Dozens of stab wounds covered the torso and arms, each of them tearing deep into the flesh and often overlapping with other cuts. Erimem guessed that there were at least thirty or forty wounds. She flinched as a priest carefully pressed back a small V-shaped fold of skin made by two stab-wounds bisecting. She wanted to not look at this terrible sight but something had piqued her curiosity.

'Erimem, will you come away?' Antranak pulled again at her arm but Erimem yanked herself free.

'There isn't much blood,' she said with curiosity. 'Why is that?'

Antranak's mouth, halfway open to chide her again, snapped shut. 'That's what I thought,' he said finally. 'I have seen many men cut down in battle. There was always more blood than this. Even the priests cannot explain it.'

The priests went about their work, putting oils onto the wounds and preparing the body to be moved.

'There's blood here.' Erimem skipped passed a priest and pointed to a broad black patch on the ground where the guard's blood had seeped onto the sand.

'Yes, I know,' Antranak muttered. 'It comes from one of the wounds in his chest. There.' He pointed to one of the cuts. 'It must have pierced his heart.'

'Perhaps,' Erimem said thoughtfully. 'But there are other wounds here that would have hit his heart. Why didn't they bleed the same way?'

'I don't know,' Antranak answered reluctantly. 'I asked the priest the same thing. They had any number of replies. Utter nonsense, all of them,' he snorted. Bluster to hide the fact that they don't know why he bled this way.'

One of the priests detached himself from the group preparing the corpse and joined Antranak. 'We have as much idea as the general here,' Fayum said sourly. Antranak glowered back.

'I didn't see you, Fayum,' Erimem said. She was glad to see her friend. With a murder taking place inside the palace, she knew she would feel more comfortable surrounded by familiar faces.

'Have you forgotten my face already?' Fayum teased. 'Or am I too lowly a priest to be a friend of Pharaoh's daughter?'

Antranak grunted. 'Better you than Horemshep or that rat-faced disgrace from the House of Anubis.'

'Antranak!' Fayum hissed, looking nervously towards the other priests. 'They'll hear you.'

'Let them,' Antranak snapped. 'My opinion of the Council of Priests is no secret.'

'Neither is their opinion of you,' Fayum countered. 'And Horemshep is bound to use this murder happening here – in the grounds of the palace you protect – to make life difficult for you.'

Antranak rubbed a hand over his eyes. He felt tired. Tired and angry. Angry with the murderer, angry with the priests for their conniving, angry with Erimem for being here... but mainly he was angry with himself because one of his men was dead and he couldn't see any way to make progress in solving the slaying. 'You're right,' he conceded. 'I'm helping no one by shouting and losing my temper. What can you tell me about the body?'

'Very little,' Fayum answered sadly. 'We're as puzzled by it as you are. He's been stabbed almost forty times but only that one blow to the heart has really produced any great amount of blood. As Antranak rightly pointed out, we have many suspicions but no solid explanation. Some of my brother priests believe that the heart is not like any other part of the body and the blood in it might be different, too.'

'Rubbish,' Antranak grumbled. 'I've cut men's hearts out myself. The blood is exactly the same as runs anywhere else in the body.'

'I agree,' Fayum continued. 'But there is something different about the blood from his heart.'

'In what way,' Antranak demanded.

Fayum rubbed his head, clearly confused. 'This blood from the wound in his heart was thinner, younger than the blood from the other wounds. It's as though he has old blood everywhere except in his heart.' Fayum dropped his voice. 'Some of the other priests are saying the guard must have been cursed.'

'He was a good man,' Antranak stated, his tone leaving no room for argument. 'I knew him for years. He served under me in the regular army before following me here.' An undeniable expression of guilt settled on his face. 'And I persuaded him to join me here. I am as guilty in his death as if I had stabbed him myself.' He held up a hand to quash any arguments. 'But I will find his killer and then there will be a reckoning.' He looked sadly at his fallen trooper a final time then turned away. 'Take him to be prepared for burial,' he told Fayum. 'Find what you can from his body but treat him with respect. He was a good man.'

'He didn't mean to insult all of the priests, Fayum,' Erimem said, consoling her friend.

'I know,' Fayum said heavily. 'He's a good man. He gets to know every man under his command. He knows their names, if they have sons... and they love him for it. He could lead them into the Underworld and they would follow him without a word. And he takes every death under his command personally.'

Erimem gazed at Antranak's broad back as he stormed towards the nearest of the palace buildings. 'He shouts and blusters,' she said softly. 'But I have never known anyone with a better heart.'

'Nor have I,' Fayum agreed. 'He has been more of a father to me than my own father ever was.'

'And to me,' Erimem echoed quietly. When she saw the startled expression appear on Fayum's face she added quickly, 'Or a favourite uncle, anyway. My father is always busy with affairs of state.'

'Ah,' Fayum nodded his understanding. 'And that is why it was Antranak who wiped your nose and told you frightening stories at bedtime.'

'Yes.' Erimem smiled wistfully, remembering Antranak bounding around her bed-chamber on all fours, bellowing as he had pretended to be a bear. 'That was a long time ago.'

'I thought it was last month,' Fayum said innocently.

Erimem's eyebrow quirked slightly but she didn't rise to the bait. 'I hear it's you and Shemek he has to tuck into bed now,' she said lightly. 'He tells me that neither of you can hold your beer.'

'That's probably true,' Fayum conceded. 'The man can drink beer like a thirsty ox at an oasis and it has no effect on him at all.' Fayum touched a hand to his scalp and it came away glistening with sweat. The sun was rising higher in the clear morning sky and the temperature was beginning to soar. Reluctantly, he accepted that he would have to return to tending the guard's body. 'I should continue my task.'

Erimem knew how important it was for a body to be treated properly before being entombed. If the corpse remained out much longer flies and insects would begin to desecrate it. 'You're right,' she nodded. 'Let me know if you find anything unusual.'

'Let *you* know?' Fayum sounded surprised.

'Yes, *me*,' Erimem insisted firmly. 'There is something unusual about this man's death and I would very much like to know what it is. So, if you find anything out of the ordinary, tell me. After you've told Antranak, obviously,' Erimem added. 'I don't think he would be very happy if you told me first.'

Fayum smiled thinly. 'I don't think he'll be happy that I'll be telling you at all. Now if you'll excuse me?' He bowed slightly and then returned to his brothers around the body.

Erimem looked away from the corpse. The priests had begun to intone prayers over the body and were moving the fallen guard into a shroud to be moved. It was time she left them to their honourable task. She looked around and saw her two bodyguards standing ten paces away, their eyes scanning the grounds for any threat to her. Slightly behind them, carefully making sure to keep the burly soldiers between herself and the sight of the corpse, was Hanek. She offered a self-conscious half-smile as Erimem returned and they began the walk back to her suite of rooms.

'I'm sorry,' Hanek said. 'But my stomach is already unwilling to hold down food. I think that seeing a dead body – especially one stabbed as often as we hear this one was – would have made my stomach sicken.'

'Old blood,' Erimem said thoughtfully, only half listening to Hanek.

'Old blood?' Hanek asked. 'I don't understand.'

'Neither do I,' Erimem answered. 'And I don't like it.' She puffed her cheeks out in exasperation. 'I am determined to know what happened to that man,' she stated. She turned to her escort. 'Prepare chariots for us. This afternoon we will cross the river to walk among the dead.'

* * *

Before leaving the palace, Erimem had an unusual encounter with Miral. It took place after Erimem had eaten a light meal of fruits and sweet bread. Ignoring her bodyguards' insistence that they should bring the chariot to her quarters, Erimem was leading the way towards the stables. Her father would have protested at her lack of majesty in deigning to walk rather than wait for the chariot, but Erimem was eager to cross the river. She had questions running through her mind that needed answers and she wasn't going to find those answers sitting in her chambers, waiting for a chariot.

The stables were huge, large enough to house more than a hundred of Pharaoh's prized horses. Among his many talents, Amenhotep was widely known as the finest judge of horses in the land and his stable was reported to contain the greatest collection of thoroughbreds the world had ever seen.

With her bodyguards puffing and sweating in their armour as they hurried to keep up with her, Erimem reached the main stable building ten paces ahead of her soldiers. She knew that she should wait and let them enter first but she was impatient and strode through into the long low building. This was where the horses were hitched to the chariots and given final feed and watering before setting out. She had expected to find the pair of chariots she had ordered prepared, but instead she saw Thutmose standing in his chariot, looking down at Miral, who had bowed low a few paces away.

'I swear, my lord that I will be the best wife to your brother that I can be.'

Thutmose nodded impassively and turned away from Miral. He flicked the reins and his chariot began to move away. Miral turned away from the sight of the disappearing chariot and stopped abruptly when she saw Erimem.

'Miral? What brought you here?'

The Mitanni girl was flustered for a moment, trying to pull her thoughts together. 'You didn't hear?'

Erimem shook her head, setting the bangs on her wig swaying. 'No. I arrived only a moment ago.'

'I thought I could appeal to your eldest brother for help with Mentu.'

'Thutmose won't interfere,' Erimem stated firmly. 'I'm sure he will see this as Mentu's business.'

Miral nodded in resignation. 'I know that now. But it was worth trying.' She forced a smile back to her lips. 'It seems that you are my only ally.'

'And I know Mentu far better than Thutmose does,' Erimem said, walking towards Miral. It was only when she was just a few paces from her friend that she noticed one of Miral's Mitannite bodyguards standing in the shadows.

'After what happened to the guard, I wouldn't have dared to come here alone,' Miral explained.

'I understand,' Erimem replied. 'My own guards are just behind me.' On cue, the two soldiers appeared in the doorway. 'I'll ask Antranak to assign two of his palace guards to protect you.'

'Thank you.' The relief in Miral's voice was palpable. 'I will feel much safer when I see them.' She took a step towards the doorway then stopped.

'Perhaps you should stay in the palace, Erimem. It will be safer here than out in the city.'

Erimem's nose wrinkled. 'I will be safe enough. No one would dare attack me with my guards by my side.'

'None of us thought anyone would be murdered inside the palace,' Miral said solemnly. 'Please go back to the palace,' she implored. 'I have only one friend here…'

'And she will be fine,' Erimem interrupted reassuringly. 'My guards are the finest Antranak could find and besides, I will be wearing a cloak so no one will know who I am.' A horrible realisation descended on Erimem. She knew that something truly awful was about to happen and she also knew there was nothing she could do to stop it. On her way to the stables, Erimem had also come to the conclusion that she would be safer going through the city incognito and had sent one of her handmaidens back to her suite of rooms to fetch a cloak. Erimem wondered if the gods were showing their displeasure at her decision to leave the city by preparing this moment for her. She offered a prayer to Ma'at, the goddess of justice, that Miral would leave quickly but it was already too late. Hanek walked through the doorway into the stables, her attention focused on rearranging the cloak she had draped over her arm.

'I chose this one,' Hanek said. 'It's not the lightest you have but it's very plain. No one will know it's you. Is that all right?' She stopped dead as she looked up and saw not just Erimem but Miral as well.

In turn, Miral stared at Hanek with a cold resentment. There was no doubt that she knew that this was her rival for Mentu. The two women stared at each other in bitter fury, neither ready to show weakness by breaking the stare. It was a small battle neither was willing to lose.

Erimem looked sadly from one to the other. Miral's jaw was clenched shut while Hanek's painted nails dug deep into the flesh of her palm and her hand bunched into a tight fist. Erimem knew that neither of her friends would give way. They had both been pushed into a position where all they had left was a veneer of pride. Whoever gave way here would lose even that thin hint of dignity and Erimem was not prepared to see either girl suffer more than they already were.

'Thank you, Hanek,' she said. 'Please take it to my chariot.' Her voice was friendly but firm enough to let Hanek know that Erimem was not to be argued with. 'Now, please,' Erimem added.

'As you wish,' Hanek said coldly. She walked towards the chariots, keeping her eyes fixed on Miral until she had no choice but to look away.

When the stare was finally broken, Miral's shoulders slumped and she let free a despairing sigh.

Erimem took her by the arm and led her to the doorway. 'You should return to your quarters.'

'I knew that I would see her eventually,' Miral muttered.

'You knew she was still in my service?' Erimem asked, surprised.

Miral shrugged. 'Very little stays a secret in this palace. Especially when I have been assigned handmaidens of my own who have little better to to than make sport of me with their gossip.'

'That will stop,' Erimem promised. 'I will see to that.'

Miral grimaced wearily. 'You are very kind to me, but I can't ask you to do everything for me. If I am to be here, I shall have to learn to stand on my own.'

'In time you will,' Erimem assured her. 'But until then, let me help. Please.'

'Very well,' Miral conceded.

'In return, I ask that you try not to be angry with Hanek.' She hurried on, seeing Miral was about to speak. 'This is as painful for her as it is for you. And she will be leaving the palace soon.'

'You are sending her away?' Miral asked eagerly.

'Not exactly. It was her own choice,' Erimem explained.

'I can't promise to change how I feel towards the girl,' Miral said. 'I know I have no right to hate her, but I can't help the way I feel.' She closed her eyes and drew a deep breath, forcing herself to be reasonable. 'But I will try to remember that this was not her fault. I can promise you no more than that.'

'That is enough.' Erimem tried to make her smile look more confident than she felt. 'And it won't be for long.'

'Good,' Miral blurted with such force that it took both of them by surprise. 'I mean...'

'I know what you mean,' Erimem interrupted and this time her smile was genuine. 'I will be sad when Hanek leaves but it is for the best.'

Miral nodded but said nothing.

'And now I must go,' Erimem said. 'Or I won't be back before nightfall.'

She waited until Miral and her bodyguard had left the stable before joining her escort and Hanek at their chariots.

At the insistence of her bodyguards, Erimem's chariots left through a small gate in the palace's west wall. It led onto a track that was only ever used by soldier and merchants making deliveries to the palace, and had no houses or farmers nearby, so they could take this route and slip into Thebes without being observed too closely. After a time, Erimem recognised it as being part of the same road she and Hanek had taken on the night they had gone into the tavern in Thebes, though she kept this to herself. She doubted if either her own bodyguard or the one sharing the other chariot with Hanek would appreciate knowing that they had been duped so easily.

The chariots were bland and carried no gold or royal crests to suggest that they carried anyone of importance and so they passed through the dusty streets of Thebes, garnering only a few disinterested glances and one outstanding burst of cursing from an old woman whose hearing was so bad that she hadn't heard their approach. Erimem was actually beginning to regret her decision to wear the cloak. While it did its job in covering her face, it also caught the heat of the sun. Sweat poured down her back and chest and Erimem felt as though she was being baked alive. Thankfully, despite Thebes's sprawl, it didn't take long before the chariots were pulling up at a small wooden jetty on the banks of the Nile. Half a dozen small papyrus boats bobbed, half in the water and half on the bank, attached by lengths of old, dirty rope to pegs driven into the dry ground. An ancient man by the name of Shonmis shook himself awake and peered at them from the shade of a reed lean-to that sat by the bank. His brown, leathery face creased a little in surprise at seeing anyone stupid enough to be out about their business with Ra the sun at his peak. He briefly considered telling them to go away and come back at a more sensible time but then a vague memory came to him. Someone had told him to hold the main boat, hadn't they? Was that today or was it some other time? He cursed his sleep-addled brain. Obviously it was today.

He pulled himself upright, trying to ignore the creaking of his old bones. Two men and two girls had got down from the chariots and were waiting for him. The men were big, muscular and had the look of soldiers or bodyguards about them while the girls were obviously from good families. There was something in the way that they carried themselves that said they were wealthy. Besides, who else could afford two bodyguards? That suited Shonmis just fine. The wealthier they were, the happier he was. He'd found that the wealthy tended to haggle less when he charged a high price.

'You're the ones who wanted the main boat?' he asked the nearest of the men, but it was one of the girls – the one wearing a ludicrous cloak much too heavy for that time of day – who answered.

'Yes,' she said. 'We wish to visit the Necropolis.'

Shonmis shrugged. What they were crossing the river for didn't interest him, as long as they paid. 'Fair enough. This way.'

Tethered to the end of the jetty was a wooden boat the length of three men stretched out head to toe, and broad enough to sit two people side by side. It was Shonmis's pride and joy, the largest boat on this part of the river. Sturdily constructed from cedar wood, he made sure it was kept clean enough to take his better-off customers across the river in comfort. It also had enough room to carry whatever the passengers would be taking to place in the Necropolis. And that was something else. He hadn't noticed it before but this group weren't taking anything across the river other than themselves. Usually people would at least be taking an ornament or something to clean their eternal homes. Still, their business was nothing to do with him. Shonmis kicked his slaves awake and had them ready the boat. Moments later, Shonmis led his passengers onto the boat. His slaves picked up the oars and began to row in long, easy strokes.

Shonmis noticed that one of the girls – the one not wearing the cloak – was looking uncomfortably at the water and had her hands clasped firmly in her lap, as far from the side of the boat as she could manage.

'Don't worry,' he said to Hanek. 'The sacred crocodiles won't attack a boat this big.'

'What about a hippopotamus?' Hanek answered nervously. 'I am told that they will attack anything.'

'True,' Shonmis agreed. 'But we are in the wrong part of the river for them. The nearest hippopotamus is half a morning's sailing away.'

'That's good to know.' Hanek relaxed a little – but kept herself as clear of the side of the boat as possible.

Shonmis chuckled to himself. He normally found that it was the big, supposedly brave men who were most nervous of river crossings. He turned his attention back to the far side of the river and briefly considered pointing out to her the crocodile he'd spotted sunning itself on a muddy patch of ground fifty paces south but he decided against it. It would have been cruel to make fun of the girl. Besides, she hadn't paid yet. Shonmis wiped a bed of sweat from his brow and looked forward to a refreshing drink of beer at the tavern while he waited for his passengers to return.

Despite being the city of the dead, the Necropolis was a busy and bustling hive of activity. Hundreds of people from Thebes visited every day to continue building and decorating the tombs that would be their homes for the afterlife. The tombs came in all shapes and sizes. The most modest of the tombs were little more than small square buildings over a hole in the ground with room for a poor man to store his few possessions to take on his journey to the West and the next life. Others were large and ornately built of sandstone into which stonemasons had carved prayers and homilies, and had space for the bodies of an entire family. But most tombs were stone and brick buildings that stood a little taller than an average man. They were sturdy enough to withstand the savage winds that regularly blew in from the south and west, and they were well-enough built that they would keep most tomb-robbers at bay. Tomb-robbing was the thing that was most feared by all the people who visited the Necropolis. The desecration of a tomb was one of the most reviled crimes in Egypt and was always punished with a brutal death if the robber was caught. To protect the dead in their eternal sleep, the Necropolis was patrolled by armed soldiers every moment of the day. The Necropolis guards proudly went by the name of 'The Footsoldiers of Anubis'. No one knew where the name had come from – it was now centuries old – but the guards embraced it. Over time, even their uniforms had altered so that each of them had an image of Anubis, the jackal-headed god who guarded the underworld and watched over the dead stitched into their kilts.

After being set ashore, Erimem led the way through the winding streets of the Necropolis towards the giant Temple of Anubis which lay at its centre. She was a little surprised at how well ordered and tidy the Necropolis was. She had expected it to be more random but everything was strictly regimented and better tended than the majority of Thebes.

A pair of Necropolis Guards stood on either side of the Temple's giant entrance, each pair with an enormous column carved into the shapes of a giant Anubis behind them. They watched Erimem's group approach and moved to block her way until one of her bodyguards raised a stone bearing carved hieroglyphs. The cartouche bore Pharaoh's name and anyone carrying the cartouche had the authority of Pharaoh himself. The guards stepped aside and let the group pass.

Once inside, Erimem gratefully let the cloak slip from her shoulders. The cloth felt heavy with her sweat and she was relieved to be in the cool shade of the temple. She ordered one of the temple attendants to fetch Fayum while she cleansed herself in a small basin of water in one of the temple's ante-rooms set aside for visiting dignitaries. With Hanek's help Erimem rid herself of most of the dust and grime of their journey and then anointed herself with oils and touched precious salts to her forehead and lips while offering a prayer to Anubis for the fallen soldier. When she emerged from the anteroom, Fayum was waiting, looking impatient.

'Princess,' he bowed.

Erimem almost scolded her friend for being so formal but then she realised that here, in a public place he had no choice. 'Fayum,' she said mildly. 'You will take me to the body of the slain guard.' It was clear from Fayum's expression that in other circumstances he would have argued against his friend seeing the body. 'Now,' Erimem added evenly.

'As you wish,' Fayum hissed. 'If the noble princess will follow me?'

Erimem almost smiled at Fayum's ability to make 'noble princess' sound like 'stubborn fool', but she kept her face a calm mask. 'Thank you, Fayum.'

With her escort and Hanek lagging a few paces behind, Erimrm allowed Fayum to lead the way. When he was sure no one else could hear them, Fayum spoke quietly. 'This is not wise, Erimem. You shouldn't be here. This is a place of death, Erimem. It's all around us here.'

'That guard was murdered in my father's palace,' Erimem argued. 'If even Pharaoh's palace isn't safe then I am well being here to offer a prayer for his ka as anywhere.'

'You're not here to pray for his spirit,' Fayum said with conviction. 'I know you too well for that. You're here because you're curious about something. There's something in this murder that's caught your attention and you won't let go till you've worked out what it is.'

'It's the blood,' Erimem admitted, trying to hide her excitement. 'Something you and Antranak said about his blood.'

'We're here. Wait a moment, please.' They had reached a large room at the heart of the temple. It had no windows and was illuminated only by torches and fires in bowls on top of long metal stands. The air smelled unhealthy, a mixture of the sweet aromas of incense, the metallic tang of blood and the stench of dead bodies. Fayum left Erimem in the doorway and hurried to a large stone altar where three bare-chested priests, all wearing the jackal masks of Anubis, tended to the soldier's body. He returned quickly. 'We don't have long, but they have no objection to a princess paying respect to a soldier who fell defending her home.'

'I will be quick,' Erimem promised, following Fayum towards the body. At the altar, Fayum dipped his fingers into a bowl containing a fine white powder and touched it to his eyelids and lips. He motioned for Erimem to do the same and she did as he instructed. Fayum Intoned a short prayer for truth to Ma'at before moving aside to let Erimem get closer to the guard.

'This is the wound that bled,' Erimem said, pointing to one of the cuts. She could have touched the corpse but with flickering shadows all around and the sickly sweet aroma of the mummification processes filling her nose, Erimem felt a sudden chill of fear. She tensed her muscles to make sure she didn't shake.

'Yes, that's the one,' Fayum agreed. He bled fresh blood from that but old, dead blood from the others.'

'I have been thinking about that,' Erimem murmured. 'It is as if he was stabbed once while alive and then many more times after he was dead.'

Fayum frowned. 'It's possible,' he conceded. 'But why would anyone do that?'

'That's a question I have been asking myself.'

Both Erimem and Fayum started violently as Antranak strode towards them from a second entrance behind Fayum's shoulder.

'Antranak!' Erimem hissed. 'What are you doing here?'

'I should ask you the same,' the soldier said. 'But I'm not surprised. Worried that you should come with only two of an escort but not surprised.'

'Now I have three of an escort,' Erimem smiled tightly.

'So, Fayum,' Antranak turned to the young priest. 'It is possible that Khofrek was killed by a single blow to the heart and then stabbed repeatedly later?'

'It would explain the blood,' Fayum agreed.

'But why would someone do it?' Erimem mused. 'Unless the killer wanted to make it look like this man...'

'Khofrek,' Antranak interjected softly.

'Yes, Khofrek,' Erimem continued. 'To make it look like he had been killed in anger when the opposite was true.'

Antranak was nodding thoughtfully. 'I had come to a similar conclusion myself,' he muttered. 'If it's true then we are dealing with a cunning murderer. One who wished to hide the manner of their actions.'

'Why would they kill Khofrek?' Erimem wondered. 'Did he have enemies or debts...?'

Antranak shook his head firmly. 'No. He was a good man. A fine soldier. He did his duty and cared for his family. He had no other women, no enemies and he didn't gamble.'

'Could it have been an intruder breaking into the palace?' Fayum asked. 'Through the gate Khofrek was guarding.'

'If it was, he was the tidiest thief I have ever heard of,' Antranak rumbled. 'The gate was still locked from inside when Khofrek was found.'

'Which means that the killer is still in the palace?' Erimem hoped she didn't sound as unsettled by that thought as she felt.

'Or was,' Antranak said thoughtfully. 'He might have slipped away before the body was discovered, though I can't be sure...' his voice tailed off and he looked sadly at Khofrek's still body. 'His wife is here,' he said softly. 'I wanted to be here when she saw Khofrek. It's going to be painful for her to see him like this.'

'I...' Erimem fell over the words. She didn't want to say them but she knew that she should, that she had to. It was her duty. 'I will stay as well,' she finally said. 'I will be here when you bring her in.'

Antranak sighed and felt a little of the burden lift from his shoulders. This was going to be unpleasant – it was a scene he had played out too often with other men who had died under his command and he had never found a way to make it any less painful or uncomfortable. He had hoped that Erimem might offer to leave her handmaiden to help Khofrek's widow. That she would stay herself was a kindness he should have expected from her. 'Thank you,' he said. 'I will go and get her now.' He turned and strode out of the chamber.

'Are you sure you want to stay?' Fayum asked uncertainly. 'This will be difficult.'

Erimem offered a tight, humourless smile. 'It will be more difficult for Khofrek's wife,' she said sadly. 'If she can gain any comfort from my being here, then it is my duty to stay. I have done nothing useful in my life so far, Fayum. It's time I did.'

Thutmose snapped the reins and urged his horses to move faster. White sweat already frothed on their black coats but Thutmose wasn't prepared to let them slow. He was troubled by his meeting with Miral and as always when he was troubled, he was losing himself in driving his horses hard. His escort of six chariots was already falling back from him. On the outward leg of his trip out to the Al-Benad Oasis garrison he had left them lagging and now, halfway back to Thebes, they were already falling into the distance. When he passed over the next rise, they would be out of view. Thutmose knew he should slow and let them catch up. How often had his father told him not to ride off alone? But he needed to think without anyone else disturbing his thoughts. He had harboured doubts about Miral when his father had announced that she would marry Mentu but he had said nothing. He was Pharaoh's son but that didn't give him the right to question Pharaoh's decisions. But the meeting with Miral in the stables had troubled him deeply. The way she had come to him and talked about Mentu left Thutmose in no doubt that the girl was unfit to marry into Pharaoh's family. He would discuss the matter with his father and with Mentu as soon as he returned to the palace.

He was so engrossed in his own thoughts that Thutmose didn't notice the large blocks of broken stone that littered the well-worn roadway between Thebes and the oasis. He couldn't have expected the stones to be there. When he had passed by that very spot early in the afternoon the road had been cleared. The first he knew of the stones was when one of his Arabian horses stumbled on one. An instant later, the chariot's wheel smashed into a large stone block and shattered. The chariot's axle snapped and the chariot dropped on one side then, as the second wheel snapped clear, the chariot's other side dropped and hit the ground. Still being dragged at full speed by the charging horses, the chariot hit a stone and flipped over, its momentum sending Thutmose over the side and trapping him under the chariot as it landed. He heard a crack and knew it was the sound of his bones breaking. He tried to release the reins but even without them, the weight of the chariot dragged him along, the sand and stones tearing the skin from his back and the back of his legs. He was already unconscious when the harnesses snapped and the hoses charged into the distance. The chariot travelled a little further before coming to a halt. He never saw the figure emerge from the gully by the side of the road or the cudgel the man carried. The man looked back in the direction Thutmose had come. He would have to be quick. He hefted the cudgel and then had a better idea. He picked up a broken piece of the chariot and hurried to Thutmose. Without pity or remorse, he raised the piece of wood and slammed it down into the side of Thutmose's head. He brought the wood down again and then twice more into Thutmose's already broken body. Then he casually dropped the piece of wood onto the dusty ground beside Thutmose and ran back to the gully. He hurried along the gulch, using it for cover. By the time Thutmose's chariot escort found the fallen prince, his killer was long gone.

Meeting Khofrek's widow, Silliba, had been even more upsetting than Erimem had expected. The woman had wept bitterly and screamed angrily at the injustice of her husband's killing. Erimem hadn't had the first idea as to what she should say to calm Silliba or offer her any comfort. She held the woman's hand and talked respectfully of Khofrek's bravery and the honour he had shown in dying for Pharaoh. She assured the grieving widow that her husband would find an honoured place in the afterlife, a special place reserved for those who met death in their king's name. Slowly Silliba's grief abated and she began to really listen to Antranak and understand who the girl holding her hand actually was. She kissed Erimem's hand repeatedly and pleaded for her to ask her father to intercede with the gods and restore Khofrek to her. Erimem had muttered and mumbled that she would do what she could but added that the ways of the Divine Ones were not for mortals like her to dictate. Erimem was ashamed at the relief she felt when Fayum and the priests returned, saying that it was time for Khofrek to be anointed. She left Silliba with the priests, massaging sacred oils into Khofrek's lifeless body.

'Thank you,' Antranak said when they reached the long passageway leading back to the entrance. 'I have never handled that duty well.'

'I don't think I did it particularly well either,' Erimem admitted wearily. 'I had no idea what I should say to her.'

'You did well enough,' Antranak replied reassuringly. 'She will take solace from Pharaoh's daughter comforting her.'

'Solace won't feed her, though,' Erimem said bitterly. 'They have children, don't they? I want them cared for,' Erimem said firmly. 'Silliba and her children. We must make sure that they never go hungry or want for clothes or a place to live. We can honour Khofrek by caring for them. The palace will pay for anything they need.'

Antranak felt a smile tug at the corners of his mouth. He wasn't amused by the earnest nature of Erimem's promise. It was more a smile of pride at the honourable, caring nature of her actions. He didn't feel the need to tell her that he had already issued orders for Khofrek's family to be cared for.

They found Hanek waiting with the Erimem's bodyguards, both of whom snapped to attention when they saw Antranak. Antranak announced that if the Princess had no objection, he and his soldiers would meet Erimem's party on the far side of the river after they had retrieved their horses from their own crossing point further downstream and Erimem had been delighted to agree. After spending so much time surrounded by death she would be happy to have as large an escort as possible. She winced at the thought of wearing the cloak again but Fayum had provided her with a more agreeable manner of staying out of the sun and keeping her identity hidden. Hanek was holding a small parasol which Fayum had sent, and Erimem and Hanek stayed in the shade of the parasol for the walk back to Shonmis's boat.

'It's a waste of time,' Erimem grumbled, looking at Antranak and his soldiers, who walked alongside them. 'I might as well have had them pay someone to shout who I was.'

'At least you don't have to wear that cloak now,' Hanek offered helpfully.

'And the parasol does offer relief from the heat,' Erimem agreed. A thought struck her. 'Why would Fayum have a parasol anyway?'

'To prop himself up with when he gets drunk,' Antranak smirked.

On reaching the boat, they found Shonmis and his slaves missing. Antranak sent two soldiers to the nearest tavern and they returned in short order bundling the three men in front of them. Shonmis, in particular, was unsteady on his feet, but indignantly proclaimed himself more than capable of seeing his boat back to the far side of the river.

Antranak's first instinct was to throw the old drunk into the river to sober him up but Erimem assured him that she and her small party would be waiting on the river bank long before Antranak and his men made their crossing. Antranak reluctantly gave way but took a measure of sadistic pleasure from telling Shonmis that his passenger was Pharaoh's only daughter and should any harm befall her the entire army of Egypt would serve out Pharaoh's vengeance. The old boatman scurried unsteadily to his boat, shoving his slaves ahead of him.

'You enjoyed frightening him,' Erimem said accusingly.

'Me?' Antranak's face was the picture of innocence. 'As if an old man like me could ever frighten anyone.'

'Old man!' Erimem snorted. 'Try not to take too long crossing the river, old man, or I shall send a search party for you.'

Antranak waited until Erimem was safely in her boat and the slaves had begun to row before rousing his men and marching them at double speed to their own crossing a few hundred paces upstream.

Hanek was the first to notice the movement in the water near the boat. Neither Erimem nor her bodyguards saw anything at the spot in the water Hanek was pointing at but the girl's fear was so genuine that none of them doubted that she had seen something.

'It was a crocodile,' Hanek said with certainty.

'Don't worry,' Erimem tried to reassure her, 'You heard the boatman. Even the crocodiles wouldn't attack a boat as large as this one.'

The first impact came just as they passed the halfway point of the journey. There was a solid thud and the back of the boat lurched outwards, turning the boat side-on to the shore.

'Keep rowing,' Shonmis yelled to his slaves. He dropped to a seat in the boat and grasped at the wooden plank for safety.

'Can you see it?' Erimem called.

Her guards swung their heads around, searching the murky water for a sign of movement. 'Nothing, your Highness,' one said.

'There.' The other guard pointed out to the back of the boat where an ominous dark green shape was moving smoothly through the water towards them.

'No, there.' Hanek's hand shot out to their left where another crocodile was gliding toward the boat.

'I thought you said they wouldn't attack,' Erimem yelled at Shonmis.

The old boatman shook his head, trying to clear the beer and confusion. 'I... I don't understand it,' he stammered. 'They have never attacked before.'

Two more shapes rose in the water nearby, moving towards the boat before disappearing into the murky water again.

'Row faster,' Erimem commanded the slaves. 'Faster.' She had barely finished giving the order when the boat was hit a second time. The great gnarled body of a crocodile surfaced under the side of the boat, tilting the craft, spilling its passengers into the river.

The first thing Erimem saw when her head broke the surface was the boat settling upside the down. The second was two crocodiles thrashing in the water, both snapping at a piece of raw meat. She knew that she had to get out of the water quickly. Everyone was taught from birth that the Nile's crocodiles became frenzied and wild when they could scent meat and Erimem knew that if she didn't get out of the water quickly she was dead. She turned for the bank and almost swam into the side of a crocodile. Her shock at the sight of the beast so close threw a question into her head. Why had the crocodile passed her by? The answer came quickly enough. One of Shonmis's slaves was desperately swimming towards the shore. The crocodile's giant bulk erupted from the water behind him, gripping one on his legs in its jaws and dragging him screaming under the water. Almost immediately the crocodile began to twist its body and spin underwater, the action ripping off the slave's leg and thrashing the river to a crimson foam. The slave's head broke the water, his mouth open and screaming in terrible agony, begging for help. He was beyond help. Before anyone could move to give aid, another crocodile slammed into his side, tearing at his ribs while another snapped its jaws around his remaining leg and began its death roll. The slave disappeared under the water again and this time he wouldn't resurface.

Erimem felt the weight of her drenched wig pulling her head towards the water, so she tore the wig from her head and hurled it back into the river. There were more crocodiles in the water than she could count. Many were congregating around the area where the slave had gone under while others seemed to be gnawing at the boat, but there were others moving towards the people in the water, preparing to attack.

'Get to the bank!' she yelled. 'Get out of the water.' She knew it was a waste of her precious breath. They all knew to get out of the water but Shonmis and Hanek in particular looked dazed. 'Hurry!' she yelled again. 'Get to the bank.' She began to swim as fast as she could, grateful for the long days she and Mentu had spent swimming in the palace pools as children. A horrifying scream ripped through the air as Erimem reached the bank and began to clamber onto dry land and then she felt a real terror run through her; a terror that she would be so close to safety only to be hauled back to the river. Her hand slipped twice as she grasped desperately for a hold and pulled herself onto the bank, expecting at every moment to feel the vice grip of a crocodile's jaws snap shut about her. Once on land, she scrambled half a dozen paces away from the edge before turning. There was carnage in the water. Shonmis's second slave was being torn apart by three crocodiles while Shonmis himself simply floated in the water, looking at the death around him in absolute terror. Erimem's bodyguards were swimming for the shore. One had his sword drawn and was bringing it down on the nose of a crocodile. He didn't see the crocodile approaching from the side until it exploded from the water and water and clamped its jaws around his torso. Erimem looked away, knowing that her bodyguard – one of the men who had trained her and who she trusted implicitly – was dead. As she yanked her head away, her eyes landed on another equally appalling sight. Hanek was close to the shore, Fayum's parasol still gripped tightly in her hand. Behind her, only its eyes and the top of its head visible was a crocodile, and it seemed to Erimem to be half as large again as any of the others. She hesitated for only the briefest instant before hurrying back to the bank. She threw out a hand to Hanek.

'Give me your hand,' she said urgently. 'Do it quickly.' Her eyes flicked over Hanek's shoulder towards the approaching beast and she knew that she had made a mistake. Hanek had seen Erimem's gaze shift and knew what it meant. She screamed and began to thrash and kick at the water, desperate to reach the shore. 'Give me your hand!' Erimem yelled again. Hanek desperately grasped for Erimem but their fingers missed by the span of a hand. 'Try again,' Erimem bawled. 'Reach for me.' This time she did catch Hanek's hand and she heaved with all of her strength, pulling the girl closer to safety. She had almost pulled Hanek to safety when the crocodile reared out of the water, its jaws snapping shut at Hanek. For a moment, Erimem thought the crocodile had missed her friend, but then she felt Hanek being pulled away from her as the crocodile backed away into the water. Hanek screamed in terror. The crocodile had indeed missed Hanek but the hem of her dress was trapped in its jaws and it was hauling her back into the water by the dress.

She fumbled at the dress but the water had made the fabric heavy and difficult to grip and fear made her fingers clumsy. Erimem hauled again at her friend but she knew that she couldn't hope to win a test of strength against this crocodile. She was sure she was going to lose Hanek, but then a second pair of hands gripped Hanek's wrists.

'Pull now,' Antranak shouted, and they heaved together. They heard a ripping sound as Hanek's dress began to tear. Spotting Fayum's parasol abandoned on the ground near her feet, Erimem released Hanek's arm. She snatched up the parasol and rammed the central wooden handle into the crocodile's eye. The monster ripped its head back in pain as blood and a clear gooey substance seeped from the eye. Abandoning Hanek, the injured crocodile slipped back into the safety of the Nile. Erimem lurched back away from the river bank. She saw Antranak helping Hanek to safety and watched in relief as Antranak's guard helped her one surviving bodyguard to the shore. Shonmis, like his slaves, was gone.

'What happened?' Antranak demanded of Erimem.

'I don't know. They just seemed to attack the boat...'

'There must be a reason,' Antranak interrupted. 'Did anyone in the boat antagonise them?'

'Of course not,' Erimem snapped. 'We're not stupid.' The burst of anger broke her free of some of the shock that had gripped her. 'There was something on the boat...'

She started back towards the edge of the river, avoiding Antranak's restraining hand so that he had to follow her.

'There.' Erimem pointed out at the upturned boat, which was now beginning to list. The last two crocodiles visible were snapping at a piece of meat tied to the underside of the boat with rope. 'I thought I saw something like that when I was in the water but I wasn't sure. Somebody hung meat under the boat.'

'Which brought every crocodile for as far as the eye can see.' He settled his gaze on Erimem. 'You understand what this means?' he asked.

Erimem nodded. 'It was deliberate. Someone tried to kill me.' She began to shake and her voice quavered. 'Someone wanted to kill me.'

'Erimem!' Antranak's voice was harsher than she had expected. 'Control yourself. You are Pharaoh's daughter. You must not show any sign of weakness.' His voice softened. 'When you are in the palace you may weep all you must, but in public, Pharaoh's daughter must be strong.'

A crowd had gathered, pulled from the nearest taverns and houses by the commotion and the rumour that Amenhotep's daughter might be involved. Some were bowing, others were just gawping, but they all expected her to do something. It felt like a weight that had suddenly landed on Erimem's shoulders. She was wet, filthy and terrified and in no mood to face this but she knew that she had no choice. She bunched her hands into fists until the nails dug into her palms and she forced herself to concentrate. 'Very well,' she forced out. 'We will return to the palace now. See that my bodyguard and handmaiden are taken care of.'

'Very wise, your Majesty,' Antranak bowed. 'You two,' he called to the nearest of his guards. 'You will stay with the princess. Don't worry,' he said quietly to Erimem. 'You'll be safe in the palace soon.'

'Good,' Erimem said with feeling. 'I will not be happy until I am safe at home.'

It was only when their chariots finally passed through the palace gates and Erimem saw the shocked faces and heard the wailing that she knew she was wrong.

# Chapter Six
## A Nation Mourns

hen the priests and physicians pronounced that they could not treat Thutmose, Pharaoh Amenhotep went mad with grief. Over and over he commanded Thutmose's lifeless body to rise. He ordered his son to rise and to live again. He commanded his brothers, the gods, to return his son to him and when his commands failed he dropped to his knees and begged. The gods ignored his pleas and Amenhotep, King of Egypt's Two Kingdoms and the most powerful man in all of the world, had to accept that there was nothing he could do for his beloved son.

His rage at that impotence was terrifying.

He went to the stables and found the horses that had pulled Thutmose's chariot. He butchered them with his battle sword, hacking them to pieces while they were still alive. And then he had Thutmose's chariot escort brought to him. For their failure to protect his son they were sentenced to execution in the most brutal manner the House of Death could conceive. It was only after Antranak's intercession for mercy that Amenhotep relented and had the men beheaded and their entire families passed into slavery.

Amenhotep raged against the world and lashed out at anyone who approached him. Word of Thutmose's death spread from Thebes and crossed the entire country in just a few days. In the country, the people mourned the prince's loss while, on Egypt's borders, her traditional enemies quaked, waiting for Amenhotep and his armies to lash out. It didn't happen. After seven days of raging, Pharaoh's anger abated and Amenhotep began to mourn. Egypt's neighbours sent messages of sympathy to the Pharaoh along with tributes to Thutmose more out of relief that their borders were safe than from any affection they had felt for the young prince. Amenhotep ignored the tributes. He made a single announcement that he had taken Techvis, the girl Thutmose had chosen to marry, as a wife himself. Everyone knew that he would never lay so much as a hand on the girl but that he had taken her into his house to honour his son. That done, Amenhotep withdrew from the world and began to grieve.

While Pharaoh mourned, Egypt waited. The depth of Amenhotep's love for his son was well known across the nation and it was expected that Thutmose's funeral would match that of a pharaoh in grandeur and scale. But no announcement or proclamation came and the country waited.

Inside the palace, tense anticipation mixed with the subdued, grieving atmosphere. A funeral of the scale that would befit a beloved son like Thutmose would take months of preparation. A mausoleum would have to be prepared for him while a permanent tomb was built, as would a funeral mask, a casket and all of the hundreds of other details that went into the organisation of such a funeral. Thousands of people would be involved and they waited for Pharaoh Amenhotep to give the word for them to begin work.

The days since Thutmose's death had been a nightmarish blur for Erimem. She had returned to the palace, her dress dried by the sun but coated with dry mud. On the journey she had held brief snatches of conversation with Antranak. He had encouraged her to hold the appearance of majesty, as though she was unaffected by her experience but inside she had wanted to scream. Someone had tried to kill her. Only she and Antranak knew that the would-be assassin had attached the meat to the boat so that the crocodiles would attack. She was sure there would be an investigation. Would it show that the attempt on her life was linked to the murder of the guard? Did it have something to do with the night she and Hanek had sneaked out of the palace? She had no doubt that Antranak would find the truth. But when she had returned to the palace and heard of Thutmose's accident, Erimem had forgotten the attempt on her own life.

The strange thing was that on the surface, Erimem's days had changed very little. Her handmaidens still tended to her needs and she spent most of her time in their company and visited Miral most afternoons. Wherever she went she was accompanied by her four new bodyguards. She even began training again, working with two of her guards while the other two stood watch. Initially she had thought that it would be an insult to Thutmose's memory for her instruction to begin again so quickly after his death but all around the palace, she saw that there was a kind of paralysis holding everyone, waiting for Pharaoh to make a move and she wasn't prepared to show that same helplessness. She knew she couldn't do that. Someone had to show an example of some kind of normality and so she stuck as closely to her regular routine as she could. Erimem also felt that she needed to show this example to make up for a vague sense of inadequacy in her reaction to Thutmose's death. On returning to the palace she had been told only that her brother was dead. Her immediate prayer had been that it wasn't Mentu. The guilt at knowing she placed the life of one brother above another gnawed at her but it was something she couldn't help. Thutmose was her brother and she had loved him, but the love had been a duty, the love a sister should feel for her brother. There was none of the friendship or affection she felt for Mentu or the protective instinct she had for Teti. There had always been a distance between Thutmose and his siblings, and yet Erimem did feel his loss for all the difficulties she had found in dealing with him. She also felt a dull guilt that she should feel a little more than she did.

Immediately after Thutmose's death, Erimem saw little of Mentu. Miral had asked her not to pressure Mentu at all about his manner towards her and Erimem found the Mitanni girl's concern for Mentu rather touching. He had acted like a bully and a brute but Miral still showed concern for him. When Erimem visited Miral she was aware that Miral was hiding her own fears and concerns in order to protect Erimem from more worry.

But Erimem did worry. She worried about the pit her father had sunk into. She worried about Mentu and about Miral, and she worried about Egypt.

The only beacon of happiness for Erimem was the return to Thebes of Teti. Her younger brother remained as she remembered him. In fact he looked exactly as he had when he left for his garrison a year earlier. He was even shorter in height than she was and still looked as if he had been dressed by a blind man. His kilt was rumpled, his pectoral was askew and the kohl around his eyes was just a little smudged. He was still mentally a few heartbeats behind everyone else in a room and he still wore that silly half-smile he always had when he saw her but Erimem didn't care. He was the most innocent ka she had ever known and she was glad that he had survived his time at the garrison, though the scars and bruises he wore showed that it hadn't been an easy time for him. Erimem saw Teti every day and hoped that once Thutmose had been put on his journey to the West and laid in his tomb, Teti would stay in Thebes. With one brother now dead, she felt more protective towards the remaining two.

On the morning she received a request for an audience from both Antranak and Horemshep, Erimem was feeling particularly protective towards her brothers. It had been requested that all three of Pharaoh's remaining children meet Antranak and Horemshep in one of the smaller halls. None of them were told that their siblings would also be attending, but each of them, even Teti, knew that this was of enormous importance if Antranak and Horemshep had set aside their differences.

'You are both insane,' Mentu stated flatly. 'Our father has never listened to us and he will not do so when he is in this frame of mind.'

'But we must try,' Erimem argued. 'Our people need their Pharaoh.'

'Egypt needs its Pharaoh,' Antranak agreed. 'We need our King to lead us.'

Mentu snorted derisively. 'If we begin to tell Pharaoh what he must do we will have to thank the gods if we are not all dead soon.'

Antranak and Horemshep exchanged a frustrated glance. Antranak was irked to see a slight hint of gloating in his adversary's eye. To their relief, Erimem wasn't giving up.

'*You* can talk with him,' Erimem pushed. 'You are now his heir and he will listen to you.'

Mentu said nothing but shifted uncomfortably. Erimem knew that the mantle of heir didn't sit comfortably on his shoulders but she also recognised the wisdom in what Antranak and Horemshep had said. She touched Mentu's arm gently. 'We will all talk with him,' Erimem said. 'We will begin by asking when we can pay respects to our dear brother.'

'I-I will talk w-with him,' Teti offered. 'I haven't seen our father since I got back.' He sounded a little hurt by Amenhotep's absence.

'We must all do this together,' Erimem reaffirmed. 'He will listen to us if we do this together.'

'Or at least be less liable to execute all of us,' Mentu muttered.

'We must do this today,' Erimem said.

Antranak's shoulders slumped a little in relief.

'You didn't think they would agree so easily.' Horemshep hissed.

Antranak hadn't heard him move closer. He wasn't surprised. He had never been able to hear snakes move. 'No,' Antranak agreed. 'I didn't.'

Horemshep chuckled mirthlessly. 'Now we must only wait to see if we have wasted our time and theirs.'

Antranak didn't reply but wondered to himself whether Horemshep wouldn't rather see this plan fail simply because it would bring more misery to the palace and he was angry for having such a jaded view of Horemshep. But he was angrier with Horemshep because he knew that his view of the priest was probably accurate.

After their fifth request for an audience, Amenhotep finally gave in and agreed to see his remaining children. They had tracked him to the Necropolis where he was again underground in the Royal Chamber overseeing the priests and embalmers as they prepared Thutmose's body for interment. His blood had already been drained and his inner organs removed and treated before they could be placed in canopic jars, which would be buried along with the body.

Amenhotep met his children at the entrance to the passage leading underground. He did little to hide his impatience at their interruption. He offered them no greeting, just a simple demand. 'What do you want?'

Erimem waited for Mentu to speak but she saw that her brother was wilting under the anger coming from their father. 'We come to honour our brother,' she said, hoping to prompt Mentu.

'I honour my son. He needs no one else.'

Erimem knew that was a signal for this audience to end. The snub had been brutally sharp. But if they left now, she was sure that he would not agree to see them again. She had to keep trying. 'Thutmose was much loved by the people.' Even if that wasn't a lie, Erimem knew it was, at least, stretching the truth close to breaking and she prayed for the gods to forgive her offence. 'Your people have asked to give respect and pay homage to Prince Thutmose as he begins his journey to the West. We thought that you should be made aware of the love your people had for Thutmose.' Erimem stopped, hoping she hadn't gone too far in proclaiming the devotion of the people to Thutmose. Most people in the palace knew the truth had been very different.

'And you felt it was your duty to tell me this?' Even though it was Erimem who had spoken to Amenhotep, the Pharaoh's question was aimed at Mentu.

'Y-yes,' Mentu stammered. 'We thought you should know.'

'Even though I had given orders that no one should disturb me under any circumstances?'

Mentu blanched. He had never liked this suggestion of Antranak's – especially given Horemshep's involvement – and now he knew it would most likely cost him his life. His father was asking him to admit to disobeying a royal command and he had no choice but to do just that. He nodded uncertainly. 'Yes, mighty Pharaoh.'

Amenhotep stared at his son for a long moment, which seemed like an eternity to Mentu. It felt as if his father was letting the moment stretch just to torture him before the Pharaoh would finally erupt with anger. Instead, Amenhotep turned away and started back down the steep stone passage back towards the Royal Embalming Chamber. 'I will think on this,' was all he said.

The audience was clearly over and Amenhotep would most certainly not tolerate a further interruption, so Erimem turned and led the way back along the corridor. She felt an odd mix of relief that her father hadn't flown into a rage and of frustration at the meeting being so short. She glanced at Mentu. From the expression on his face she guessed that he was simply relieved his ordeal was over. She turned to Teti and found him lagging several paces behind. He looked close to crying.

'What is it, Teti?'

Teti sniffed. 'He didn't speak to me.'

Erimem made a move towards Teti but Mentu was already there, comforting the younger man. 'His mind was probably just on Thutmose,' Mentu said and, for the first time, Erimem began to think that he might actually be suited to being Pharaoh.

Early the following morning, Antranak was both surprised and delighted to be summoned to the throne room to meet his Pharaoh. His delight was tempered more than a little when he saw that Horemshep was already present, along with Nesmut, the inept vizier, and a number of others of the court's highest dignitaries. Antranak bowed low but Amenhotep waved for him to rise quickly.

'Let us not waste time on formality, my friend,' Amenhotep said quickly. He was brisk and determined. Antranak knew the Pharaoh's moods well and knew that his King was eager to be busy. That, in itself, was something he could praise the gods for.

'As my Pharaoh commands.'

'I have mourned my son alone,' Amenhotep said, speaking briskly to keep the sorrow from showing in his voice. 'My son was my most beloved. He was the prize of all Egypt and his loss tears out my very heart. But I cannot mourn my son alone.' He snapped to his feet. 'I spoke with my son on this yesterday,' he said, dropping the crop and flay, the symbols of his position onto the throne.

'Your son?' Nesmut asked. Antranak swore that he would cut the vizier's head from his shoulders if he asked if Pharaoh had spoken with Thutmose's corpse or communed with his dead spirit.

'Mentu,' Amenhotep said, and Antranak noted the pride in his king's voice. It was the first time in many years he had spoken of any of his children except Thutmose with that tone. 'He came to me yesterday and spoke wisely on this matter,' Amenhotep continued. 'He reminded me that the people of my land deserve the opportunity to show their love for Thutmose.'

'That is wise indeed, Majesty,' Antranak agreed easily, ignoring the sly, knowing glance Horemshep threw at him. 'Prince Thutmose deserves the respect and prayers of all of your people.'

'I agree,' Amenhotep said vigorously. 'It would be selfish of me to mourn alone any longer and it would be a disrespect to Thutmose if I did not order that his funeral be the most memorable our land has seen. Something of a scale that befits a son of Pharaoh.'

'He deserves no less, your Majesty,' Horemshep agreed slickly. 'Wouldn't you agree, Nesmut?'

The vizier started slightly, uncomfortable at being asked his opinion. 'Oh, yes,' he agreed quickly.

Amenhotep strode back up the steps to his throne. 'Preparations must be made. We have less than sixty days to make ready for Thutmose's journey to the afterlife.'

According to tradition, a body should be placed in its tomb within seventy days of death and by Antranak's reckoning they now had fifty-five days to send Thutmose on his journey. 'I am sure all of Egypt will praise your wisdom on this matter and give homage to Thutmose.'

'Egypt isn't enough.' Amenhotep's statement took the assembly by surprise.

'Majesty?' Antranak asked. 'I'm not sure I understand you.'

Amenhotep sat in his throne again and crossed the crop and flay across his chest. 'I will have it known to the leaders of all nations that I expect their highest envoys to attend the ceremonies for my son Prince Thutmose, and that I expect them to send appropriate tributes for him to carry into his next life. If any country fails to comply with this, I will see their actions as an insult to Pharaoh and to Egypt and will consider it an act of aggression to which I will respond in the harshest manner.' He paused, waiting for any reaction. None came. 'Let that message go out today.'

Nesmut nodded dumbly, wondering how many men he would be sending to their deaths for carrying so provocative a message. He forced a politician's smile. 'It will be done before the afternoon dies, your Majesty.'

'See that it is.' Amenhotep looked round the men in front of him, the highest-ranking men in his kingdom, staring at each one in turn, letting them know that he was watching them. These men would give only their best if they thought that Pharaoh had them under scrutiny. 'Your task is set,' Amenhotep said finally. 'You may all go.'

'May I ask a question, your Majesty?'

The men had begun to bow when Horemshep's voice stopped them. They looked up at the priest, startled.

Amenhotep gazed down at the priest with interest. 'What is it, Horemshep?'

Horemshep bowed from the waist. 'I apologise for interrupting your Majesty but I had wondered on the subject of Prince Mentu's marriage.'

Amenhotep all but cursed out loud. He had forgotten the Mitannite princess, although he could never admit as much.

'That must be delayed,' Antranak stated firmly. 'Or cancelled altogether. It would be an outrage to think of a marriage while the land mourns.'

'Normally I would agree,' Horemshep answered swiftly. 'But this is an unusual time for Egypt.' Horemshep spoke in a low, persuasive tone. 'We have fought a war in which many of our young men have died in bringing triumph to the land, and now we have lost our most beloved prince. The hearts of your people can take only so much sorrow, your Majesty. A marriage would give them an opportunity for some joy at this terrible time.'

'But the girl is a Mitannite,' Antranak snapped. 'How can you think of the heir to the throne taking a Mitannite wife?'

'Because Pharaoh agreed to the marriage,' Horemshep said smoothly and Antranak knew instantly that he had walked into the trap Horemshep had laid for him. 'Pharaoh gave his word on this marriage,' Horemshep continued. 'And our Pharaoh has always kept his word.'

'But she is a Mitannite,' Antranak repeated, frustrated with his stupidity in being led to the slaughter by Horemshep.

'I am aware that she is a Mitannite,' Horemshep said. 'And an alliance with a traditional enemy, an alliance that ends the possibility of another bloody war...' he left the thought to hang tantalisingly. 'That would be good for the people's spirits at a time of great sadness.'

'But the boy will one day be Pharaoh,' Antranak argued. 'Would you have Mentu take a Mitanni as his queen?'

'I didn't say he should take her as his queen,' Horemshep countered. 'I, more than anyone, would be against an outsider becoming queen, but when he eventually becomes Pharaoh, hopefully many years hence, he will have many wives. What harm will it do for one of them to be this Mitannite girl?'

'Because she will be his first wife, you idiot,' Antranak snarled.

'Does that matter?' Horemshep asked. The thin smile showed that he had manoeuvred Antranak into exactly the position he wanted and Antranak could do nothing but wait for the blow to come. 'As I recall,' Horemshep went on, 'our current Pharaoh did not take his first wife as queen.'

Antranak felt as if he had been kicked. He should have seen the way Horemshep was playing him, but whether he had let his guard down or whether Horemshep had simply taken him by surprise, Antranak knew he was beaten. 'I am uncomfortable with this idea,' he said. 'But I will, of course, follow my Pharaoh without question.'

Amenhotep offered a wry smile to his old friend. 'As ever, the loyal Antranak seeks only to protect your Pharaoh and his family. But on this occasion, I believe that Horemshep is correct. We must continue with the life of Egypt. And,' he added. 'I gave my word to the Mitanni that there would be a marriage binding our lands. Pharaoh does not break his promises. The marriage will go ahead as planned.'

Pharaoh had given his decision and Antranak knew he had no option but to accept it. He bowed and waited for Amenhotep to leave. When Pharaoh was gone, Antranak made sure he intercepted Horemshep. 'You had every argument for the marriage prepared,' he growled.

Horemshep snorted dismissively. 'I needn't have bothered. You were so predictable, Antranak.'

'Why?' Antranak demanded. 'Why are you so keen for this marriage to go ahead?'

'For the good of Egypt, obviously,' Horemshep said sarcastically.

'The truth!' Antranak demanded. He grasped the handle of his sword menacingly. 'For once tell me the truth, if you can.'

Horemshep laughed derisively. 'You won't harm me, you old fool. Not in Pharaoh's palace.' He turned to leave then stopped. 'But I will tell you why I favour the marriage. Our Pharaoh has lost a son. What could be better for him than for his new heir to provide him with a grandchild? The Mitanni girl is beautiful enough and I'm sure Mentu won't object to his part in producing children. And so, when Mentu gives Pharaoh grandchildren, they will be closer than before and both will be happy.' He smiled a jackal's smile. 'And they will remember who suggested the marriage and who spoke out against it.'

Antranak pulled a deep breath as Horemshep left the throne room. Even when they had shared a goal, the priest had been plotting. Antranak cursed his stupidity in relaxing his guard against the priest. One day, he promised himself, he would see the priest grovelling in the sand. The thought cheered him greatly and he almost cracked a smile as he set off for the barracks.

Word that Pharaoh had made his decision regarding Thutmose's funeral spread across Egypt almost as quickly as the bad news which had preceded it. The Egyptian people breathed a collective sigh of relief and offered prayers for their Pharaoh's wisdom. Egypt's neighbours breathed a little easier and while in council they talked in outraged terms about Amenhotep's demand for tribute, every one of them knew that they would send just a little more treasure than was necessary. Dignitaries prepared for the long, arduous journey to Thebes and armies were mobilised to escort the caravans to Egypt's borders while out in the deserts, bandits sniffed opportunity in the wind.

The palace became a hectic buzz of constant motion. Wig-makers and dressmakers passed stonemasons and artists while soldiers drilled constantly so that during their long march escorting Thutmose's coffin not one step would be out of time. Everyone in the palace was busy every moment of the day.

Everyone except Erimem. While all the activity carried on around her, she felt lost and at a loose end. There was little she actually could do and she sank into her normal routine with a vague feeling of frustration. Even the training with her new bodyguards did little to help her mood and she found that she was pushing herself harder with each training session to work out her anger.

Most days she visited Teti. Initially he had been happy to see her and they had talked about the past. Teti always talked about happier times when they were children. She knew that in his heart Teti would always be a child and that he would never belong in the adult world so she let him talk of games they had played long ago. However, as the month drew to its close, Teti was struck by the sickness which still lingered in the palace. Fayum brought a healer who called the condition 'a slight fever which he would treat', saying that the fever was probably related to Teti's broken heart at his brother's passing. He gave Teti various potions of honey and ox blood while saying that Teti should be 'moored at his mooring stakes'.

'That means keep him on his regular food as well as these treatments,' Fayum had explained.

Erimem had listened and watched the physician treat Teti, first alone and then with priests and other healers, but Teti didn't seem able to shake the fever. The physicians told Erimem not to worry. Teti had always been a sickly boy and they would restore him as they had always done.

Teti wasn't the only person struggling to break free of the fever. Erimem noticed that as the time came closer for Hanek to leave Thebes, the girl was spending less and less time tending to her duties, though she chose not to tackle Hanek on the subject. The other girls rallied around their friend, covering her tasks and spending their evenings sitting with her. Since the murder of the guard, none of them had dared to sneak out. Like Erimem, the handmaidens had reached the conclusion that Hanek leaving was for the best. They reported that Hanek had taken the news of the marriage going ahead very badly, something which Mentu had confirmed when he intercepted Erimem on one of her walks in the garden.

'I need to talk with you, sister,' he had said, drawing Erimem away from her handmaidens, who took their cue and began to walk the other way. Only their bodyguards had followed them through the grove, though at a discreet distance so that the conversation couldn't be overheard.

'What is it?' Erimem asked.

Mentu came straight to the point. 'Hanek will not see me.'

'He cannot see you,' Erimem corrected him. 'Our father has forbidden it.'

'Forbidden it,' Mentu snorted derisively. He glanced around nervously before carrying on. 'The day father made the announcement that I would marry that Mitanni...'

'Miral,' Erimem interrupted. 'Her name is Miral.'

Mentu carried on, ignoring the interruption. 'The day father said I would marry Miral, Hanek spent the night in my bed.'

Erimem stopped dead in her tracks. She stared at her brother, appalled. 'You disobeyed an order from our father?'

Mentu grabbed Erimem's arm and yanked her along the path so that they were walking again. 'Keep your voice down,' he hissed. 'Or would you have everyone in the palace know?'

'Father should know,' Erimem snapped. 'How could you do something so stupid?'

'Because I love Hanek.'

'And do you not love our father?' Erimem responded angrily. 'Do you not love your Pharaoh?'

'Of course I do,' Mentu answered, his face flushing with temper. 'But I am entitled to chose who I love. Even the lowest man in the city has that right.'

'Not if his Pharaoh tells him otherwise.' Erimem's anger was boiling over as well. 'And neither does Hanek. Have you thought what he will do to you if he finds out that you have disobeyed him?'

'I am his heir, he will not harm me.'

'No,' Erimem bunched her hands into fists and willed herself not to hit him. 'But he would send Hanek to the House of Pain without a second thought.'

'I would not let that happen,' Mentu stated grimly.

'And how would you stop it?' Erimem asked, as if she was talking to a simpleton. 'He is the Pharaoh. He is a living god. We all live by his command, even you and I.' She reigned in her anger. 'Everyone is subject to Pharaoh's law, Mentu. When you are Pharaoh, we will be ruled by your word, but for now, we obey our father's commands.'

Mentu wanted to argue. He wanted to shout that Erimem was wrong, but he couldn't. She was right. 'It doesn't matter now,' he sighed heavily. 'Hanek will not talk to me.'

'At least one of you finally has sense,' Erimem snapped, then immediately regretted the harshness of her tone. 'I'm sorry,' she added quickly. 'But it will be for the best this way. I am sure of it. You know that Hanek will be leaving the palace soon?'

Mentu nodded sadly. 'She will not talk with me before she leaves.'

'Then you are lucky many times over,' Erimem said, affection returning to her voice. 'She has saved you both from more suffering if father found out.'

'Will he find out?' Mentu asked bluntly.

Erimem thought for a moment before answering. 'Not from me,' she replied finally. 'At least I will not seek to tell him of this. If he asks I will not lie to him, but I don't think he is likely to ask.'

'Thank you,' Mentu sighed. 'For Hanek, I thank you.'

'You are also lucky that Miral is still prepared to marry you,' Erimem continued. Seeing the sour expression appear on Mentu's face she cuffed him about the arm. 'You have treated her like a slave or worse, an animal.'

'She is here because she was sold to us as a peace offering,' Mentu sneered. 'She has nowhere else to be.'

'And still she asks me every day if you are well and how you are dealing with Thutmose's death.' Erimem prayed to the gods to forgive her for embellishing the facts with 'every day'. 'And every day she asks if you have spoken of her.'

'Does she?' Mentu sounded disinterested.

'Yes!' Erimem answered, anger seeping back into her voice. 'Though why she wastes her time asking after you only the gods would know. I should tell her to marry Teti and leave you to wallow in feeling sorry for yourself.'

'I came to you for help, not a lecture,' Mentu snapped.

'It's the only help I *can* give,' Erimem shot back. She forced herself to stop before saying anything more. 'I don't want to fight with you, Mentu,' she said quietly.

'That's not what I want either.' Mentu turned and headed back towards his bodyguards. 'I will marry Miral but I can't force myself to be happy, not even if our father commands it.'

Erimem woke the next morning and found that a determination had settled on her in her sleep. She had spent too long doing nothing.

The sun was beginning its daily climb from the horizon when Fayum arrived. He blushed a little under the scrutiny of Erimem's maids, and she stifled a laugh as she saw her friend puff his chest out and pull himself up straight. Oddly, Erimem had never thought of her friend with girls before. He was a handsome enough young man and his prospects were good, so she had no doubt that he would be seen by many families as an ideal husband for their daughters but she had still never imagined Fayum as being interested in a wife.

He bowed, making a show for the watching handmaidens. 'Princess,' he said affably. 'You summoned me?'

'I asked you to come,' Erimem corrected. 'Because I thought you might appreciate a break from your labours. And because the last time I visited you...' She paused, remembering the crocodiles turning the Nile red with blood. 'Well, it did not go well.'

Fayum's usual, reassuring expression returned. 'I thought as much. And I must admit that I am more careful than before when I cross the Nile now.'

'I am pleased to hear it,' she relaxed a little. 'Please continue to do so. Now, if you can bear to be parted from your admirers, I will tell you why I asked you to come?'

'Admirers?' Fayum asked innocently. 'I don't know what you're talking about.'

'The reason you're holding your stomach in and throwing your shoulders back,' Erimem said dryly. She turned briskly to her handmaidens. 'You may all go. Now,' she added. The girls giggled from the room leaving Fayum looking rather disappointed. 'You can stop puffing yourself out like a peacock now,' Erimem told him.

Fayum feigned a sour look before breathing out and relaxing into a more normal – and comfortable – pose. 'If you insist. Now may I ask why I am here.'

'The murder.' Erimem's eyes sparkled with eagerness. 'I think I know why the murder was committed.'

'He has slipped from most people's thoughts, and that is not going to give his ka rest in the afterlife.'

'I haven't forgotten him,' Erimem admitted. 'But through the night a thought came to me in my sleep and I remembered it when I woke.'

'A dream?' Fayum sounded intrigued. 'Shemek is always saying that dreams are important. They open our eyes to thoughts we would not dare to consider when we are awake.'

'It wasn't a dream,' Erimem corrected him. 'But I would think one of the gods must have smiled on me to give me the thought.'

Fayum felt himself being swept along by Erimem's excitement. 'Tell me more.'

Erimem began pacing, gesticulating with her hands and talking so fast that Fayum struggled to keep pace with her. 'It's obvious,' she said. 'So obvious Antranak should have seen it straight away and so should we. The blood and the locked gate were so clear. Khofrek was found stabbed beside a locked gate,' she stated. 'He had many stab wounds but only one had bled freely. The others had bled what you called "old blood".' Fayum nodded and she continued. 'The gate was locked and barred which can only be done from inside. That means the killer remained inside the palace grounds.'

'Antranak has already surmised all of this,' Fayum protested, but Erimem waved him to be quiet.

'Antranak also surmised that a single wound killed Khofrek and the others were done to the dead body later. But why would someone do this?' Her voice was becoming faster again and her hands danced, pointing and gesturing as she spoke until she clasped them together to keep them under control. 'They would do this to the body only for one reason – to hide the single wound that killed Khofrek. The rest is obvious. The murderer sneaked close to Khofrek, slew him and then slipped out of the palace, returning some time later through the same gate. He stabbed Khofrek repeatedly to make it look like an attack by a wild person rather than a deliberate assassin's blow. And then he went back to his business in the palace.' She held her breath, waiting for Fayum to tell her what nonsense she had spoken, but her friend said nothing. He only looked thoughtful.

82

'Have you told Antranak of this?'

Erimem shook her head. 'Not yet.'

'Then you should,' Fayum said solemnly. 'And I think he will have something to tell you.'

Something in Fayum's tone left Erimem with a sick feeling in the pit of her stomach.

# Chapter Seven
## Revelations and Decisions

ayum should have kept his mouth shut!' Antranak rounded angrily on the young priest, who took an automatic step backwards but refused to wilt under the soldier's stare.

'She has a right to be told,' Fayum retorted.

'A right to suffer because of my suspicions?' Antranak shouted, angrily wiping sweat from his face with the back of his hand. 'I told you that I have no proof.' Disappointment was etched on his face. 'And I told you in confidence.'

Erimem had let the confrontation between the friends take its course but now she felt compelled to intervene. 'Perhaps you can tell me in confidence, Antranak.'

The soldier thought for a moment then shook his head. 'I would rather not, Erimem. It…'

Erimem's voice cracked across her friend, her unusually imperious tone putting him short. 'And I would rather not have to order you to tell me the truth, Antranak but I will certainly do so if I must.' She paused, raising an eyebrow haughtily. 'Well?'

Antranak said nothing, taken aback by Erimem's superior manner. Occasionally their friendship meant that he forgot that she was the daughter of his Pharaoh and carried the living god's blood in her veins. Her rebuke was a sharp reminder of that fact. 'Very well,' he said sourly. 'But remember that I warned against this.'

Initially it looked like junk or firewood, a pile of broken timber strewn carelessly around one of the larger rooms in the building that housed Antranak's palace guard, but as soon as Erimem saw the golden crest on a curved panel of wood, she recognised it and felt herself gripped by an icy chill. 'Thutmose's chariot,' she  said through gritted teeth, her jaw clamped tightly shut. It took every bit of strength she had not to shake.

'Yes,' Antranak nodded. 'I had it brought here after his... incident in the desert,' he finished weakly.

'Death,' Erimem said. 'The word you tried so hard not to say is "death".'

'Yes, it is,' Antranak agreed reluctantly.

Being so close to the wrecked chariot that had killed Thutmose, and probably still wore his blood, was desperately unsettling for Erimem, as if it was a living thing that had slain her brother and might reach out a broken wooden tendril for her. 'Show me what you found,' she instructed Antranak, eager to be out of the room as quickly as possible.

Antranak seemed to think for a moment before picking up two pieces of a long round pole.

'The chariot's axle.' Antranak said, laying the two pieces on a table under a high window to give a better view of the broken wood. 'We thought the axle had broken, causing the chariot to flip over.'

'You *thought* that?' Despite the painful emotions pulling at Erimem, she had forced herself to concentrate on Antranak's explanation. 'Does that mean you think differently now?'

Antranak turned the two pieces of the axle over so that the splintered ends lay close together. Had he wanted to, the soldier could have pushed them together, back into the form of an axle. He pointed to one end of the break. 'It was one of the soldiers who brought the chariot in who spotted this.'

Erimem followed the line traced by Antranak's finger along the wood to the end of the break. For most of the split, the wood was rough and splintered but for the span of a hand at the beginning of the split, the wood was smooth and even as it cut diagonally across the axle. For a moment, Erimem peered at the wood in confusion before the terrible realisation struck. She gripped the edge of the table tightly and Antranak moved across to rest a hand under her arm. She felt numb, even more so than she had felt when she had heard of Thutmose's death. The clean lines on the wood could have only one meaning – the axle had been cut deliberately. 'Thutmose was murdered.'

'I can't be sure,' Antranak said, but there was no conviction in the denial. 'But when I inspected the chariot I found similar marks on the wheels.'

'But you think he was murdered,' Erimem demanded. 'That is what you think. Answer me, Antranak. Tell me!'

Antranak had to force himself not to take a half step away from Erimem. He had known her all her life but he had never heard her so shrill or demanding. 'Yes,' he admitted. 'I do think that our beloved Prince Thutmose was murdered. I have spoken with Shemek and we are both of the opinion that the axle and wheels were damaged so that they would fail when the chariot was travelling at speed.'

'And what does my father think?'

Antranak shuffled uncomfortably but refused to wilt under Erimem's angry scrutiny. 'I have yet to tell my Pharaoh of my suspicions. He has suffered enough pain at this loss. I will not bring him more suffering on the strength of suspicions I can't back up with facts.'

'Is that the reason you kept it from me as well?' Erimem demanded.

'Yes,' Antranak agreed. 'You would all have been told when I knew the truth. You have been through enough. You must remember there was an attempt made on your life that same day.'

Erimem thought for a moment, rolling one half of the broken axle around in her cupped hand, taking in every aspect of the split wood that was responsible for her brother's death. 'You were kind to do this for us,' she said finally. 'And you were right not to tell my father. He has endured too much with Thutmose's death.' She dropped the wood and turned on Antranak. 'But you should have told me.'

'No, I should not,' Antranak answered angrily. 'You should not even know now. Not until I am sure of the facts.'

'I think the facts are obvious, Antranak,' Erimem stated blankly. 'Thutmose was murdered and an attempt was also made to kill me. Those are facts.' She pushed one end of the splintered axle towards Antranak. 'And it is a fact that if you do not tell my father this then I will.'

'Erimem, I...'

'*Princess* Erimem,' Erimem cut across him. Their eyes locked, both angry and both convinced that they were right. They knew each other well and each knew that the other was not likely to back down and admit to being wrong. Finally Erimem broke the silence. 'He *will* hear this, Antranak.'

Her tone left Antranak in no doubt that Erimem would carry out her threat. He looked away, failing to hide his disagreement with her actions. 'Very well,' he said quietly. 'But I will tell him. It is my responsibility. I will do it.' He half turned then stopped and bowed stiffly to Erimem. 'If I have your permission to leave?'

Erimem nodded. 'You may go.'

Antranak spun on his heel and marched from the room.

'You were harsh with him,' Fayum said softly. 'He has been kind to you all of your life. He was only looking to protect you and your...'

He was cut short as Erimem grabbed one of the pieces of the broken axle and screamed with uncontrollable anguished rage as she hurled it against the wall with all her strength. When he saw the torment in Erimem's face and the tears welling in her eyes, Fayum began to doubt his actions for the first time.

To Antranak's surprise, Pharaoh Amenhotep held his grief and anger in check as the soldier told the Pharaoh of his suspicions. Amenhotep had demanded to see evidence and Antranak had shown the damaged axle and wheels to his Pharaoh as evidence for his fears. Mentu and Horemshep, who had been present when Antranak had found Pharaoh and whom Amenhotep had demanded join them, were in do doubt that Antranak was correct in his assumptions.

'The timber shows clear signs of being tampered with,' Mentu said and Horemshep had nodded.

'I see no other explanation for this,' he concurred. 'Antranak did well to find this evidence.' Antranak's eyebrow twitched upwards in surprise at the compliment but he didn't interrupt. 'The question he must now ask, though, is who is responsible for this action and for the murder of our Prince?'

'The Mitanni?' Mentu suggested.

'No, your Highness,' Horemshep replied thoughtfully. 'Although I hear that some of their people are against this union – as indeed are some of our own – the Mitanni have too much to gain from the marriage of their princess to you.' His lips pursed in concentration. 'The Nubians have been aggressive of late, attacking our outposts in the territories they dispute with us.'

'That is true,' Antranak agreed. 'Although they have not attempted anything so aggressive this deep in the heart of Egypt since the time of your great father, Pharaoh.'

Amenhotep rubbed his chin thoughtfully. 'The thought that my son was murdered is not one I wish to entertain,' he said. 'But you make a convincing case for it, Antranak, while Horemshep has the wisdom to see who is likely to be responsible. But I will not go to war with the Nubians without proof of their guilt.'

'A wise judgement,' Horemshep nodded. 'But might I suggest that a sign of their guilt would be if they continue to attack our southern garrisons?'

'Is that enough?' Antranak asked. 'Surely that is only a sign that they are disputing these southern lands?'

'A dispute they chose to make more aggressive just as the noble Thutmose was taken from us in a tragic accident?' Horemshep left his question in the air. 'Surely that would be too great a coincidence?'

'I agree,' Amenhotep stated firmly. 'It is unlikely that this is a coincidence, but I will not go to war without further proof.' He looked at Antranak. 'Have our spies in the south find all they can of any involvement the Nubians may have had with Thutmose's death. And have them also look for any further attacks by the Nubians on our garrisons. No,' Amenhotep caught himself. 'Have our spies in all our neighbours look for any involvement with Thutmose's death. If he was murdered I swear that I will cut out his killer's heart and feed on it.'

On returning to her apartments, Erimem dismissed her handmaidens. Describing it later, she would say that she had thrown them out, chasing them from her rooms until she was left alone with the distant but steady presence of her guard the only humans nearby. Left alone, she had lurched back and forth from outrage to shock to terror to misery and back to outrage again. Even though she had never felt close to Thutmose as she did with

Mentu or as protective of him as she felt of Teti, Thutmose had been her brother and would, one day, have been her king. Sorrow, anger, guilt and a hundred conflicting emotions ran through Erimem's mind. She dropped onto a couch and wept angrily.

She lost track of time and only found herself drawn back her surroundings when she heard light footsteps moving towards her.

'Go away,' she yelled, without bothering to look up. The footsteps were light enough that they could only belong to a girl. Obviously one of her servants had returned. 'I told you to get out!' Erimem yelled again.

'You didn't tell *me* to leave.'

Erimem looked up abruptly. Miral was standing by the couch, an expression of concern on her face. 'There is a rumour in the palace that Thutmose was murdered,' she said gently. 'For you to be like this I think it must be true.' Erimem nodded and the other girl sat by her. She put a comforting arm around Erimem's shoulders and pulled close. Erimem buried her head against her friend's shoulder. 'Normally it's you who is comforting me.'

Another set of footsteps approached. These were heavier, the steps of a man. There was an uncomfortable silence before Miral spoke. 'I will stay with her tonight. She will be all right.'

Mentu cleared his throat. 'Very well.' He turned to leave then stopped. 'Thank you, Miral,' he said quietly, and then strode for the doorway.

Erimem pulled herself away from Miral in time to see Mentu disappear through the door. 'Was that Mentu?' she asked, pushing tears away with the heels of her hands.

Miral nodded. 'It was.'

Erimem tried to force a smile. 'He spoke to you.'

'He did,' Miral replied. She sounded surprised, as though the thought hadn't occurred to her. 'Although they were hardly the romantic first words a woman dreams of hearing from her future husband.'

'I'm sure you will hear those words from him in time,' Erimem's voice was little more than a croak.

'Are you?'

'No,' Erimem replied honestly. 'He's as stubborn as a camel.'

'But much more handsome,' Miral said wistfully.

Erimem peered at her friend through smudged, tear-filled eyes. 'Are you losing your heart to my brother?'

Miral smiled ruefully. 'I think I gave it willingly long ago. Perhaps that is why I have endured so many insults from him.' She shrugged. 'Not that I have any real choice in the matter.'

Erimem sniffed and dabbed away her tears. 'My brother will come to love you. I'm sure of it.'

Miral's eyebrow twitched. 'You are more certain than me,' she said drily. 'And you sounded far from convincing.' She leaned forward and kissed Erimem on the forehead. 'But thank you for saying it.'

Erimem managed a rumpled smile. 'Another day I would have been more convincing.' She looked at Miral's dress. Black smudges of kohl stained the green linen. 'I've ruined your dress.'

'I have many others,' Miral said reassuringly. 'I believe my husband's father is quite wealthy.' They both laughed. It was brittle but served to ease the tension. 'I will have another sent,' Miral added. 'I would ask for one of yours but I think it would be tight in certain places.' She glanced at her chest meaningfully.

'It would certainly make Mentu take notice of you.'

'I would rather he noticed me than my breasts,' Miral sniffed. 'Men are obsessed with them.'

'I don't think that's a problem I'm likely to have,' Erimem said sourly.

'Then you're lucky. Men will look at your pretty face.' Miral sniffed and screwed up her face. 'Though I would advise you to be washed and to have fresh make-up applied before that happens. Your tears and the smudged make-up are a mask hiding you. When they are repaired, you will be my beautiful friend again. But we can deal with your appearance in the morning. You are tired and you should rest.'

'You told Mentu you would stay.'

'I will.' Miral reassured her. 'I won't leave you alone.'

'Thank you.'

'You are my friend. Before long you will be my sister. You don't have to thank me. Now, you will go to bed.'

'You sound more like a mother than a sister.'

'By this time next year, I pray that I am both.'

By the time Mentu reached the sleeping quarters of Erimem's handmaidens, he had worked himself into a foul temper. He knew that it was mainly because of Thutmose's murder, but he was angry that his sister had been abandoned to the extent that Miral had had to comfort her. He found the door he was looking for and pushed it open without announcing his intention to enter. Hanek lay on her bed, a small bowl beside her. She looked pale, evidently another victim of the fever that was working its way around the palace. She struggled to sit upright.

'Mentu,' she said. Her voice was thin. 'You can't come here. We can't meet.'

'Don't worry, I won't be staying,' Mentu said sourly. 'I came to find out why you had left my sister alone when she needed someone she trusted to be with her.'

Hanek pulled herself from the bed. 'We left because she told us to,' Hanek replied angrily. 'She was upset and in a foul rage and demanded that we leave her alone.'

'And you left her?' Mentu yelled. 'Even though you saw that she was distressed? She needed you and you abandoned her.'

'I did as my mistress instructed me,' Hanek yelled. 'And you have no right to question me on my loyalty to Erimem.'

'I have every right,' Mentu snarled. 'And you would do well to remember that you no longer have the right to talk to me in that manner.'

Despite Mentu's warning, Hanek's anger was still boiling. 'Pharaoh decided that, not me. We had disobeyed him for too long. It was dangerous.'

'How could it be dangerous?' Mentu yelled. He pounded his chest in frustration. 'I will be Pharaoh. I will be able to take as many wives as I see fit. I could have made you my queen!'

Hanek shook her head. 'Your father is strong and healthy. You will not be Pharaoh for many years.'

'I pray that you are right,' Mentu agreed. 'I trust in Ra that my father will have a long life ahead of him.'

'As do I,' Hanek agreed. 'But I cannot stay here waiting for those years to pass until your father journeys to the West so that we might be together.'

'You sound as though you wish my father a swift death,' Mentu said, an accusing edge in his voice.

'No,' Hanek said defensively. 'But I can't stay here until you become Pharaoh... how long? Ten years from now? Twenty? Longer, perhaps?'

Mentu sucked a deep breath. He had spent countless nights alone running through the arguments he would use to persuade Hanek to stay near him when this meeting finally happened, but now that the time had come, he found that he had no urge to use any of them. If Hanek was unwilling to wait a little for their relationship to continue, he wondered how real was that 'great love' she had spoken of so often? Was it a love of him or of the power she could gain through him? He knew that families sent their daughters into the palace as handmaidens in the hope of finding a good marriage. Was that all that had happened with Hanek? Either way, there was no doubt that this was the end and he had no wish to prolong it further. 'Then there is nothing more for us to say.'

'No,' Hanek murmured softly. 'You're right, your Majesty.' She reached for a cloak, as eager as Mentu for the torment to finish. 'I will attend your sister now.'

Mentu quickly stepped to the side, blocking her path as she tried to move around him. 'There is no need. Miral is with her. She will take care of my sister tonight.' Mentu felt a surge of satisfaction at the look of pain and surprise on Hanek's face. He knew it was petty to take any joy from it but he wanted her to feel the same sense of betrayal and abandonment that he had felt when she had turned away from him. 'Make certain that your mistress is properly attended in the morning. If you abandon her again you will answer to me for it.' He turned and swept from the room, carrying himself with the confidence and certainty of a king. It was only when he had left the building and turned the corner that his shoulders slumped and he punched a wall in fury.

Erimem woke feeling disoriented. Her mouth was dry and her head felt fuzzy, as though a wet blanket had been wrapped around her dully aching skull.

She stretched and arched her back – and stopped when her shoulder bumped into something solid behind her in her bed. She spun around and saw Miral's bleary eyes looking at her from under a wild tangle of dark hair. Erimem's momentary confusion disappeared as she remembered her friend's promise to stay with her. Miral blinked a few times, trying to blink away the sleep from her eyes and Erimem felt a slight tingle of pleasure that Miral didn't wake up looking as beautiful and elegant as she was whenever Erimem normally saw her. She imagined that she looked considerably worse. With Miral's help she had removed most of the smudged make-up that had marred her face the night before but she knew she would be a long way from her normal self.

'Did you sleep well?' Miral asked. 'You look much better for some rest.'

'I think you are just being kind,' Erimem replied. 'I am, sure I look like some terrible vengeful demon.'

'No,' Miral said in an easy, friendly tone. 'You look much worse than that.'

'Thank you,' Erimem choked out a laugh and Miral joined in. 'And thank you for staying with me.'

'You would have done no less for me,' Miral shrugged. 'Although I think you would have received a warmer greeting from my handmaidens than I will receive from yours.' She nodded towards the door where one of Erimem's attendants peered in before scuttling away again. 'It's no one's fault. It's just the way that fate has decided we must be.' She swung out of the bed and stretched. 'It would be best if I returned to my own quarters now. I have a great deal to do today. Besides,' she ran a hand through her unruly hair. 'If Mentu saw me with hair like this before our marriage he would take a chariot and hide in the desert until I gave up and went home.'

After Miral had borrowed a hooded cloak and set off for her own quarters, Erimem slipped back into her own routine. She was aware of the odd looks her handmaidens gave her but she held back from apologising. She had come to think of them as friends but she knew that Hanek was one of their number. They had looked at Miral with contempt and Erimem had been tempted to throw them all out again. But she needed them to help her bathe and dress. Antranak's revelation the day before had shaken her but Erimem was now more convinced than ever that Khofrek's death was somehow linked to both the attempt on her own life and Thutmose's assassination. As she ate a light breakfast of dates, bread and a wine, an idea began to form in Erimem's mind and she started making a mental list of those she would need to help her.

While Erimem was eating breakfast, Amenhotep and Mentu were also sitting down to their morning meal. Since soon after Amenhotep had emerged from his deepest wave of mourning, he had insisted that Mentu join him for breakfast each morning. He would then spend his day teaching his son how to deal with the politics of the court, of how to deal with foreign nations and domestic questions such as the harvest or taxation. In the afternoons, he and Antranak would instruct Mentu in military tactics and improve his basic fighting skills. Even though taxation bored him close to tears and he had no interest in politics or war, Mentu gave himself over completely to his lessons. It was the first time in a dozen years that his father was actually seeking to spend time with him and Mentu was relishing the attention from his father. He knew that this interest was his by default, that his father was using him to replace Thutmose, but Mentu embraced it anyway.

Breakfast had followed its usual path of pleasantries followed by Amenhotep laying out the day's agenda. Midway through detailing the visit to the tomb-builders' village outside the Valley of High Kings that they would be making in the afternoon, Amenhotep broke off abruptly and pushed aside his food.

'Is something wrong, my father?' Mentu asked.

'I think that is a question you should answer,' Amenhotep replied. A servant came forward to collect his plate, assuming he was finished eating but Amenhotep waved the servant away. 'When I first announced your marriage to the Mitannite…'

'Miral,' Mentu supplied.

Amenhotep nodded his thanks. 'When I first announced your marriage to Miral, you were violently against the idea.' He raised a hand to stop Mentu from protesting. 'You came to me and asked me to cancel my orders, to let you marry someone else.'

'I remember that day very well. You refused my request.'

Amenhotep reached out and placed a hand over his son's. 'If you asked me again today, I would delay the marriage to the Mitannite and allow you to marry this other girl.'

Mentu's stomach lurched. He was being offered the one thing that he had so desperately wanted… but Hanek had chosen to finish their affair and in truth he wasn't certain any more that she was all that she had seemed. The suspicion that he had been a target for a profitable marriage rather than a man Hanek had fallen in love with still clung to him. One day he would be Pharaoh and he couldn't allow himself to be tricked into a marriage. Neither could Pharaoh ever be seen to give in to a mere woman. And then there was Miral. He had treated her badly but she had acted with dignity and he would not forget the kindness she had shown to Erimem. A thousand conflicting thoughts ran through his mind, pulling him one way and then the other. But for all that he could remember the scent of Hanek's skin close to him, the feel of her around him, the taste of her soft skin, he couldn't bring himself to say the words that would bring her back to him. He sensed that his father was watching him, waiting for him to reach a decision and he suspected that there was more to this offer than a simple act of love from a father. It felt like a test.

'My father is most kind to make this offer,' Mentu said carefully. 'But I am aware that my marriage to Miral will end a conflict that has raged for hundreds of years. I cannot put my own wishes above the needs of Egypt.'

'When you are Pharaoh, your wishes and the needs of Egypt will be the same thing,' Amenhotep said imperiously. 'Never forget that.'

'I do remember that,' Mentu assured his father. 'Just as I remember that until I am Pharaoh, my task is to serve you and Egypt as best I am able. In this matter, I believe I can do that best by taking Miral as a wife and ending the bad blood between our people and the Mitanni.'

Amenhotep thought for a moment then nodded his approval. 'A wise answer,' he praised, a smile pulling at the corners of his mouth and a slight twinkle appearing in his eye. 'And it won't hurt that she is a most agreeable-looking girl. A remarkably womanly figure for one so young.'

'Really?' Mentu feigned ignorance. 'I haven't noticed.'

Amehotep barked a laugh, the first real laugh anyone had heard from him since Thutmose's death. 'My son, you made an honourable decision and made it wisely, but you will have to learn to lie more convincingly if you are to deal with the Council of Priests.'

Mentu nodded and laughed. 'Tell me,' he said after a moment. 'What would you have said if I had accepted your offer?'

'I would have given you a chance to reconsider,' Amenhotep replied. 'And then I would have asked you how long your eyesight has been failing.'

'She is beautiful, isn't she?' Mentu said thoughtfully.

'Young and strong,' Amenhotep agreed. 'She will give you many strong sons. And many happy nights making them.'

Mentu was intrigued to find that he didn't hate the idea quite as much as he had expected.

Shemek was the last to answer Erimem's summons. He shuffled into her rooms, complaining that the Princess was acting more like a Pharaoh every day... *didn't she know how old he was...? Did she know what time of day it was...?*

Erimem simply smiled and welcomed him, asking him to join Fayum and the handmaidens who were already waiting. Hanek had asked to be excused, saying that she was still suffering from the effects of her fever, and Erimem had agreed, making a mental note that she should remember to visit Teti. Like many in both the palace and Thebes at large, Teti was still struggling to overcome the fever.

She would ask Shemek to visit Teti when they were finished here. The astrologer had more learning on more subjects than any one man had a right to. He would grumble and moan but hopefully, he would be able to help Teti recover.

Looking round her gathered group, Erimem thought ruefully that it wasn't exactly a force to match the Isis Squadron. An old man, a young priest and half a dozen pampered handmaidens plucked from Thebes's highest families. She had thought briefly of taking her thoughts to Antranak or at least of asking for a dozen men to be assigned to her, but she knew that she had hurt her friend when she had spoken to him so harshly. She had been right to insist that he tell her the truth but he had deserved better than to be spoken down to as if he was no better than a slave. She would have to make amends to him for that. She noticed that Fayum was fidgeting, probably remembering what had happened when he had been summoned the previous day. And today, he wasn't flirting with the handmaidens.

Erimem began by describing the details of Khofrek the guard's murder and of the theory she and Antranak had come to, that the sentry had been murdered with a single thrust of a knife to his heart and that the other wounds had been added later to disguise the precision of the fatal wound to make the slaying look like it had been committed by a maniac and hide the killer's actions in leaving and then returning to the palace. She finished by saying that Khofrek was a man of good character with no debts or enemies.

When Erimem had done she looked to the small group for their reaction. Fayum had heard it all before and looked stoically back at her. The handmaidens looked understandably uneasy and some made little gestures, invoking the protection of the gods but it was Shemek's reaction that Erimem was most interested in seeing. His head was lolling forward and his heavy eyebrows masked his eyes. For a moment, Erimem wondered if the old man had fallen asleep but he raised his head, his eyes looking sharply at her. 'That all makes sense,' he mused, sucking his bottom lip thoughtfully. 'But it gives us no idea as to who committed this terrible crime. We can assume that this wasn't a personal act of murder. This poor Khofrek was simply in the wrong place when the killer had to pass.'

'That is the conclusion we reached as well,' Erimem blurted eagerly, relieved that her old tutor hadn't simply laughed at her conclusions.

'I taught you well,' Shemek chuckled. 'Antranak as well. Although he was much more difficult to teach than you. His mind was always wandering. So were his eyes. He had an eye for a pretty girl in his youth. But so did I at one time, and I took the eyes of the girls as well. Not that you'd believe it to look at me now.' He sighed wistfully, his memory slipping back through the years.

Erimem gently moved the conversation back on track. 'If this murderer was prepared to slay Khofrek,' she said, 'then it must have been important for him to leave the palace and return.' Fayum and Shemek nodded assent while the handmaidens looked more confused than ever as to why they were at this gathering. 'And that has made me wonder if there have been other nights when this killer has slipped out of the palace into the night.'

'No,' Fayum protested. 'That can't happen. 'Every entrance is guarded. No one can pass unseen and the gates are never opened except...'

'If a pretty girl asks the guard to do it,' Erimem cut in. She looked to her handmaidens, who began to understand why they were present and they started to squirm. 'And there are stories of other entrances to the palace. Ancient ones that are long forgotten.'

'I assume that's why I am here,' Shemek said pithily. 'I'm the only person in the palace ancient enough to remember all these secret entrances.'

'The only man *wise* enough,' Erimem corrected. 'You know this palace better than anyone. You also know the legends and rumours about the palace better than any hundred people.'

Fayum nudged Shemek. 'She means you're an old gossip.'

'She's right,' Shemek said ruefully. 'I am a gossip. It's one of the few things I can still do that's actually worth doing.' He turned to Erimem. 'You want to know where these secret entrances are because you think they'll try to slip out again?'

'Why would it happen just once?' Erimem asked. 'If they had to go out once, it's at least a possibility that they've had to do it again.'

Shemek couldn't argue with the logic. 'What do you want me to do when I have this list of entrances?' he asked. 'It shouldn't take long. There aren't many left. Should I tell Antranak?'

This was the time Erimem had been most uncertain of. She gathered her courage and forced confidence into her voice. 'No, you will tell me and we will deal with it among ourselves.' No one replied but their startled expressions spoke volumes. Erimem knew that if she hadn't been Pharaoh's daughter they would have been saying she was mad. Instead they were just thinking it. 'There will be no danger to anyone,' she reassured them hurriedly. 'We will simply watch these entrances as a precaution. If we see anything, we will summon the palace guard and let them deal with the intruder.' She mentally gave herself a pat on the back for not using the word 'killer'. Her little group was nervous enough without her reminding them that they would be tracking a murderer. 'No one who is not here now must know of this. No one. It must remain secret or we will frighten our prize away.' And, she added to herself, if nothing happens I won't look quite so foolish in front of the entire palace. And if she did discover an intruder, she would have something to pass to Antranak as a peace offering.

Even though the palace was centuries old and had been built up and embellished by successive Pharaohs and dynasties, it didn't take Shemek long to list the sites of possible breaches in its security. There were four in all. Two were instantly dismissed as being too close to the army's barracks. That left two options, both of which Shemek described as perfect for anyone seeking to slip in and out of the grounds.

One was a slight gap in the wall where a carved stone had been damaged and had been removed for a stonemason to repair. The gap was small but enough that a man could just about squeeze through. The other was a grated water pipe where water from the Nile was diverted along a canal and into the grounds to fill Pharaoh's pond and used to water his gardens. A heavy, metal mesh covered the canal to stop the sacred crocodiles from entering the palace grounds but Shemek assured them that a determined man could bend the copper mesh and make it look as if it had never been tampered with. Erimem agreed that these were the most likely places for an intruder – if such an intruder still existed – to come and go.

She congratulated the old man and he glowed under the praise. It was a long time since he had been given such glowing tributes by a member of Pharaoh's own family. He was relieved when Erimem excused him the last part of the duty and summoned a chariot to take her old tutor home.

Once she was sure that Shemek was being taken to his rooms like an honoured dignitary, Erimem turned her attention to the remainder of her gathering. 'We will find places from which we can watch these breaks in the wall,' she announced. 'There are eight of us here so four will watch each of the breaches.'

'But we need sleep,' Linsis, the most vocal of the handmaidens, complained.

'And how can we defend ourselves?' Valu asked. She was the youngest and smallest of the handmaidens and barely looked capable of fighting a breeze.

Erimem was prepared for the question. 'Each group will have two of my personal escort with them. No one man can defeat two of Pharaoh's finest warriors.'

'And I will protect you, 'Fayum promised earnestly.

'You will be with me, Fayum,' Erimem said snippily. 'It's the only way I can protect my girls from you.'

Fayum scowled.

# Chapter Eight
## The Enemy Uncovered

he first night's watch yielded nothing but a dozen very tired people who yawned through most of the next day at court. Those set on watching the gap in the wall caused by the removed stone had settled behind a wall leading to steps up to the top of the palace wall while Erimem's group had commandeered a large pagoda on an island in the middle of the pool closest to the channel which brought the Nile's water in and led outside.

Both parties had split into two watches of two who split the night evenly between them. The only moment of interest for any of them came with the first light of dawn when Erimem woke, huddled deep in a cloak to see Fayum and Linsis in a most intimate embrace. Evidently they had grown tired of the watch and found another way to pass the time. Erimem had closed her eyes, feigned a yawn and stifled a smirk at the sudden gap that had grown between Fayum and Linsis when she opened her eyes. They had returned to the palace and gone about their business lethargically, most of them relishing the gap in the day's business when the sun was at its height to catch some more sleep. Only Erimem's ever-present bodyguards seemed oblivious to the need for sleep and she contemplated asking Antranak for an extra detail of guards so that these men could get some rest.

The day itself was swelteringly hot, unusually so even for Thebes, and Erimem struggled to find the energy to perform even the most mundane tasks. She skipped training with her guards as a kindness to them and to herself, and visited Teti, who had improved a little with the advent of a new serving girl who brought his food and made sure he actually ate it. Erimem kept the visit short, partly because she knew that Teti needed to rest and partly because she felt that she was intruding on something with Teti and his servant. She slept and ate heartily before making her daily visit to Miral where, for once, her welcome was less than warm. Two of Miral's Mitannite bodyguards stood at the doorway, blocking the entrance. When Erimem approached they stood their ground until she was forced to stop.

'I am here to see Miral.' The guards looked back sourly but didn't move. Erimem met their surly gazes with just a hint of contempt. She was tired and in no mood for this kind of nonsense. 'Move aside,' she commanded witheringly. 'Or my escort will move you. There are four of them and only two of you. They are armed, you are not, now move!'

The force of Erimem's anger took the Mitannite soldiers by surprise but they looked set to stand their ground and accept the consequences until Miral's voice came from inside her room.

'What is happening?' Miral emerged, radiant in an emerald green dress which dipped daringly low at the front showing more than a hint of her considerable cleavage and was slit high at the side revealing a shapely, tanned thigh. Ornately designed golden rings and bracelets decorated her fingers and wrists. She took in the situation at a glance and threw an icy stare at her guards. 'Move aside you cretins and let my sister pass. Or should I have your entrails fed to the jackals for insulting the daughter of Pharaoh?'

Reluctantly, the sullen guards moved aside letting Erimem pass. Her own bodyguards moved past the Mitanni as well and stood guard between their mistress and the foreign soldiers.

'I apologise for my countrymen,' Miral said wryly. She looked past Erimem and raised her voice to make sure her guards heard. 'Today they have acted like idiots!' But her anger didn't last. It disappeared and was replaced by a huge, happy smile.

Erimem peered at her friend intently. 'Something is different today.'

'I'm smiling?' Miral offered with an impish gleam.

'No,' Erimem said with a hint of puzzlement. 'You look different... your dress is...'

'Revealing,' Miral said cheerfully. 'Almost immodestly so, especially for one about to be married.'

'I was going to say, "Your dress is beautiful". But it does show more than I would have expected, so I suppose you're right. But it's not the dress. It's...' she looked her friend in the eyes – and gazed straight into the answer. 'Your eyes!' she exclaimed. 'You're wearing kohl.'

Miral wafted fingers at her eyes where the black powder had been applied in the traditional sloe-eye design. 'I was informed this morning that I would be receiving an honoured visitor, so I asked the handmaidens to help me look more like a bride fitting for a prince of Egypt.'

'Who was it?' Erimem asked. 'It wasn't the vizier, was it? I know he's wanted you to become more like us and...'

'It was your brother,' Miral blurted happily.

'My brother?' Erimem repeated dumbly. It took a moment for the words to sink in. 'Mentu visited you?'

'No,' Miral said, as though talking to an idiot. 'It was Teti.' Her beaming smile returned. 'Of course it was Mentu.' Miral grabbed Erimem's hands and hauled her to a low seat. 'He welcomed me to the palace and said that if I had any concerns that I should see him personally.' She jangled her hands in front of Erimem, showing off the gleaming gold jewellery. 'And he brought me these as a gift.' She wafted a hand towards her bed-chamber. 'There are caskets of them through there. Gold, precious stones, ornate carvings...' She stopped and eyed her friend suspiciously. 'Did you talk with him?' she demanded.

'You asked me not to,' Erimem replied evasively.

'You didn't answer my question,' Miral replied.

Erimem shifted slightly. 'I may have mentioned a few things,' she said uneasily. 'But I hated seeing the way he was...' She yelped as Miral flung her arms around Erimem and pulled her into a tight embrace.

'Thank you,' Miral whispered. She pulled Erimem's hands to her lips and kissed them. 'I am in your debt forever.' She leaned over and pressed her lips gently to Erimem's. 'And I am your sister forever,' she said, pulling away. 'That is a custom of my people. From the expression on your face I think it's not a custom here.'

Erimem shook her head. 'No, but I am pleased that my brother has seen sense at last. The only option I had left was to beat it into him.'

'I think you'd win,' Miral whispered conspiratorially.

Erimem glanced back at the doorway and at Miral's guards who still stood, surly and miserable beyond the doors. Her own guards were facing them with their backs to Erimem and Miral. 'I assume that your happiness has something to do with why they are so aggressive?'

Miral grimaced. 'Not everyone is happy with this marriage. There are some among my people – and in Egypt too – who dislike the match.' She nodded at her guards. 'Those two have fought Egyptians for so long that they despise the idea of me taking one as a husband.' She pursed her lips thoughtfully. 'But if I am to spend more time with your brother, it would be better if my countrymen weren't nearby, sulking. Should I arrange to have your Egyptian soldiers as escort when I see your brother?'

'I think that would be wise,' Erimem nodded. 'Have you arranged to meet my brother again?'

Miral nodded excitedly. 'Tonight. He will join me here to eat and we will talk alone.'

A look of understanding appeared on Erimem's face. 'Ah. That is why you have dressed like this?'

'Not only dressed,' Miral whispered. She peered past Erimem to make sure that none of the guards could see them. She leaned forward and less her dress fall open. She pulled the material aside to reveal a breast, its nipple painted gold. She slipped the material back into place quickly. 'I won't know him in my bed until we are married,' she said firmly. 'But I will let him glimpse what is waiting for him.' She giggled. 'Accidentally, of course.'

'Of course,' Erimem agreed with mock sincerity. And then she began to laugh as well. Her brother, the notorious womaniser, was about to be seduced into waiting until he was married. There was a delicious irony to it. 'I think,' she said slowly. 'That you and Mentu are well matched.'

By the time Erimem left, Miral's Mitannite guards had been replaced by four of Antranak's finest soldiers, two of them carrying spears and the others armed with swords. Miral herself was having the finishing touches put to her appearance for her meeting with Mentu and Erimem mused happily that Miral was going to have a much more enjoyable night than she was.

The second night followed the same dull pattern as the first, even down to Linsis and Fayum keeping a rather closer watch on each other than was necessary. Midway through the night, just after Erimem had taken watch, she had heard a noise but it had only been drunk charioteers cutting through the gardens to return to barracks. One had stopped to relieve himself in the pond and Erimem had made a mental note not to dip her feet in the pond for the rest of the month. But apart from that, the night passed without incident.

The weather that day proved to be both a blessing and a curse. The sun was again unusually hot and a scalding, dry wind blew in from the desert. It made the day unbearable and those who could gave in and did nothing, lying and suffering through the heat. Only slaves and servants struggled about their normal tasks in the baking conditions. So, while the heat and dryness were uncomfortable, it allowed Erimem and her little band to catch up with rest and sleep without anyone noticing anything untoward and it was early in the afternoon that Erimem decided she was feeling refreshed enough by sleep and food to venture out into the sun. When she had asked Linsis to fetch her a parasol so that she could pay her daily visit to Miral, she had caught a hint of resentment in the girl's eyes.

'You don't approve of me visiting Miral?' she asked bluntly.

Linsis's eyes dipped to the floor. 'It's not my place to approve or disapprove of your actions, my lady. I am your servant.'

'I thought you were my friend,' Erimem replied swiftly. 'I thought you were all my friends.'

'We would like to be,' Linsis answered eagerly. 'But each day you visit Miral and each day we see Hanek sickening in her bed.'

'How is she?' Erimem asked, suppressing a pang of guilt for not asking after Hanek earlier.

A concerned frown appeared on Linsis's dark face. 'Like many in the palace, she is unable to shake the fever. But I think her soul sickens more than her body. She has given her heart to a man who is now giving his affections to another girl. But at least she will be gone before the marriage.'

'Good,' Erimem replied. She could hardly imagine how Hanek would be feeling. Spending her days alone in her room while she was sick with fever, she would have nothing to do but think on what she had lost. 'It will be best for her to be away from here.'

Linsis nodded in agreement. 'But it's hard not to feel…'

'I understand,' Erimem interrupted. 'But we must live with what will happen, not with what Hanek would want. It was my father's choice.'

Thankfully, Erimem's visit to Miral was a far happier occasion than her conversation with Linsis. After a leisurely stroll to Miral's apartments – during which one of her bodyguards had looked scandalised when she had handed him the parasol to hold over her head – Erimem found Miral looking as radiant as ever and if anything, even happier than the day before.

'I assume your evening with Mentu went well,' Erimem asked with mock innocence.

Miral beamed. 'It was wonderful.' she was virtually bouncing with glee. 'We ate as the sun died and then we talked long into the night. The women of my people told me that a man should be encouraged to talk about himself.'

'You won't have found that difficult with Mentu,' Erimem said wryly. 'He has always enjoyed talking about himself.'

'No,' Miral disagreed. 'He spent the night asking questions about me, about my life before I came here, about what I like to do…' Her eyes gleamed with happiness and Erimem didn't have the heart to tell her that Mentu had used the same trick of seduction on Miral that she had been taught to use on him. 'And then we walked in the gardens,' Miral continued.

'The gardens?' Erimem asked, wondering how close Miral and Mentu had come to her hiding place. The gardens were vast so the chances of them being near were remote.

'Yes,' Miral said. 'The sun had set when we went out and I began to feel the cold bite through me. When he saw I was shivering, Mentu put his cloak and his arm around me as we walked.'

'That was most thoughtful of him,' Erimem said, trying hard to keep the smile from her voice. She had been right. Mentu had played Miral at her own game and won.

'He's very generous,' Miral agreed. 'And very kind. But he didn't stay with me through the night,' she added hurriedly.

'I didn't think that he would,' Erimem answered quickly, surprised by her friend's outburst.

'I just wanted you to know,' Miral said defensively. The twinkle returned to her eyes. 'Though from the way he held me against him when we were walking and the way he looked at me, I think he wanted to stay.'

'Given how much of you that dress you were wearing let him see I'm surprised you didn't have to fight him off,' Erimem grinned.

Miral's eyebrow raised slightly. 'What makes you think I would have tried to fight him off?'

Erimem's jaw dropped open. 'Miral!' she exclaimed. 'You…'

'Hussy?' Miral supplied. 'Harlot? Loose woman?' She sighed. 'Or a woman in love? Last night I could have been all of those for him.'

'But instead he respected you and left,' Erimem said with approval.

'Yes, he did,' Miral said regretfully. 'But not before he had seen a good deal of what is waiting for him when he is my husband.' She patted her chest, which was now concealed beneath a far more demure dress. 'I have often wished these were smaller but last night they were my allies.'

'Miral, you are no better than one of the temple girls!' Erimem scolded. 'You flaunted yourself.'

'I did,' Miral smirked. 'And it worked.' She looked worriedly at Erimem. 'But I think you had a less pleasant night.' She gently touched the weary puffiness around Erimem's eyes. 'You didn't sleep well? Tell me you haven't been struck with Teti's fever?'

'I'm all right,' Erimem reassured her. 'I don't have a fever.' She puffed her cheeks out and blew despairingly. 'Though I think some people would think I have a brain fever.' She saw the confused look on Miral's face and thought of dismissing her statement to Miral with a glib comment, but she had the feeling that the Mitannite girl would see through any deception, so she gave a concise report on how she had spent the past two nights.

'You were right,' Miral said when Erimem was finished. 'I do think you are mad and should see a physician to have your brain cured.' She grasped Erimem's wrists. 'Do you know how dangerous what you are doing is? If this man exists, what will he do if you corner him? He will lash out.' Concern creased her beautiful face. 'You could be hurt or worse.'

'I will be safe with my guards to protect me,' Erimem said confidently.

'Did they help you when your boat was attacked by crocodiles?' Miral demanded. Her voice softened. 'These are dangerous times. You should be more careful.' She caught Erimem's chin between her thumb and forefinger. 'I couldn't bear to see something happen to you.'

'I will be careful,' Erimem promised. She sighed wearily. 'Besides, I think this is a waste of time. If we see nothing tonight, I will abandon the the thing as a stupid idea.' A wry smile tugged at the corners of her mouth. 'Besides, I don't think I could face another night of Linsis and Fayum's... activities.'

'Activities?' Miral asked. 'Oh,' she said as realisation dawned. 'Activities. Perhaps I should come along tonight. I may learn something.'

'You know enough already,' Erimem answered. 'Besides, won't you be spending your evening gazing into the eyes of my brother?'

Miral's mouth quirked into an unhappy grimace. 'Not tonight. He and your father are visiting an army camp. But he must do his duty. He told me that he and your father are spending a great deal of time together.'

'So I hear,' Erimem agreed. 'Everything that my father taught Thutmose, he must now teach to Mentu.'

'It will be difficult for them both,' Miral mused. 'I think Mentu feels uncomfortable at taking Thutmose's place. He hasn't said as much but I know he relishes his time with your father. He said as much to me last night.' Miral wrinkled her nose. 'I'm worrying for no reason, aren't I?'

'Probably,' Erimem said.

'I worried that he would never forget the servant he preferred to me,' Miral said with surprising bitterness.

'You have nothing to fear from Hanek,' Erimem promised. 'She will be gone in a few days. I will be visiting her in her quarters to say our farewells after I leave here.'

'You are visiting a servant?' Miral asked, clearly shocked by the thought. 'Why not summon her to your apartments?'

'She has been sick with the fever,' Erimem explained.

'And sickening from losing Mentu?' Miral asked.

'That too,' Erimem conceded.

'I am not sorry that she is leaving,' Miral stated flatly. 'But I have no real grudge against her. She has no more control over her heart then I have over mine. Oh!' Miral exclaimed with a look of surprise. 'I haven't shown you the present Mentu brought me last night. Come with me.'

She dragged Erimem by the hand through to the bedchamber. Lying asleep on a rug at the foot of the enormous bed, with a chain around its neck, was a tiger cub. Miral knelt and tickled the cub under the chin. The tiger shifted slightly but didn't wake.

'I told Mentu two nights ago that I had always wanted to see a tiger and last night he brought me this little one.' She stood up. 'He sleeps a lot, then when he wakes he eats and cries.'

'Are you talking about the tiger or Mentu?' Erimem asked innocently.

Miral scowled at her, then a huge grin lit up her face and she hooked her arm through Erimem's. 'If you are going to spend your night out in the dark, you will need to eat. And if I am to spend my night with only handmaidens for company then it would suit us both to eat together early.' She glanced back at the tiger. 'Besides, it's much better to eat when he's asleep. He's very sweet but still quite wild.' Her eyes twinkled. 'And so is the tiger he gave me.'

The sun was well on its journey back to the horizon when Erimem left Miral's quarters. She gave a small prayer that the sun would rise again the next day. With an aggrieved-looking bodyguard again holding the parasol to protect her from the last of the sun, Erimem quickly made her way to the low building that housed her handmaidens' rooms. She had stayed longer with Miral than she had intended and would have less time than she wanted to say goodbye to Hanek. At the doorway she met Linsis, who was clearly surprised to see her mistress.

'I am here to see Hanek,' Erimem explained. 'Which is her room?'

'Follow me and I will take you there.' Strict rules dictated that no men could enter so Erimem left her bodyguards. She followed Linsis into the building and she was surprised by how large and bright it was. Regular windows let light into the spacious rooms and the sweet smell of flowers came in on the breeze. The furnishings were more ornate than Erimem had expected as well, but she reminded herself that her handmaidens were from good families who could afford craftsmanship for their daughters.

'Hanek's room is at the back of the building,' Linsis explained ruefully. 'And it's the biggest. We're drawing lots to see who gets it when she leaves.'

They had reached the end of the building's central passage, where the corridor turned at a right angle. Erimem stopped short as she saw a large figure ahead, his back to them as he pulled a door shut. Linsis opened her mouth to speak but Erimem pulled her back around the corner and hustled her into the nearest room. They heard heavy footsteps and then the nearby creak of a door.

Erimem waited a moment before speaking, to be sure that the man wasn't lying in wait. 'Is there a second entrance?'

Linsis nodded and warily led her mistress back into the corridor. A small door leading to a path was lying open. 'That man,' Linsis said nervously.

'I know,' Erimem interrupted. 'He was a Mitannite. One of Miral's bodyguards.' She indicated along the corridor, to the door the Mitannite hade been closing. 'Is that Hanek's room?'

'Yes,' Linsis confirmed. She was shaking and Erimem had to grab the girl's wrist to make sure that she didn't run.

They made their way along the corridor, moving slowly and quietly until they reached the door. Unsure of what she might see inside, Erimem gingerly pushed at the door. The shutters were closed across the windows so that only shafts of light illuminated the room, but Erimem and Linsis both saw clearly enough. Four or five empty wine jars lay discarded on the floor while two goblets sat on a table by the bed alongside plates of bread and fruit. Hanek lay sprawled on the bed, the top of her dress pulled down so that her breasts were uncovered and the lower half of the dress was rucked up around her waist so that the dress looked like little more than a belt. She was sprawled with her legs apart with one draped over the side of the bed, her foot resting on the floor and her most intimate parts were exposed. She was breathing deeply, her chest rising and falling regularly in sleep. Leaning against her breast was an empty goblet. Erimem pulled the door shut slowly.

'I don't understand,' Linsis gasped. 'Why would Hanek take a Mitannite into her bed?' She said she hated the Mitanni.'

'A Mitannite stole her lover.' Erimem grasped Linsis by the wrist and pulled her away. 'Perhaps Hanek decided to repay Mentu by taking a Mitannite lover of her own.'

'No,' Linsis protested. 'He must have forced himself on her.'

'By bringing wine to get her drunk?' Erimem asked sarcastically. 'And food enough for a small feast?' She shook her head. 'I don't think it's fever that has been keeping Hanek in bed recently.'

'We should wake her,' Linsis said urgently. 'We should ask her what she has been doing.'

'We will do nothing,' Erimem commanded firmly. 'We will forget that we saw any of this and go about our own business.'

'But Hanek...'

Erimem's hand cut down sharply, quieting Linsis. 'Hanek is leaving us in a few days. She is not the first girl in Thebes – or this building.' She stared at Linsis meaningfully. 'Who has made a bad choice of man.' Linsis looked away, a blush spreading as she remembered the night Erimem had saved her at the tavern. Erimem softened her voice. 'She has suffered enough with her heart being broken. It would be cruel and petty of us to make her suffer more by asking her to explain this. So we will forget this happened and the next time you see Hanek, you will smile and tell her that I will visit her tomorrow morning. You will not mention this, is that understood? Or would you rather I told everyone about you and Fayum in the pagoda?'

Linsis flushed but had the decency not to try to deny her actions.

'Come,' she said, slipping into a more friendly tone. 'We should return to my rooms. The sun is almost set.'

Linsis nodded and they set off, Linsis slipping into her own room to collect a cloak, wondering how much Erimem had seen over the past few nights. Her blush grew just a little warmer.

By halfway through her watch, Erimem had decided that this would be the last night of watching. It was wasting people's time and, more importantly, she was cold tired and uncomfortable. An icy wind had picked up from the north east and was cutting through her heavy cloak. She pulled the garment tighter around her. Linsis had given up hiding her attachment to Fayum and was snuggled against the priest's side and Erimem felt a hint of jealousy that she had no one. Fayum had Linsis; Miral had Mentu (who had, she had learned, returned early from his trip so that he could see Miral); Teti had a serving girl making eyes at him and even Hanek seemed to have cast aside her misery and found herself someone to warm her through the night. Erimem snorted. She didn't even have a tiger cub to cling to.

'Is something wrong, Princess?' Fayum's voice almost made Erimem leap.

'Fayum!' she scolded. 'Are you trying to frighten me to death?'

'No,' the priest replied. 'I was having difficulty sleeping so I thought I would talk with you.'

Erimem was grateful for the company. The bodyguard, with whom she shared the watch, was hardly fascinating conversation. 'You should sleep,' she said, desperately hoping Fayum would ignore her advice. He didn't fail her.

'Linsis is sleeping on my arm,' he explained. 'The arm feels as though it has a thousand pins pricking it but I haven't the heart to waken her.'

'You're fond of her?' Erimem asked cautiously.

'You know I am,' Fayum replied. 'She told me that you know we have become...'

'Friendly?' Erimem offered.

'Very,' Fayum confirmed. 'She also let slip that you were angry with her this afternoon. And then she tried to cover it as a nothing.'

'It was a nothing,' Erimem assured her friend. 'I am not angry with Linsis now and I wasn't really angry with her then.'

On cue, Linsis moved restlessly in her sleep and turned tighter into Fayum, sliding an arm inside his heavy dark cloak. 'Good,' he said. 'She likes you. She tells me that they all like you. All of your handmaidens. Even the ones you make sit out in the cold all through the night.'

Erimem humphed quietly. 'This will be the last night of it. Tomorrow we will all sleep in our own beds.' She ducked her head forward to peer past Fayum at the sleeping Linsis .'I did say *your own* bed.'

Fayum chuckled. 'I don't think she and I have sleep in mind.'

'Fayum!' Erimem whispered hoarsely. 'You are a respected priest at one of the most venerated temples. You shouldn't talk like that.'

'And you know that it's only in the act of sexual love that priests are truly close to our gods. That's why we have the temple prostitutes.'

'That's why so many men choose to be priests,' Erimem grouched. A movement on the far side of the pagoda caught her eye. Her bodyguard was tapping his colleague on the shoulder. Together, they peered out into the night. Erimem glanced at the sky and cursed the high clouds that were skidding across the heavens. There was little enough moon that night without clouds hiding it from view. She put a finger to Fayum's lips and moved across to join the two soldiers. Fayum gently eased Linsis away from his shoulder and followed Erimem. The bodyguards didn't speak but held two fingers to his eyes and then pointed out towards the palace wall. Erimem shook her head in confusion. She could see nothing. But then, on cue, the clouds parted and the crescent moon shone its meagre light – just enough for Erimem to make out a single figure in a heavy black cloak which even covered his head as he reached the broad alcove that housed the copper grating that allowed water to enter. He stopped and looked around, concerned by the moon's appearance before dipping into the alcove.

'Go!' Erimem pushed her bodyguards hard. 'Alive if you can.'

Her escorts leaped from the pagoda and charged towards the grate but before they were halfway to the alcove there was a metallic creaking as the metal moved.

'Hurry,' Erimem yelled. She grabbed Fayum's arm. 'Get Antranak,' she commanded. 'Tell him what has happened.'

'Where will you be?' Fayum demanded, but Erimem had already slipped over the low wall of the pagoda and was running after her bodyguards. Fayum cursed and shook Linsis. 'Wake up!'

By the time Erimem reached the grate, both the intruder and her two bodyguards had passed through a gap caused by the gate being pushed slightly at one side. Footsteps were running into the distance to her right. Squinting into the darkness she could just about make out some kind of movement and she ran towards it. The moon escaped from the clouds for an instant and she recognised the figures of her two bodyguards running across an open stretch of ground towards a distant black shape she took to be houses or huts for boats. They had to be approaching the Nile. Sure enough there was a definite tang of the river in the air and Erimem was sure she could hear water flowing not too far ahead. A niggling worry began to pester Erimem. Finding these buildings in the dark would be almost impossible unless the intruder already knew of their existence. Which asked the question of why he was going to them? To escape in a boat? If she was right, he had returned to the palace before, which meant it was likely that he would have sought to return again. So why go here? Unless, perhaps, he was meeting accomplices. That niggling worry turned swiftly to dread. If she was right, Erimem had ordered her bodyguards to run straight into an ambush. She called for the soldiers to stop but she was running and breathing hard, and her voice was little more than a choked gasp.

'What is it?' Fayum's voice sounded breathless and Erimem was relieved to see a murky shape running towards her in the dim light. The clash of metal on metal from ahead came as an answer.

'He must have been meeting allies,' Erimem explained. The sound of swords clashing again sounded along with shouts and cries in a language Erimem didn't understand.

'Go back,' Fayum gasped. 'Go back to the palace. I'll help them.' He ran forward into the night. Erimem stopped and half turned. Should she run back to the palace as Fayum had said? Who knew what was waiting for her in the darkness? But if she went forward, she knew exactly what was waiting. Whatever she did, she knew she couldn't stay where she was. Reaching inside her cloak, she grasped the hilt of a fighting dagger and pulling a deep breath, she ran forward.

Oil lamps burned dimly outside two small fishermen's huts and in the small flickering pool of dull yellow light Erimem saw that her bodyguard, with Fayum by their side, were fighting off at least twice as many men. She had been right. The intruder had been meeting allies and now they were going to kill Fayum and the bodyguards to protect their secrets. She could count at least six of them in the half-light, most of them ebony skinned showing that they hailed from the south. They had formed a sort of circle around the three Egyptians and were edging towards them, prodding with spears and swords, looking for the chance to attack. Fayum was clearly the weak spot in the Egyptian force. He was small in comparison to Erimem's escort and while they were armed with swords, Fayum only had a hooked fishing pole he had grabbed as he ran to join the fight. Two of his black-skinned adversaries were probing his defences and already it was all Fayum could do to fend off this tentative attack. When they attacked in earnest, he would be cut to pieces and when the odds stood at six against two, her guards would also be cut down, no matter how bravely they fought. One of Fayum's attackers lunged and he swung the pole to parry the oncoming attack. It was the opening his opponents had been working for and the other attacker swung his sword at Fayum's mid-section. At the last moment Fayum managed to shift his balance and swing the fishing pole back, deflecting the sword so that it only caught him a glancing blow to the arm. Ignoring the sharp pain from the cut in his arm, Fayum spun the pole back towards the other assailant. This time the fishing pole took the full force of an oncoming sword and was sheared in two. Half of the pole was ripped from Fayum's grasp and sent flying. He swung the other half violently back and forth, desperately holding his pursuers at bay.

Erimem could see that her bodyguards were struggling to hold their attackers off, but Fayum was in a more desperate position. He could have only moments before he was cut down. Snatching up the discarded half of the fishing pole Erimem charged at the nearest of Fayum's attackers. She ducked low and swung the fishing pole with all her strength at the man's knee. There was a sickening scrunching sound of bone, muscle and gristle as the knee joint folded from the side. Taking his opportunity, Fayum slammed the other half of the fishing pole into the reeling assailant's face and the man fell, blood and broken teeth spilling from his mouth. Behind him, Fayum's other tormentor had raised his sword, ready to bring it slashing down across the priest's back but Erimem raised her piece of fishing pole and slammed it down through the attacker's foot, deep into the ground. He screamed and tried to pull himself free but Fayum was on him, beating him viciously with the wooden pole. Distracted by their colleagues' sudden reversal, the remaining four attackers let their guards fall slightly and Erimem's bodyguards took full advantage. One drove his sword through the chest of the nearest enemy and turned the dying attacker as a shield until he could pull his sword free. Another of the ambushers toppled as a sword hacked into his midriff, almost tearing him in two and letting his innards spill to the dust.

In just a few heartbeats, the odds had swung in their direction and Erimem began to feel confident that they would win through when she heard Fayum's alarmed voice call her name and felt a rough arm clamp around her throat. It had to be the intruder from the palace who had led them here. For a moment he had slipped her mind. Yellow light caught the edge of a polished knife as it was brought to her throat and then she felt the blade's sharp edge press against her skin, cutting until she was sure she could feel the blood trickling from the wound. She knew she was going to die. Fayum and her bodyguards, who had by now dispatched the last two attackers, were all standing ready to kill the man holding her, but it wouldn't matter. She knew that she would be dead. She offered her spirit, her ka, into the protection of the gods and waited for the final slashing movement of the knife across her throat. But before the killing blow could come, the sound of dozens of running feet charging towards them distracted everyone. In that instant, Erimem reached for the dagger she held inside the sash of her dress. She grasped it with both hands and pushed backwards. She felt the flat of the blade slide against her side and then the resistance as it dug into her captor. Shocked by the sudden pain, his grip loosened further and Erimem managed to heave the hand holding the knife away from her throat far enough for her to drop down like a dead weight, sliding through his flailing grasp. She hit the ground and dived towards her escort. Suddenly alone and outnumbered, with no means of defence, the intruder kicked over a large oil lamp, spilling burning oil in front of Erimem and her guards, making them leap backwards as the oil caught light. Through the flames they saw the intruder run towards the river and onto a boat. Despite his wound, he began to paddle quickly and within a few moments had been eaten by the night.

The source of the thundering footsteps finally emerged from the darkness as Antranak led a dozen of his men into view. He was breathing hard and sweating heavily despite the chill in the air, but he didn't make any effort to pause and catch his breath before hurrying to Erimem.

'Are you hurt?' His eyes dropped to her neck and widened in horror. 'You are. He cut you.'

Erimem held a hand to her throat and it came away, her hand coated with a thick liquid and she wondered at how black her blood looked in the darkness. She touched the wound again but Antranak pulled her hands away and turned her so that he could use the burning oil to see better.

'It's wide but shallow,' he said with clear relief. 'It won't kill you. You probably won't even be left with a mark. You've been lucky.'

With the excitement fading, Erimem could feel the sharp pain and the throbbing from her throat. 'That's easy for you to say. It's not your throat.'

'No, but my throat would have been cut if you had died tonight,' Antranak snapped angrily. 'What were you thinking, setting a trap like this? Why didn't you tell me what you had discovered?'

'Because I hadn't discovered anything,' Erimem answered sharply. 'And because...' she trailed off self-consciously. 'Because I talked to you like a servant, not a friend.'

Antranak's face softened. 'I am just relieved that you are still able to talk. Here.' He grabbed Fayum and tore strip from the priest's tunic. 'You should have known better,' he snapped at Fayum before handing the strip of cloth to Erimem. 'Use that to cover the wound.'

As Erimem tied the cloth around her throat, she became aware of an unusual, unpleasant smell. 'Antranak, is that...'

'Burning flesh,' Antranak confirmed. The burning oil had spread across the ground and was engulfing three of the dead attackers. 'Get them out of there,' Antranak instructed. 'We will learn nothing from them if we are left with charred husks.'

'At least two are still alive,' Erimem said, pointing to the two she and Fayum had dealt with.

Antranak eyed them with interest. 'The one with the smashed jaw won't be saying anything for a time and the other...' His eyebrow shot up as he saw the pole pinning the man's foot to the ground. 'You?' he asked Erimem. She nodded. 'Unusual,' Antranak said thoughtfully. 'But effective nonetheless.'

Erimem beamed at the praise, and at the return of her easy friendship with Antranak.

'I don't like this,' Antranak said suddenly. 'Look at them. All of them. The colour of their skin.'

'I noticed that,' Erimem agreed. 'They're Nubians, but the man we followed from the palace wasn't. His skin was lighter. Lighter even than mine.'

'That makes it worse,' Antranak mused darkly. He turned to his men. 'Have the bodies brought back to the palace. The priests may prove useful for once and learn something from them.' Fayum ignored the bait, and let himself be pampered by a concerned Linsis. Antranak pointed at the two injured Nubians. 'And take those two to the House of Pain. I will have answers from them before they die.' He turned back to Erimem who was securing the cloth around her throat and glowering at Linsis, silently cursing the girl for fussing over Fayum instead of helping her. 'Your father will have to be told of this,' Antranak said. 'And I won't be able to keep your involvement from him.'

Erimem smiled wryly. 'He should know everything,' she agreed. 'He has been angry with me before but he forgives me.'

Antranak set a huge hand on Erimem's shoulder. 'If he rages at you because of this, remember that he is your father and that he will be afraid that he could have lost you, too. He loves you a great deal.'

'Does he?'

'The girl has lost her mind,' Amenhotep hurled a goblet of wine across the room and it crashed off a wall a hand's breadth away from a slave's head. 'Leave it!' he yelled as the slave knelt to picked up the cup. 'I said leave it! Get out!'

The terrified slave ran for the door in relief. When Pharaoh was in this kind of rage, he knew it was safest to be as far from the King as possible.

'Erimem is aware of the danger now, Majesty,' Antranak said, trying to smooth over his king's rage. 'She will not place herself in danger again.'

Mentu spoke up. He was the only other person present thus far. Others had been summoned but had yet to arrive. 'But you must admit, my father that she showed great courage to face the Nubian assassins.'

'What use is courage if she is dead?' Amenhotep snapped.

'But she did uncover that there are Nubians plotting,' Antranak said, picking up on Mentu's statement. 'Plotting with someone within the palace walls.'

'Within *my* palace walls,' Amenhotep snarled. 'I want that intruder found, Antranak, and I want you to burn answers from him.'

Antranak nodded grimly. 'The city guard are already searching with every man they have. The palace guard are helping but we must maintain the security of the palace itself. However, I have sent for every soldier we have to help and when Horemshep gets here I will demand that his temple guard assist as well.'

'Don't wait for him,' Amenhotep said quickly. 'On my divine command, the temple guard will help.'

'Yes, Majesty.' Antranak turned to leave and felt his mood sour further as he saw Horemshep scuttling along the throne room's marble floor. 'Have your temple guard join the search,' he told the high priest. 'Pharaoh's orders.'

Horemshep ignored Antranak and bowed before Phraroh. 'I answered you summons as swiftly as any man could, mighty Pharaoh. I have heard what happened tonight. My temple guard are at your disposal.'

'*My* temple guard are always at *my* disposal,' Pharaoh barked.

'Why now?' Mentu asked. 'Why are the Nubians doing this now?'

'To capitalise on their actions in the south,' Antranak said. 'They have taken disputed lands from us while we mourn your brother and now they plan something in Thebes. Perhaps in the palace itself.'

'I believe Antranak is, as always, half correct,' Horemshep said, his voice as slick as oil.

'Explain yourself,' Antranak demanded, looming over the smaller priest.

Horemshep refused to be cowed. Despite the enormous difference in bulk between them, he showed no fear of Antranak. 'I mean that the Nubians are moving now because we are mourning Prince Thutmose and also because of Prince Mentu's forthcoming marriage.'

'He could be right,' Antranak said thoughtfully. 'If the Mitanni and Egypt are allied by marriage and blood, the Nubians will be isolated.'

Amenhotep rubbed his chin thoughtfully. 'I see your point,' he said to Horemshep. 'The Nubians would be against this marriage and seek to stop it happening.'

'How?' Antranak asked. 'Prince Mentu is always heavily guarded.'

'Two people are required for a marriage, Antranak.'

'Miral?'

Mentu was already racing for the exit before anyone had time to react to his cry.

Erimem felt terrible. The wound on her neck stung, and the balm of honey and oil that the physician had applied to the cut stung even worse. She wouldn't sleep but she couldn't do anything either. She knew that her father would summon her some time during the day. He would shout at her, he would call her stupid and he would banish her to her apartments not to show herself again until he gave her leave to do so. And in a few days he would relent and things would return to normal. Except things weren't normal. In the past she had been guilty of minor misdemeanours, a child's offences. This time, she had almost been killed, and had put the safety of the palace in danger. Pharaoh would have every right to rage at her. The thought brought on a wave of nausea – which she was sure was made worse by the pain-numbing poppy potion the physician had made her drink – and she lay back on her bed. He had said it would give her memorable dreams, even when she was awake. The potion had tasted vile and she had thrown most of it away. She wanted to be sick and returned to her bed to lie down. A short time later, she heard footsteps hurrying through her apartments and she thought with relief that her handmaidens were finally returning. Instead, when she looked up, she saw Miral running towards her, alarm and concern on her face.

'Erimem? They told me you were hurt.' Erimem tried to sit up and say that she was fine, but Miral pressed gently at her shoulders. 'Stay still. You must rest.'

Erimem pushed her way up onto her elbows. 'I am fine,' she protested, then winced as the motion of talking set her neck stinging again.

'You don't look fine,' Miral rebuked her. She straightened the bandage around Erimem's throat. 'Perhaps you can begin a fashion wearing a cloth around your throat like this,' she joked. 'Perhaps in a bright colour.'

'As long as it's not blood-red,' Erimem half-smiled.

Miral set her hand on Erimem's brow, gauging her temperature. 'Don't joke about that,' she said seriously. 'You could have been killed and you will be lucky if you don't catch a fever from that wound.'

'I'm more worried about what my father will say,' Erimem muttered. She peered past Miral and for the first time saw the large man standing in the doorway. He looked vaguely familiar and it took Erimem several moments to work out why she recognised him. Finally it came to her. He was one of Miral's Mitannite bodyguards – the one she had seen leaving Hanek's room after their passionate encounter the previous afternoon. An Egyptian soldier would have discreetly glanced around the room, ensuring that nothing threatening or untoward was happening but this one was staring straight at Erimem, an expression of recognition on his hard features. He must have seen her when she had tried to hide at the handmaiden's quarters. For him to recognise her was one thing but to brazenly stare at her while she lay in bed was another altogether. It was unacceptable and there was something predatory in his gaze that made Erimem very uneasy. The sound of running footsteps distracted them both and Mentu pushed the guard aside and ran into the room. Miral rose from the bedside and moved to intercept him.

'She's isn't badly hurt,' Miral said in her most reassuring tone. 'The wound isn't deep.'

'Good,' Mentu nodded his approval and smiled encouragingly at his sister before taking Miral by the arm. 'But I was looking for you.'

'Me? Why?'

Erimem tried not to listen as Mentu explained his concerns to Miral. She looked away to give them some privacy and caught the Mitannite guard at the doorway shifting uncomfortably, bending slightly to the side. He moved his hand and Erimem saw that where Mentu had pushed him, the bodyguard's tunic was marked with a spreading crimson stain. For a moment, she thought that Mentu must have cut the Mitannite but then the realisation came – he was bleeding exactly where she had stabbed her assailant earlier that night by the Nile. The Mitannite caught the direction of her gaze and a malicious grin spread across his face. Reaching into his tunic, he pulled a long knife with serrated edges on both sides of the blade and moved quickly towards her.

'It's him,' Erimem choked. 'He's the one I stabbed.'

Miral and Mentu both snapped round to see the bodyguard charging towards them. Mentu instinctively pushed Miral towards Erimem on the bed before meeting the bodyguard head on, clutching the knife-hand with both of his hands, pushing the blade away from his face. He tried to force the Mitannite backwards but he was outmatched in strength and experience, and the Mitannite heaved the Prince backwards, sending him crashing against a broad dark wood chest. The impact drove the wind from Mentu but he forced himself to stay on his feet. He saw Erimem's fighting daggers sitting on the chest and grasped for them but the Mitannite was too quick. He slammed his own blade down across the daggers, trapping them against the roof of the chest, jarring them from Mentu's grasp and then swung his blade wide at Mentu.

The Prince leaped back but the serrated blade dug into his chest cutting a deep gash over a hand's width across his skin. Erimem had pulled herself from her bed and ran at the Mitannite, slamming both of her hands into his bloodied side. She heard him gasp in pain before she felt the back of his hand smash into the side of her face, sending her reeling across the floor. She tried to pick herself up but her body had become slow in responding to her mind's commands. She saw the Mitannite turn back to Mentu, who had fallen across a low couch. The Mitannite raised his knife to strike down the Prince but then stopped, a look of puzzlement of his face.

Miral was holding the handle of one of Erimem's fighting daggers, its blade buried in her bodyguard's chest. She pulled the blade from the man's chest and then drove it into his heart. Erimem was vaguely aware of voices – familiar voices like Antranak and her father – and of soldiers pouring into her rooms, hacking at the Mitannite with their swords. She could also see Miral cradling Mentu's head but when she tried to stand and join them her knees buckled and everything went black.

# Chapter Nine
## A Deep Wound

The first face that Erimem saw when she woke hardly came as a surprise. Antranak was standing by her bed, looking concerned and munching on a wooden bowl of figs while staring miserably out of a window. She shifted slightly in her bed and turned. The figure sitting on the side of her bed did come as a surprise.

'Finally,' Amenhotep said with relief. 'I had worried that it would be another day before you were returned to us.'

'Another day?' Erimem croaked and instantly wished she hadn't. Her throat was dry and rasped as though it had been filled with sand while her head felt as if it would burst from the pain inside. The side of her face ached as well and refused to move as it should when she had spoken.

'Don't try to talk,' Amenhotep instructed quietly. He took a wet cloth from a bowl of water and laid it gently on Erimem's cheek. 'Fayum assures us that the swelling to your face will begin to disappear in a few days.'

'And he will mix a brew to dull the headache he expects you to have,' Antranak added. 'With your permission, Pharaoh, I will fetch him.' Amenhotep nodded his assent and Antranak strode off to find his young friend.

'You had Antranak worried,' Amenhotep said, lifting the cloth and dipping it in the bowl of water before putting back across Erimem's cheek. 'For a time, we thought you might not wake again. You slept for two full days.'

'I'm sorry, father…'

Amenhotep touched a finger to Erimem's lips. 'Quiet, child. You have nothing to be sorry for. Miral told us how bravely you attacked her bodyguard. I would have lost a second son if you hadn't been so brave.'

'Mentu's not dead?'

Amenhotep wiped the tears of relief away from his daughter's eyes. 'No. The cut on his chest will leave a scar but he will survive. Miral has sat with him almost every moment since he was injured.'

'She killed her bodyguard,' Erimem croaked. 'At least I think she did. I can't remember properly. I can only remember small pieces of what happened.'

'My guards cut him to pieces but her wounds would have been fatal for him had the guards not arrived. She deserves to claim the kill.'

'Why?' Erimem croaked. 'What was he doing?'

Amenhotep held a goblet of wine to her lips and let the liquid trickle into her mouth. 'Because a small group of Mitanni oppose this union between our lands and they have allied themselves with the Nubians. The Mitannite king arrived today. He offered me his life for this attack.' A slight smirk flitted across the Pharaoh's face. 'I let him suffer for a while before telling him he was safe. But he has promised to put the soldier's family to death as a warning to anyone who stands against this alliance.' He stood and handed the goblet to a handmaiden who was hovering a little way from the bed. 'And now you must rest,' he said to Erimem. 'You will need your strength to choke down whatever foul-tasting potion Fayum conjures up.'

'The guard who attacked us.' Erimem coughed but forced herself to continue. 'I saw him leaving the chamber of one of my handmaidens the day we followed him.'

'Which one?' Amenhotep demanded.

Erimem paused, aware that every one of her handmaidens would be watching. Hanek might even be there, but they would all know that she had no choice but to answer her father. 'Hanek,' she said. 'The girl Mentu wanted to marry.'

Amenhotep pulled a deep, angry breath. 'And she took her revenge for being set aside by conspiring with our enemies.'

'Hanek would never have done that.' Erimem protested. 'I think... I am sure that she and the Mitannite were lovers. He must have used her to learn about the palace.'

Amenhotep stroked his daughter's forehead. 'You have a good heart, Erimem, but you prefer to see only the best in people. In this girl you see a spurned lover in search of comfort with the Mitannite. I see a jealous girl set on revenge. She betrayed her people, she betrayed Mentu and she betrayed you, little chicken.' He leaned over and kissed the top of her head. 'She will not escape my justice.'

Erimem watched her father leave and wondered how long it was since he had called her little chicken.

'Go to the handmaidens' dormitories and bring the girl to us. If she's not there search the palace and send men to her family home. Bring her family to the House of Pain. Search the entire city if you have to but bring her to me. And make sure she's alive. She can't answer questions when she's dead.'

Antranak's lieutenants bowed to Pharaoh and ran to carry out Antranak's instructions. Antranak followed half a step behind Pharaoh as he strode back through the gardens towards the Throne Room. 'They will find her, Majesty,' he assured Amenhotep. 'They know the skins on their hides depend on it.'

'Good,' Amenhtoep said blandly. 'What am I to do with the girl, Antranak?' he asked suddenly.

'Leave her to me,' Antranak replied. 'I will take her to the House of Truth and find out what happened. If that doesn't work, then it will be the House of Pain.'

'Not the handmaiden,' Amenhotep said quickly. 'Erimem. What am I to do with her?' He stopped and looked out at the garden. 'She spends her days here in the gardens letting Shemek fill her head with his nonsense or hidden away in the mornings learning to be a warrior.' He turned quickly to catch Antranak's surprised expression. 'I am Pharaoh, old friend. I know everything that happens in my palace.' He sighed heavily. 'At least I used to. Now I don't even know what is going on in my own daughter's head.'

'May I speak honestly, Majesty?' Antranak asked.

'Always.'

'She loves you, Majesty,' Antranak replied simply. 'Let me explain. She doesn't love you because you are Pharaoh or because you are a god living among us. She loves you because you are her father and more than anything she wants to be a child you can be proud of.'

'So she runs wild, learning fanciful rubbish and acting like...'

'Like a prince rather than a princess,' Antranak spoke before he could stop himself and instantly he regretted it. No matter how often Pharaoh called him a friend, he still knew there were limits to that friendship. 'My apologies, Pharaoh. I spoke out of turn.'

'You did,' Amenhotep snapped. 'But,' – his voice softened – 'I think you also spoke honestly. When I was raised I was told by my father that I must in turn raise my own heir. I know how to raise a son, Antranak, even if I failed to father enough of them. I know how to prepare my son for the challenges he must face in replacing me.' He shrugged, a helpless gesture completely at odds with his usual unshakable self-confidence. 'What do I do with a girl, Antranak? She's long past an age when she should have been married.' He turned to his friend. 'Perhaps I should give her to you as a wife. I would be honoured to bring you into my family.'

Antranak held his breath, gauging whether Amenhotep was serious or simply venting his frustration. 'Pharaoh does me great honour,' he said carefully. 'But my heart was taken long ago. I married once and I will not do so again. But if I did, I am not the man for Erimem. I could never be her husband but, had I been her father, I could not have been more proud of her.'

Amenhotep put a hand on his shoulder. 'Perhaps you are more her father than I am,' he said quietly. 'You have spent more time raising her than I.'

'Have I ever told you why?' Antranak asked.

'No.'

'She found me in the gardens on the day my wife bled to death in childbirth. My daughter had died, strangled by the cord inside her mother and I wanted to die as well. I wanted to join them in the afterlife. I had chased everyone else away from me. I'm sure they thought I would have killed anyone who approached me. But Erimem – she could have been no more than two summers at the time – climbed into my lap and put her arms around me. She didn't know why I was unhappy. She just knew that I was sad and tried to make me feel better. I have loved the child since that day, but it could never be as a wife.'

Amenhotep tightened his grip on Antranak's shoulder. The old soldier rarely spoke of his wife. Even after more than a dozen years, Antranak had never come to terms with her loss. 'Then think of Erimem as your brother's child,' he said. 'And advise me what is best to do with her.'

'Do nothing,' Antranak replied. 'For now at least.' Seeing Amenhotep's quizzical look he continued. 'There is no one of a royal house outside of Egypt that you would find suitable for her.'

'I wouldn't taint our blood-line with most of them,' Amenhotep agreed dismissively.

'Then wait a year,' Antranak urged. 'Wait until Mentu and Miral have been married a year and let Mentu take Erimem as his second wife. They are well matched in personality and would keep the line pure. Miral knows that she will have to share Mentu with other wives in future. Surely she would be happier to share him with someone she already calls her sister.'

Amenhotep stroked at his chin in a gesture Antranak recognised. Pharaoh tended only to stroke his chin that way when he thought favourably of an idea. 'I will think on it,' Amenhotep replied. 'But first we must find this Hanek girl. She has many questions to answer.'

The rat's nose twitched and it peered at this monstrous intruder in its larder. Hanek stared back at the creature but didn't dare make any effort to chase it away. The soldiers she had heard outside of the grain store where she was hiding would still be close enough to hear any disturbance, so she tried to relax and ignore the rat. In due course, the rat lost interest in her and scuttled off across the top of the grain. Hanek settled deeper into the grain and let it flow over her until only her head and shoulders showed. She would wait until darkness fell and then make her move.

Erimem woke late the next morning and was pleasantly surprised to find that her headache had faded. The side of her face still felt swollen and she could see the puffy cheek in the bottom of her vision but she felt stronger and in far less pain than she had been when she had finally succumbed to sleep the night before. Even the stinging pain in her neck had faded to a dull throb. She summoned her handmaidens and with their assistance was bathed, had her head and body shaved and was anointed with sweet-smelling perfumes before they helped her dress and tied another bandage around her wounded throat, adding gold and precious stones to the bandage to give it the appearance of a piece of high fashion. The girls worked proficiently but were subdued and Erimem knew that it wasn't just her weakened state that had affected them. Each of the girls would be wondering if Hanek had really betrayed Egypt? Erimem knew that none of the girls would hold any ill-will towards her for saying all that she knew about Hanek. She had really had no choice.

Once dressed and with a magnificent new wig placed on her head, Erimem began to feel like herself again. The only thing she missed was make-up to the swollen side of her face. The puffiness made the skin too tender for her to let anyone apply kohl.

After eating a light meal of a sweet fruit bread and fish, Erimem announced that she would visit Mentu. Linsis announced that Pharaoh had expected Erimem to try to visit her brother before long and had prepared for it. She led Erimem outside to where four eunuch slaves sat in the shade beside a large carrying chair covered with a linen roof to keep the worst of the sun at bay.

'If you go anywhere, Pharaoh has ordered that you are to be carried.'

A small part of Erimem wanted to rebel and announce that she could walk for herself, but her father's act of kindness warmed her and so she settled into the chair and allowed herself to be carried on the slaves' shoulders to Mentu's quarters. By the time she arrived, Erimem was relieved that she had agreed to being carried. The sun was mercilessly strong and the air was as dry as the desert sand itself. Even shaded under her canopy she was uncomfortably hot. She was also relieved that she didn't weigh much. The eunuchs were sweating profusely from the exertion of carrying her chair and she wondered if she should have stronger slaves assigned.

Mentu was being attended by priests and physicians. He looked pale but Erimem was sure that was to do with the physician, who was drawing together the two sides of the livid gash on Mentu's chest using an acacia thorn and fine hemp thread. Mentu gasped as the physician pricked the thorn through the skin and gently pulled the wound closed. Miral sat with Mentu's head in her lap, stroking his brow and whispering comforting words to him. Erimem had been fascinated by the physician's actions. She had heard of people having wounds stitched closed as a dressmaker might repair a piece of cloth but she had never actually seen it before. She made a mental note to track down this physician later and quiz him about it.

The physician cut the thin twine and handed the thorn to a younger priest, possibly an acolyte only learning his master's trade. In return, he took what looked like a strip of bandage no longer than a forearm. He handled it with care, touching only the edges and, as the bandage turned, Erimem could see that one side was coated with something wet that glistened as it it caught the light. The priest's careful handling suggested that it was sticky on that wet side and that was confirmed in her mind when the priest intoned a soft prayer and applied the strip of bandage over the stitched wound. He smoothed the edges but avoided putting any pressure on the wound itself.

'In five days the flesh will have rejoined and the covering will be removed,' the physician said in a dull tone. 'Once the wound is uncovered and the twine removed, you must wear a poultice of honey and oil and treat the wound regularly with meat.'

'I am to be married in six days,' Mentu growled at the physician. 'I do not intend to go to my wife with a slice of meat strapped to my chest.'

'You will wear a goat's carcass around your neck if he tells you,' Miral chided. 'As long as it heals you.'

Mentu growled but didn't argue. 'Leave us,' he told the priest. 'Get out and leave us in peace.'

'Should I leave as well?' Erimem asked as the physician harried his young disciple from the room.

'Erimem!' Mentu began to stand but Miral held his shoulders down.

'Stay still, or you will tear the stitching and the healer will have to do his work again.'

'Miral is right,' Erimem said, hurrying to join them. 'You should rest.'

'And why aren't *you* resting?' Miral asked, anger clearly rising in her voice. 'You are as bad as your brother. Is there no sense in your family at all? You could both have been killed but you act as if nothing had happened.' Her voice cracked and she pulled a deep breath to steady herself.

Mentu and Erimem exchanged a swift, knowing look. Miral had almost lost the only two people in the city she loved and had been forced to kill someone she had trusted to save them. Her pain was of a different kind to theirs.

'You're right,' Erimem said softly. 'We are both lucky to be alive. I came to thank you for that. I have lost one brother and I couldn't bear to lose another – even one as annoying as Mentu.'

Miral smiled limply. 'He's not so bad once you get used to him.'

'Have you ever heard a bride talk so proudly of her husband before?' Mentu asked.

Miral bent and kissed his forehead. 'I am not your bride yet, so I can say what I like.' She looked at Erimem's swollen cheek. 'Your face already looks better than it did two days ago. I visited you while you were in your long sleep. Your father spent a good deal of time with you as well. As a father should. Mentu will give love and care to all of our children, whether they are male or female.'

'*All* of our children?' Mentu asked. 'How many children do you plan to have?'

'That is my secret,' Miral said sweetly. 'But I promise to keep you informed of my progress.'

The gentle teasing between the couple brought a smile to Erimem's face. She winced with pain as her cheek protested at the movement. 'I'm going to be a dark cloud at your marriage with my face like this,' she grumbled.

'Perhaps if you wore a veil...' Mentu said.

'Don't tease her,' Miral scolded him. 'The swelling will go down in a few days, Erimem,' she promised. 'You will look like yourself again in time for the marriage.'

'Don't say that,' Mentu protested. 'She's had enough bad luck already.'

Erimem glared at her brother. 'Maybe we should get the physician to stitch your mouth shut.'

The sun had dipped beneath the horizon and entered into its daily battle in the underworld when Erimem returned to her apartments. The eunuchs had carried her back with more ease in the cooler evening air and she spent the short trip reflecting on the happiness she had seen in both Mentu and Miral. They had barely moved more than a few paces apart in the time Erimem had spent with them and they had constantly shared glances and small touches. It seemed that some good had come of the attack in Erimem's rooms.

Mentu and Miral had cemented their affection into something that seemed more lasting. So, despite the continuing aches in her jaw and throat, Erimem was in good spirits when she re-entered her quarters and she didn't immediately notice the tense atmosphere in her apartments. The handmaidens were fussing just a little more than usual, but she put that down to her injuries. And she was sure that the forced humour they were showing was simply there to keep her spirits high but, after a time, she became aware of the nervous little glances and fleeting looks that were passing back and forth among the handmaidens. Linsis in particular seemed especially skittish.

For a time, Erimem convinced herself that the other girls had simply found out about Linsis's dalliances with Fayum and were teasing her for becoming involved with such a lowly priest but the other girls were nervous as well and showed no sign of the friendly goading they used when teasing one of their number. Intrigued by the cause of the tension – and equally fascinated by the fact that the girls had chosen not to talk with her about it – Erimem began to study her apartment.

On the surface, everything seemed normal, exactly as it should be. Nothing precious was broken and nothing seemed to be out of place. Unusually, her gown she wore to bed was already set out ready for her, and she noticed that a selection of dresses had been prepared for to wear the next day, along with jewellery and even a pectoral which she rarely wore. Several pairs of sandals in various designs sat by the dresses on a low chest. Normally this wasn't prepared until morning when she and several handmaidens would go into the various rooms where her clothes and wigs were stored to choose her clothing for the day. Nearby, a selection of her wigs had been placed discreetly on a table. If she hadn't been looking for something unusual, she was sure she wouldn't have noticed them. Something was definitely wrong and the handmaidens' unwillingness to talk about it, meant that Erimem would have to force the matter.

'I will sleep tonight in the Palace of Concubines,' she announced casually.

'It is many days since I saw my mother and I would like her to know that I am well.'

'That would be a kind thing for you to do,' Linsis said. 'Your honoured mother would have a great deal of comfort from seeing you are well.'

'I shall go now,' Erimem said, rising to her feet. 'But I shall need a cloak to guard me from the night's chill.' She set off for the door leading to the rooms where her clothing was stored, ignoring the protests of the handmaidens. On the way she swept one of her three-pronged fighting daggers from a marble and ivory table. She flicked the point of the dagger back towards her handmaidens. 'I will get it myself – stay where you are.'

The arched door led into a small passage with doors leading off on either side. Each door led to a room specifically set aside for a particular section of Erimem's appearance. One room contained only wigs, another was for sandals. Dresses filled one room and other, more informal clothes had a room of their own.

Erimem pushed open each of the doors and peered into the rooms. The light from the oil burners in the corridor was dull but enough to show that nothing unusual was in any of these rooms. Only two doors were still unopened. On the left, a room which held her toiletries – the sacred oils used to bathe and anoint her as well as small things like the blades used to shave her head and body. The other room was where her make-up was stored and prepared for use. The room holding the cosmetics was larger and would have been more comfortable for an intruder to hide in but Erimem was uncomfortable at the thought of turning her back to a room that contained something as deadly as her shaving blades.

'Linsis, bring a light here,' she ordered. 'Now.'

The servant shuffled along the short passageway, holding a small oil lamp. 'Princess, please. You don't need to...'

'I know very well what I need to do, although I think some others may need reminding of their duty. Now hold the lamp still.'

Erimem pushed the door open and stepped back, her dagger pointed towards the doorway. Hanek sat on a stool, staring at her with a kind of resigned terror. 'Get up,' Erimem ordered in a hard voice as an icy anger began to grow in her. 'I am Pharaoh's daughter and you will stand in my presence or kneel at my feet but you will not sit. Get up! Stand up now!'

Tears ran from Hanek's eyes as she stumbled to her feet. As she moved into the light Erimem could see that the girl was filthy. Her dress was dusty and covered with all manner of stains. 'Please,' she began but Erimem wasn't prepared to listen.

'Fetch my bodyguards,' she instructed Linsis. 'Do it now or suffer the same fate as this one.' She flicked her dagger menacingly towards Hanek's throat. 'You will all be sent to the Hall of Truths for my father's judge to decide your fate for harbouring this traitor but the punishment will be much worse if you disobey me now.'

Linsis was shaking with terror. She knew the sentences served by the

Pharaoh's judges were harsh and often brutal, but from somewhere she dredged up what little courage she had. 'Please let her speak, Princess. Let her tell you what happened.'

'I know what happened,' Erimem spat. 'She betrayed Egypt and almost caused both Mentu and me to be killed. Let her tell her story to Antranak. He will get the truth from her.'

Hanek dropped to her knees and clutched at Erimem's legs. 'I didn't betray you,' she whimpered. 'I didn't betray anyone. I know what is being said about me but none of it is true. Please believe me. It's not true.'

'What isn't true?' Erimem asked, pushing away from Hanek's grasping hands. 'That you took a Mitannite soldier as your lover to get some kind of revenge against my brother? That you plotted with your lover to stop the marriage?'

'No,' Hanek pleaded. 'None of it is true. I never saw this Mitannite soldier you're talking about.'

Erimem's open hand cracked against Hanek's face. 'Don't lie to me! I saw you. So did Linsis. We saw him leave your rooms. We saw you sleeping drunk with your dress up around your waist like a whore. We saw you, Hanek! You can't deny that.'

'No,' Hanek sobbed. 'I know that was how you saw me – Linsis told me – but I swear to you that I don't know how I came to be like that.'

'You don't remember your lover's visit,' Erimem snarled sarcastically. 'That doesn't say much for him.'

'He wasn't my lover!' Hanek screamed. 'I have never been with a man apart from Mentu.' Erimem snorted derisively but Hanek continued. 'I have been unwell for some months now and had stayed in bed most of the time. That afternoon I heard food being delivered outside my door but when I went to fetch it, no one was there. I thought one of the other girls had taken pity on me and brought me food.'

'None of us did,' Linsis said. 'Nor did anyone else. The food didn't come from any of the palace kitchens.' She quietened at Erimem's look.

'I ate the food and drank some of the wine,' Hanek continued. 'And then I woke, feeling tired and confused and spreadeagled as if I had spent the afternoon making love.'

Erimem's hard expression didn't change. 'Which you had.'

'No,' Hanek objected. 'I had not been touched in that way. Even though I was asleep, I would know if I had been touched that way.'

'You claim you slept through this man being in your rooms?' Erimem asked. 'While he undressed you but didn't molest you?'

'Not asleep,' Hanek argued. 'I told you that I was confused when I woke. My head ached and I couldn't concentrate. My thoughts were a jumble. I think there was a drug of some kind in the food I ate.'

'Why would a man drug you and then not have his use of your body?' Erimem demanded.

'I don't know,' Hanek whined. 'But I know that I never saw this man and didn't take him as a lover. I wouldn't dare with the sickness I have had. I haven't had the fever. I am sick every morning because I see your brother falling in love with another woman while I am carrying his child in my belly.'

Erimem felt her own stomach lurch. With her words Hanek had changed everything. This was no longer a question of whether a handmaiden had betrayed her mistress or even her country. If Hanek was telling the truth, it was possible that she carried in her belly the child who should be Mentu's heir and one day sit on the throne of Egypt.

'Come into the light. I need to see you better.' Erimem grabbed Hanek by the wrist and dragged her along the corridor into the main room. 'Linsis, go to the door and see that we are not disturbed.'

'Yes, my lady.' Linsis ran off, relieved no doubt to be able to get out of Erimem's sight.

'Take off your dress,' Erimem instructed Hanek.

'Princess?'

Impatiently, Erimem took her dagger and cut through the shoulder straps on Hanek's grimy dress and pulled the dress down to Hanek's waist. 'Keep you hands at your sides,' Erimem ordered. 'I will have the girls hold your hands to your sides if I have to.'

Hanek did as she was told and squirmed as Erimem scrutinised her body. There was a slight swell to Hanek's belly and her breasts were a little fuller than they had been a few weeks earlier and while Erimem was no physician she knew enough to recognise those signs. She turned to one of the other handmaidens.

'Bring her a dress to wear. One of mine. And bring oils to clean her.' The handmaiden ran off to do as she was told. 'Sit,' Erimem said to Hanek, who was struggling to pull her dress back over her breasts. She waited until Hanek had taken a seat on a couch before sitting herself on another couch several paces away. She kept the dagger firmly clasped in her hand. Intrigued as she was by Hanek's story, she was still wary of the girl and wasn't ready to take a chance on trusting her.

'Does Mentu know about the child?' she asked.

Hanek shook her head. 'I found out after your father had ordered us not to meet any more.'

'Though you were still seeing my brother in secret after my father forbade it,' Erimem countered accusingly.

Hanek's eyes dipped, unable to meet the accusation in Erimem's gaze. 'Yes,' she admitted. 'But I stopped it when I found out that I was pregnant. Mentu and I had broken your father's law and disobeyed his command. I was afraid of what he would do if he found out.'

'Mentu would have protected you.'

'Mentu couldn't protect you and his Mitannite girl from one soldier,' Hanek said bitterly. 'How could he protect me from Pharaoh's rage? He is a caring man but I would trust you to protect me ahead of him.'

'I can't protect you,' Erimem said starkly. 'You have told me a story but offered me no proof of any of it. You are clearly carrying a child but how can we know if the father is Mentu or the Mitannite we saw leaving your room or perhaps another man altogether?'

'Because I have never been with a man other than Mentu. He was my first. He will tell you as much.'

'But how can we know he was your only lover?'

'Because I love him,' Hanek said simply.

Erimem sat and stared at the girl. The evidence against her was strong but there had been something in the way she had stated her love for Mentu that had rung true. She desperately wished that she could go and ask Antranak what to do, but she knew that Antranak was convinced of Hanek's guilt.

So was her father. He would simply order Hanek's execution. Fayum, she knew, would simply tell her to see Antranak. She wondered briefly about seeing Mentu and telling him what Hanek had said, but he was inseparable from Miral. And how would this affect Miral? She and Mentu had only begun to find some happiness together. Did she have the right to throw that into doubt on the word of someone who was probably a traitor?

'I can't protect you,' she repeated. 'And you can't stay here. It's too dangerous, for me as well as for you. And you can't go into the city. Every soldier and guard is looking for you.'

'Then what can I do?' Hanek asked helplessly.

'That's not my concern,' Erimem stated calmly. 'Too many people tell me things that are nothing to do with me. For instance, someone told me that a trading boat would be stopping near here tonight before continuing north to beyond Giza with the first light. It's of no interest to me who travels on that boat.' She reached across to a table and grasped a golden statue in the shape of an falcon – a depiction of the god Horus. She threw it to Hanek. 'There is enough gold in that to buy you passage, shelter and food for a lifetime. If I am ever asked about it, I will assume that you stole it.' She paused briefly. 'If you choose to send me a message in code a year from now calling yourself a fisherman's wife, perhaps using Linsis as a vessel to carry this message, I will see how things have changed here and decide whether I should tell Mentu any of this. By then we will know more of the Nubians and their plans and I will have a better idea of whether I can trust you.'

'Y-You're letting me go?' Hanek stammered.

'You're escaping,' Erimem corrected. 'I had no knowledge that you were ever here. If you are caught before you reach the boat and talk of this meeting, I will call you a liar to your face and demand your execution. And if you run to the Nubians, I will know of it,' Erimem promised ominously. 'I will find out if you betray me, and I will see you die. But if you are telling the truth, I will do what I can to help you.'

'I am telling the truth,' Hanek said desperately. 'I have done nothing wrong apart from fall in love with a man I can never have. My family are also innocent but have been taken to the House of Truth. Antranak will be torturing them for answers they can't give.'

'If they know nothing, Antranak will discover that.'

'Through torture?' Hanek demanded. 'They have had their house and all my father's possessions seized by Antranak's order. They might be executed for something none of us did.'

'I can't stop that,' Erimem said. 'My father's word is justice. The best I can do is ask that he has them passed into slavery. I think he will see that as reasonable. I will buy them myself if I can but I will make no promises.'

'Thank you.' Hanek began to move towards Erimem but the princess moved her dagger into her lap ominously and Hanek stopped. 'Thank you,' she repeated, a broken edge in her voice.

'Bring me a cloak,' Erimem ordered and a handmaiden scuttled off to collect the garment. 'If what you've told me is true,' she said to Hanek, 'then I will see you again. But if you have lied to me then I will see you dead.' She settled into her cloak as two handmaidens set it on her shoulders. 'You two stay with Hanek and make sure there is no evidence that she was ever here. The rest of you will escort me to visit my honoured mother.' She paused and looked back at Hanek. 'I hope we meet again.' And then she was gone.

Hanek looked at the exquisite gold falcon in her hand and then at the beautiful dress Liram was holding out to her. And then she burst into tears.

# Chapter Ten
## A Time to Rejoice

n Egypt there was no actual ceremony when a couple married. A contract was drawn up between the two families, usually detailing how much was being paid for the bride, and then, after as lavish a feast as could be afforded, the husband moved his new wife into his home. Among the common people of Egypt, these feasts often lasted deep into the wedding night and through into the next day. When the bride was marrying the heir to the throne of Egypt, the banquet in the palace was expected to last five or six days with the people of Egypt also expected to celebrate for at least two or three full days.

The Mitannite delegation led by King Gadamare had arrived and set up camp outside of Thebes. Under normal circumstances, a visiting king would have been invited to stay in the palace, but Miral had spoken at length with Pharaoh Amenhotep and suggested that it might be best to let her father have his own camp outside of Thebes. She argued that letting the Mitanni have their own camp would let her father retain the illusion of being in control of his people while in Egypt, which would help to silence those who would now see the Mitanni as a puppet force for Pharaoh. She suggested quite forcibly that it would be wise to have plenty of soldiers on duty near the Mitannite camp, in case hostility from the wars spilled over. She spoke eloquently, persuasively and with charm, as she had done on each of the many occasions she had met Pharaoh since she had saved Mentu. Whether it was out of gratitude for saving his son or because he was swayed by her charm or simply because he agreed with Miral's thoughts, Pharaoh had agreed to her suggestions.

In private, he had asked Antranak, 'Have you seen how she reacts to her father? She is afraid that he will do or say something to spoil her marriage.'

'She doesn't trust him. Or doesn't like him. Or both. And he has a pitiful history with diplomatic journeys,' Antranak had snorted. 'When he travelled to Ghosh to secure a trading alliance he came back with a war instead because he got drunk and insulted his host.'

Amenhotep had chuckled. 'His inability to hold his drink is as legendary as his inability to win a war. They would do better with Miral as their leader.'

'I think she and Mentu have other plans,' Antranak had said. 'They were talking earlier of how many grandchildren they would give you.'

'They can fill the palace with them. I can always build a bigger palace.'

The day of the marriage turned out to be swelteringly hot yet again. The temperature rose with the sun and by mid-morning the city was groaning under the baking heat. Any final preparations for feasts to celebrate the wedding were left to slaves, while free citizens took shelter in the shade. Some took the unusual heat as a sign from the gods that they should cool themselves with beer and begin their festivities early. Of course, these were mainly the people who treated every day as a day to start drinking early. As the sun reached its height and the dry heat became unbearable, the Mitanni emerged from their camp in the desert by an oasis to the west of the city.

Their party was smaller than had been expected. King Gadamare had brought only a dozen or so of his most trusted advisers – enough to show the respect due to Pharaoh but a small enough number that they wouldn't alarm the people of Egypt – or the large contingent of Egyptian soldiers sent as their escort. The Mitanni and their escort entered the city through the giant northern gate. The king and his advisers rode in chariots. Behind them, some of their slaves herded livestock while others struggled to carry the vast array of gifts the Mitanni had brought. Gadamare's council had blanched at the expense but the king had been resolute. No price was too great to pay to ensure that Egypt had no reason to attack his people.

Gadamare's procession was watched with curiosity by those people of Thebes who were prepared to risk the sun's ire but, for the most part, Gadamare was disappointed – and more than a little insulted – by the general lack of interest in his presence shown by the Thebans. Typical Egyptian arrogance, he had snorted before catching himself and reminding himself of exactly why he was in Thebes. And so he had adopted a resolute, kingly expression and continued on his way.

Other processions of foreign dignitaries followed through the day until, when the Ethiopian king was last to arrive, even the most curious of the onlookers had lost all interest in the foreigners prancing through the streets and had gone off to find a celebration to join.

As was to be expected for the marriage of Pharaoh's son, the banquet was extraordinarily opulent. The grandest and most imposing of the many banqueting halls was the only place in Thebes – in the world – fit for such an event. Exotic fruits from the furthest reaches of the world had been brought to Thebes by the shipload along with outlandish foreign animals, slaughtered and set on the tables in an outrageous display of wealth and power. Every fragment of every table's surface was covered with a vast amount of food, far more than these guests could ever hope to eat while there was enough wine and beer waiting to keep Egypt's entire fleet of warships afloat. At the end of the hall, Pharaoh and those closest to him dominated the room from a raised platform, from which they could look out over the entire length of the banquet hall. It was another statement of power. Pharaoh was looking down on kings.

Sitting at Pharaoh's right hand was Mentu. He was exhausted. Nesmut had come up with the idea of having Mentu ride his chariot from the palace to the main square and then back again so that the people could see the Crown Prince and his bride. Mentu had known it was idiotic but his pride had made him agree even though only Miral's support had kept him on his feet. Someone – Miral he suspected – had arranged for a sturdy wooden block inscribed with Mentu's name to be placed behind his cushion so that he could lean back and relax. He was far more at ease once he had been able to sit down.

Miral herself sat at her husband's right hand and positively glowed. Away from the direct glare of the sun the purple threads that had been weaved through her dress became obvious, dividing the dress into sections that looked like the scales of a snake when she moved but when the orange rays of the late afternoon sun caught the dress the material caught the light and shimmered like a flame. She was elegant and beautiful and had eyes only for her husband. As the procession of gifts from the various nations was paraded in front of them, Miral gave them only the most cursory of glances and offered a nod of thanks to the king responsible before her eyes were drawn back to Mentu.

Seated on the other side of Pharaoh, beyond a very weak-looking Teti, Erimem wondered how it must feel to be so in love. Perhaps one day she would find out but for now, she was content to see Mentu and Miral so happy, and she was relieved to see that her father had recovered most of the energy that Thutmose's death had stolen from him. She was also relieved that he had welcomed Teti to sit by him. No one had expected the youngest prince to attend the marriage banquet. His had been weak but steady for some days but he had insisted that he felt stronger and, aided by the servant girl who had been so attentive to him, Teti had taken his place.

Erimem was surprised to have been placed in such a prominent position alongside Teti. She had expected to be seated at the head of a table alongside Mentu's mother and a number of the most respected court women, with only her father and the married couple to have such an exalted position with the most noted kings close by but Amenhotep had chosen to make a statement to the world about his family. He had put his children on a level above kings.

The procession of gifts, which had initially intrigued Erimem, quickly became a bore with each nation trying to outdo its neighbour in generosity and hoping to buy Pharaoh's favour. For them, the politics mattered but to Erimem it was mind-numbing and so she started scanning the crowd for familiar faces. She spotted Horemshep and his miserable shrew of a wife at a position far too prestigious for her liking. Further back she saw various members of court that she recognised and she was sure she even caught a glimpse of Shemek and Fayum.

She stifled a smirk as Shemek's head began to loll forward and only jerked upright when Fayum's elbow dug into his ribs. Eventually she spotted Antranak walking casually around the outside of the hall, watching the assembly for any hint of trouble – and given that almost every country present had been to war with each of the others at some point there was a fair chance that some disturbance would flare up sooner or later, but probably not until much more wine had been drunk.

There were no great speeches or proclamations. Nesmut the vizier spoke very briefly, saying that Pharaoh welcomed his guests into his home and Miral into his family and that was an end to it. The feasting could begin in earnest. As quickly as food was eaten and wine was drunk more was delivered. Musicians played muted music on a mixture of horns and drums and after a time topless dancers began to spin through the hall, gossamer thin strands of a silky material trailing from their arms like transparent wings. With ease they skipped free of any wandering hands. If any of the men wanted that kind of entertainment, there would be plenty of girls made available to oblige later in the night and for those whose tastes were slightly different, there would be boys on hand to cater for their needs.

As the night wore on and more wine was drunk, the voices became louder and the discussions more heated but there was no trouble. The conspicuous presence of Antranak's guards saw to that. The various kings took turns in paying respects to Pharaoh and to the young couple. Early in this procession, Teti had begun to weary and Amenhotep ordered that he be taken to his chambers. For the first time since Teti's mother – Amenhotep's favoured wife – had died, he spoke to the boy with genuine affection.

At the same time he released Erimem from any duty to sit and endure the politics he would have to talk with the various kings but she stayed by his side for each king's visit until only the Mitannite king had still to pay his respects. It would be the first time Miral had spoken with her father since he had arrived and Erimem felt that she would have been an intruder on the moment. So she excused herself and joined the women of the court. She was aware that some of the men from the various visiting nations were eyeing her with interest but she put it down to the last vestiges of the bruising on her cheek.

'Foolish girl,' her mother said. 'They are looking at the prettiest girl in the hall. You are a beautiful girl and they would swarm around you like a pack of jackals if you were anyone else's daughter.'

'Then I must give the gods even more praises and offerings for my parents,' Erimem said sweetly. 'I don't think I like the look of any of them.'

The women were returned to their quarters early, before the night became raucous, and Erimem drifted from one familiar face to another until she saw Mentu helping Miral to her feet. She skipped up the stairs and caught them as they began to leave and wished them her love, prayers and happiness. When they had gone, she caught a melancholy expression in her father's eye and she understood it immediately. Despite all his efforts with his remaining children, Amenhotep's heart was still broken from the loss of Thutmose. Oddly, she found the mood had settled on her as well and she asked Amenhotep's permission to leave. She ordered a servant to deliver food and wine to her apartments and then, alone in her own rooms, Erimem got very, very drunk.

Erimem was dreaming. She had to be. She was dreaming that Miral was standing by her bed, looking excited and unkempt and irritatingly beautiful. She blinked a few times and then cursed her dream for being so vivid. Her tongue felt as though it had been fitted with a rug and her head ached almost as badly as when she had been beaten by the Mitannite guard. In her dream, Miral was speaking to her and shaking her. It took a few seconds for her to realise that she wasn't dreaming at all.

'What are you doing here?' she grumbled.

'Mentu was called to see your father,' Miral answered. 'There was news delivered overnight that the Nubians have attacked and taken two cities in the south. I didn't hear which ones but your father has sent the kings back to their own lands already.'

Erimem groaned and sat up. She felt the sheet soft against her skin and she peeped under the cover. She clearly hadn't bothered finding her sleeping gown before crawling into bed. 'I must have been drunk. I never sleep naked.'

'I did last night,' Miral whispered excitedly. 'I was terrified. At first I was afraid that Mentu would be too tired or in too much pain to make our marriage real last night.' She gnawed at her bottom lip. 'And then I was afraid that he would.' She sat on the bed and dropped her voice as though afraid of being overheard. 'All the time I've been here I have known what would happen. I've joked about it with you, but it wasn't a joke last night. It was real and I was terrified. I almost ran here to hide with you.'

Erimem blinked and looked at the empty goblet by her bed and the small jars of wine lying on the floor. The stale smell of the wine was turning her stomach. 'I think I was past helping anyone.'

'The women of my people had told me what to do. They spent months telling me how to behave on my first night with my husband. I felt like a fool but I was so nervous I didn't know what else to do. So I did what they told me. I danced for him and then I went to him.' A hint of uncertainty showed in her eyes for a moment. 'It hurt, Erimem. He was kind and gentle but it hurt. And there was blood.'

'I don't think I need to hear this.' Erimem squirmed uncomfortably. 'But it's all right now?' she asked hopefully.

Miral nodded. 'The pain stopped after a little and Mentu was very gentle.' A happier memory came to her. 'Well, until he couldn't control himself any longer.'

'Enough!' Erimem wafted her hands at her friend. 'There are some parts of last night you should keep between you and Mentu.'

'I know,' Miral sighed. 'But I had to tell someone how happy I am.'

'I think everyone who saw you yesterday will know how happy you are,' Erimem said blearily. 'But you probably shouldn't tell them any of things you just told me.'

'You're probably right,' Miral laughed. 'I have him, Erimem. I have him.'

'It's not fair,' Erimem grumbled. 'You have a husband who loves you and I have a headache.'

'I have a husband who is already abandoning me for affairs of state,' Miral contradicted. 'But I know what will cure you.'

'So do I,' Erimem muttered. 'Sleeping until tomorrow.'

'Nonsense.' Miral yanked the sheet away from Erimem. 'You have a pool near here. If we swim that will wash your aches away.' She skipped away towards the door. 'I'll be waiting for you. If you fall asleep again I'll have your escort carry you there and throw you in.'

Erimem watched her friend pass through the doorway and out of her bed-chamber. 'Mentu,' she muttered softly, 'I'm going to drown her.'

The entire council of priests was already present, along with all of Pharaoh's closest advisers when Erimem and Miral arrived at the council chamber. Their swim had been interrupted by Linsis, who had delivered a message summoning them to Pharaoh's presence. With every member of Pharaoh's advisory councils in attendance, it was clear that there could only be one announcement. Shuffling uncomfortably at the centre of the assorted advisers and council members were King Gadamare of the Mitanni along with his own advisers. Each of them looked as if he would rather be anywhere else instead of in the council chamber.

Amenhotep was in his customary position on the throne, flanked by Mentu and Teti with Horemshep, Nesmut and Antranak slightly to the side. Pharaoh's arms were crossed across his chest, holding the crop and the flay. Resting on his head and sending an unmistakable chill through the chamber was the legendary blue battle crown. Amenhotep noticed the girls enter and nodded for them to join him. Miral looked quizzically at Mentu. He remained impassive except for a slight shake of the head. Miral slipped her hand into his and waited for Pharaoh to speak.

'Egypt is a peaceful country,' Amenhotep began. 'We act only to defend our own borders and the lives of our own people. We do not attack our enemies without reason and we hold no malice towards any nation or their people. We are a peace-loving people, generous to our neighbours and honourable in our actions.' His voice turned cold. 'But we are not a weak nation. Those who move against us will face the consequences and those who attack us will find that we are brutal in our righteous vengeance. Last night, as we celebrated the union of my son and his bride, word arrived that the Nubians had overrun two of our cities to the south, murdering hundreds of our people.'

The assembled councils rumbled their anger but quietened respectfully as Amenhotep continued.

'For months they have taken advantage of the nation mourning the loss of my exalted son, Prince Thutmose. That would have been unforgivable enough in its own right but recently my respected and loyal friend, General Antranak, with the assistance of my beloved daughter, Erimemushinteperem, has discovered evidence proving that the Nubians have been plotting against this palace. More than this, they have uncovered proof that my divine son Thutmose did not die in an accident. The axle of his chariot was deliberately damaged to snap when his chariot travelled at speed. This sabotage cost Thutmose his life.' Amenhotep paused, letting his words sink in. 'My son was murdered, taken from me by those who have chosen to plot against Egypt and against her Pharaoh. They have chosen to attack us and now they must pay for their actions. I have given my word to the ka of Thutmose that his soul will see his enemies' blood turn the desert red. I have ordered my armies to be mobilised. Every man who has served in my armies in the past ten years will again fight in my name. Thebes and Egypt will be defended but with my son, Prince Mentu, I will take an army such as no one living has ever seen and I will crush our enemies until they are no more than a distant memory cast to the winds. My brothers, the gods, will travel with us and with their blessing my son will be avenged.' He stood, keeping the crop and flay across his chest. 'We will march in three days.' He turned and found Miral had stepped into his path.

She bowed as low as she could manage. 'May I speak, mighty Pharaoh?'

Amenhotep tapped the flay irritably against his chest. 'What have you to say, girl?'

Miral breathed deeply and charged on. 'Egypt's army is the mightiest the world has ever known and has no need of assistance, but on behalf of King Gadamare, I offer you the Mitannite army. They will serve under your command and I swear that they will fight as loyally as any man.'

'Miral!' On the floor of the hall, Gadamare started forward in shock, but was pulled back by his advisers.

Amenhotep spun to stare at Gadamare. 'Is this true? Do you offer me your army?'

Gadamare squirmed under the scrutiny of every pair of eyes in the hall. If he refused, he would be a figure of ridicule and probably murdered before nightfall for insulting Pharaoh. 'Yes,' he stated, appalled at how badly his voice shook. 'Our countries are joined by marriage and we will stand by our new allies.'

'Then I accept,' Pharaoh nodded. 'You will join me in my chambers.' He turned to Miral. 'And so will you,' he said quietly. She bowed and stood aside to let Amenhotep pass.

Gadamare caught up with Miral a dozen paces from the door to the room Pharaoh had near the council chamber. 'Have you lost your mind?' he demanded, grasping Miral's wrist.

'Let her go!' Mentu demanded.

'She is my daughter,' Gadamare snapped. 'And an ungrateful one.'

'She is my wife,' Mentu argued, yanking Gadamare's hand free of Miral's arm. 'And you will not lay a hand on her again if you wish to leave this palace alive.'

'Is this the way of it?' Gadamare demanded. 'You sell us into slavery to Egypt and then have your husband threaten your own father?'

'Slavery?' Miral rounded on him angrily. 'You sold me into slavery here when you sent me here as a wife for anyone who would have me. You made me a slave. Worse, you turned me into a breeding cow, little more than a whore to buy a peace your constant failures as a king had made impossible any other way.' She pulled herself upright and stared at him with unmistakable contempt. 'But I have prospered here. I have a husband I love and who loves me. I have a sister who has shown me love and kindness and here I have a father worthy of the name.' She left the barb to hang in the air before continuing. 'This is a chance for you to make the alliance with Egypt real and solid. For the sake of your people, don't waste it.'

Gadamare watched his daughter turn her back on him and stride into Pharaoh's chamber. He knew that he had no choice other than to send his troops south for the coming battles and he hated it.

# Chapter Eleven
## The March South

he Mitannite troops caught up with the Egyptian army on the eighth day of their long march south as the Egyptians settled for the night at the Oasis El Boerka, the largest watering hole for several days. The Mitannite army arrived after marching double fast through the heat for days without more than a few hours' respite per night and collapsed into the sand, exhausted. But the next morning, they were ready to break camp alongside their Egyptian counterparts and even the most bitter of Egyptian soldiers had to give the Mitanni credit for their determination.

As ever, Pharaoh Amenhotep was the first to take to his chariot. It was good for morale if the troops saw him lead the way. Amenhotep rode his chariot alone, preferring to take the reins himself instead of having a charioteer drive for him. He would only surrender the reins when battle commenced and he would need his full concentration for the fighting. A few moments later Antranak's chariot drew level with Amenhotep. 'We are ready to move out, Majesty.'

Amenhotep's eyes scanned the enormous mass of men around him, stretching so far that he couldn't see the horizon. 'What of the Mitanni? Are they with us or is their king still asleep?'

'He won't do that again. Princess Miral paid him a visit last night to tell him that it was unacceptable for him to slow Pharaoh's march.' Antranak chuckled. 'I think most of the camp heard. She has spirit.'

'And a loud voice when she chooses to use it,' Amenhotep laughed. 'I hope Mentu is wise enough to keep her happy.'

'I don't think that is a problem, your majesty,' Antranak said, pointing to a chariot slowly moving towards them. Mentu and Miral stood side by side until Mentu stepped behind his wife and dropped an arm around Miral bringing her across in front of him. She leaned back and rested her head on his shoulder, utterly contented.

'If the gods are favourable, she will make me a grandfather, Antranak,' Amenhotep murmured. 'Soon, I hope.'

'The Mitannite king has no sons, has he?' Antranak asked lightly. 'Which would make Miral his only heir, at least until she has a son when the Mitannite crown would go to the child. And he would also be heir to the crown of Egypt.'

'And Egypt would then gain control of the Mitanni,' Amenhotep joined in the game by feigning surprise. 'I hadn't thought of that.'

'Of course not, Majesty,' Antranak agreed, a definite twinkle in his eye.

'It's good to have you with me again, old friend,' Amenhotep sighed.

'Where else would I be other than by my Pharaoh's side?'

Amenhotep nodded towards Mentu, who was still engaged in a whispered lovers' conversation with Miral. 'He's not ready to command an army yet.'

'He will be,' Antranak said confidently. Seeing Amenhotep raise an eyebrow in surprise, Antranak continued. 'With you and me tutoring him, how could he be anything else?'

'I assume that you have the chariot to yourself today,' Amenhotep laughed. Too often recently Antranak had thought he would never hear that sound again. 'Because I doubt if there would be room for anyone to share it with your swollen head.'

Antranak slapped at his waist, held in by the leather girdle that hung down over his leather battle kilt. 'Majesty, there is barely room for anyone else with my girth. I'm not as slim as I once was.'

'Still the finest warrior in my land,' Amenhotep said proudly. A movement over Antranak's shoulder caught Amenhotep's eye. 'Your passenger is coming.'

Antranak twisted his head to see Erimem hurrying towards them. She wore a boy's kilt that reached to her knees and a boy's winter tunic covered her torso. She had a leather cuff on each wrist and a coiled golden cobra twined around her left bicep. If it hadn't been for the delicate, pretty features and the slight swell of her breasts she could have passed for a boy.

'I'm not comfortable with her being here,' Antranak muttered. 'It's not safe. She should be at the palace with Teti.'

'Don't worry, Majesty,' replied Antranak. 'If she comes face to face with a Nubian, it's the Nubian who's in danger.'

'My Pharaoh.' Erimem bowed deferentially to Antranak before nimbly leaping up beside Antranak on his chariot. She eased the reins from the soldier's hands. 'I'll drive.'

Amenhotep turned his head and coughed to hide his grin. Mentu drew his chariot alongside his father. Straggling some way back, Amenhotep could see

Gadamare trundling towards them. He was in no mood to wait for the fool. 'Give the order, Antranak. We move out now.'

The march continued for six more days. The Egyptian and Mitannite armies remained separate entities, despite Miral's stated hopes that they would begin to bond as allies. However, the two armies did begin to show signs of mutual respect by taking turns singing songs to their kings in their camps at night. Neither army tried to drown the song of the other and neither sang a song of winning a battle against the other. It wasn't much but it was a beginning and, as Amenhotep told Miral, 'After decades of war, a beginning is all we could hope for.'

At the end of the sixth day, the advance scouts returned with news that the Nubian army was camped half a morning's march ahead on the far side of an open plain outside of the city of Khesh, one of the cities the Nubians had recently taken. The message was clear. The Nubians had chosen this as the battleground and were waiting. Amenhotep had immediately ordered camp to be set up with perimeter sentries trebled from the previous night and then had called a war council.

Pharaoh's tent was, for someone marching long distances every day, vast and spacious, at least as large as most of the rooms a normal family lived in. But large as it was, the tent was in danger of proving too small for Pharaoh's council of war. Soldiers who were unable to squeeze inside stood at the tent's open flap listening. Pharaoh had already explained his battle tactics. The chariot squadrons would be split into three major groups and so would the foot soldiers. The first group of foot soldiers would draw the Nubians onto the field.

Once battle was joined one of the chariot squadrons would sweep in to wreak havoc among the enemy before another wave of infantry joined the fray. Another chariot attack would follow that and then the cavalry – elite soldiers on horseback – would mop up the enemy. If resistance was firmer than expected, he still had a third wave of both chariots and infantry at his disposal. Amenhotep had outlined his plan briefly and concisely but everyone in the tent knew precisely what was expected of them. For the second time, Miral spoke volunteering the Mitannite army.

'I would ask that the Mitannite army lead the way onto the battlefield.' The tent fell silent with shock. Everyone present knew that the heaviest casualties would come in those early engagements. Miral had volunteered her countrymen for the bloodiest stage of the battle.

'No!' Gadamare finally choked out. 'You do not speak for the Mitanni, girl.'

'Perhaps,' Miral snarled. 'But when courage is required, you don't speak at all. You want an alliance with Egypt but you are not willing to prove the Mitanni worthy of an alliance. Prove you are worthy in battle.' She paused dramatically. 'Unless you are afraid.'

Gadamare's hand flew to the hilt of his sword but Mentu was faster. His sword was drawn and held to the Mitannite king's throat before Gadamare had begun to draw his weapon. 'I warned you once. Never threaten my wife. I will not warn you again.'

Very carefully, Gadamare removed his hand from his sword. 'You have betrayed your people and your father,' he spat at Miral.

She stared back imperiously. 'I betray my people by giving them an opportunity to cement an alliance with Egypt? You would betray them by denying them that chance. And I am no longer Mitannite. I am a daughter of Egypt and my only father is my Pharaoh. I have no other father.'

The stark finality of Miral's dismissal shook Gadamare into silence and he took a faltering half-step backwards away from his daughter.

'Enough,' Amenhotep said finally. 'We are allies here and we will not argue among ourselves.' He pointed to his map, picking out the positions to be held by two of the infantry divisions. 'King Gadamare, we will be honoured to have half of your troops included in the first wave of soldiers onto the field. The remaining half will form part of the second wave. Is that agreeable?'

Gadamare nodded dumbly.

'Then it is decided,' Amenhotep said firmly. 'Tonight we can sleep well, knowing that we will have our gods by our side in battle and that they will lead us to victory tomorrow.'

He dismissed them and watched the tent empty. Before she could leave, he caught Miral's arm. 'What is more important to you? Your hatred of your father or your love for your people?'

'Egypt is my home now,' Miral replied automatically. 'Her people are my people.'

'Don't play word games with me,' Amenhotep said sharply. 'You were born a Mitannite and you still hold them in your heart.'

'I want them to prosper,' Miral conceded. 'Is it wrong of me to want them to have a real, lasting peace with my new home in Egypt?'

'No,' Amenhotep said. 'But insulting their king is not the way to achieve that.' His expression softened as he saw Miral's crestfallen face. 'Your ambition was honourable. Only the manner you chose to achieve it was flawed. You must control your anger. Your father will forgive you,' Amenhotep said kindly. 'As I forgive you, my daughter.' He glanced at Mentu. 'Now take her to your tent and dry her eyes.'

Amenhotep waited until the tent flap closed, leaving him alone with Antranak and Erimem before speaking. 'I wish Miral had been with us on some of our campaigns over the years, Antranak. We wouldn't have needed to raise a sword.' He clapped his old friend on the back. 'Now go and rest. We have the battle tomorrow. You too, Erimem. And Antranak, don't keep her awake all night with stories of past battles.'

'As you wish, father,' Erimem bowed and left, with Antranak behind her.

Amenhotep stretched. He would give prayers and then he would walk among the men. They liked to see that their Pharaoh was among them. Then he would sleep, certain that he would win a victory the next day. He was confident, determined and completely at ease. His mood would have been very different if he had known that just before sunset on that day, his youngest son Teti had been forced back to bed by another wave of the fever.

# Chapter Twelve
## The Battle of Khesh

he plain of Khesh, where the battle was to be fought, was bordered on one side by a steep cliff which led up into barren, rocky mountains. The other side of the plain bled into marshland leading to a river leaving the plain as a corridor between the two inhospitable opposites of nature – the wet marshlands and the arid rocks. The plain itself had rises at either end of this corridor and dipped away in the centre, more of a bowl than the flat plain that had been expected. With plenty of moisture from the river and protection from the worst winds provided by the rocky mountains, the plain was carpeted with thick, lush grass and a few young trees had begun to sprout. Under normal circumstances, it would have been a beautiful place but none of the warriors gathering for the battle had time to think of the scene's beauty. Instead, they noted only that it was a perfect battleground. From their positions on the rises, the respective leaders would be able to watch the battle's progress while the inhospitable terrain on either side of the plain meant that there would be no chance of the enemy launching a surprise attack from the flanks. The battle would be fought head-on and no one doubted that it would be vicious.

The Egyptian army had moved into position just after dawn, eager for the fighting to be over and finished by the time the sun reached its height and sapped their strength. Commanders ordered their troops and issued final instructions while charioteers fed and watered their horses, talking to the beasts to calm their nerves. These horses were all experienced in warfare and knew what was to come. Amenhotep moved through his forces, waving to them from his chariot and promising them glory and eternal luxury in the afterlife if they fought for him. As usual, he was alone in his chariot and, as well as the blue battle crown, he was wearing heavy, leather armour covered with small plates of metal. His chariot, studded with jewels and painted with golden images of the gods and of Amenhotep's previous victories, glinted in the early morning sun giving the impression of something ephemeral and god-like moving among the troops.

Erimem watched it all from the very top of the rise. Like her father she was aboard a chariot but unlike Pharaoh, she wouldn't be involved in any of the action. Despite the chariot being armed with swords, spears and a bow and arrows, her charioteer had been ordered to get the Princess away from danger if anything unexpected happened. The same orders had been given to Miral's charioteer and the Mitannite princess had reacted as badly as Erimem.

'Majesty!' Antranak's voice broke through the morning air. His chariot was approaching Amenhotep's and Pharaoh followed the soldier's outstretched finger. On the far side of the plain, a vast dark wave was spilling over the rise and moving onto the edge of the battlefield.

'I hadn't expected so many,' Amenhotep said without any real concern. 'They might make a battle of it yet. Send in the infantry.'

Antranak nodded and signalled to the commander of the first wave of foot soldiers to head onto the plain. The commander relayed the signal and the soldiers began their steady, ordered march forward, walking in unison. The ground shook with each step they took and a chant began. At first it was difficult to make out what was being said but as more soldiers picked up the chant and their voices became louder, the word became clear.

'THUTMOSE! THUTMOSE! THUTMOSE!'

The soldiers had made their feelings clear. They would fight for the memory not just of a fallen prince, but also of a fallen soldier. One of their own. Amenhotep forced himself to ignore a swell of emotion. Now there was only the battle. 'Watch the Mitanni,' he said to Antranak. 'Gadamare is an opportunist. He doesn't share his daughter's dreams.'

'If they betray us in any way, I will give you his head,' Antranak promised.

Amenhotep nodded and quickly scanned the troops. He saw Mentu in his place among the elite Anubis chariot squadron. Their eyes met for a moment and Mentu raised his spear in salute before they both returned their attention to the plain.

The two armies moved towards each other in lines, stopping around a hundred paces apart. Each side waited for the other to break and make the first move. And then, reacting to some unseen signal or action, both armies moved as one, surging forward and roaring intimidation and obscenities at the opposing forces. And then, with the horrendous crash of metal on metal and the screams of men being butchered, the two armies locked in battle.

Amenhotep leaned forward in his chariot and Antranak held his breath, waiting for the Mitanni to turn on them, but it didn't happen. Gadamare's army poured forward, cutting and hacking at the Nubians with brutal

144

efficiency. Only the vast numbers of Nubians had prevented them being overrun in the first encounter and a second wave of Nubians rolled over the hill, charging to join their comrades. Their presence would swing the battle into the Nubians' favour. As soon as he saw the reinforcements move, Amenhotep signalled to the Anubis chariot squadron. An instant later, the horses reared and the chariots surged forward, hurtling down the incline into the battle.

At the top of the rise, Erimem watched Miral with concern. Her friend clutched at the rail on her chariot as soon as Mentu's chariot squadron had begun to move. Erimem's tent was placed near to Mentu's and she had heard Miral plead with her husband not to be involved in the battle so early and then weep when she had lost their argument. Later, Erimem had heard the couple share a desperate passion filled with the knowledge that it could be their final night together. Erimem could understand Miral's fears but Mentu had to be part of the battle. He had to fight for their dead brother and just as importantly, he had to replace Thutmose in the eyes of the army. To do that, he had to take the blood of the enemy and share the risks that the soldiers faced. Frustration welled in Erimem again. She was more accomplished with the spear and bow than Mentu was and she should have been fighting to avenge Thutmose, but instead she was a spectator.

The battle roared ahead of him and his chariot thundered towards the mêlée but above it all, Mentu could hear the pounding of his heart. He had never wanted to be a soldier, never wanted to be in a battle, but the gods had chosen this path for him and he had no choice other than to fight. He wiped his hand on a cloth Antranak had tied to the chariot's rail. The soldier had warned Mentu that his hands would sweat in battle and he would need the cloth to dry the sweat away. Mentu allowed himself a grim smile. He wasn't actually in battle yet and already his hand was drenched. The chariots were swinging out wide in an arc, coming close to the sheer cliff face before turning in sharply. The line of Egyptian soldiers parted to let the chariots thunder through. The faces of the soldiers on the ground became a blur, passing too quickly for Mentu to notice. He saw the passenger in the chariot directly ahead jab out with his spear, slashing and stabbing Nubians. Shifting the spear in his hand, Mentu lashed out, tearing through the neck of the nearest Nubian. He yanked the spear back and felt the dying man's hot blood spray across his arm. He wanted to be sick but instead he lashed out again, thrusting his spear through an ebony chest.

High on the rise, Amenhotep watched the chariots cut through the Nubians with pride. He could see Mentu working with efficiency in the middle of the squadron. The commander of the Anubis squadron had been given clear orders to protect the Prince at all times, though Mentu had no idea of the fact. A movement high on the opposing ridge caught Amenhotep's eye. More

Nubians were being sent into the cauldron below and with them were Nubian chariots. If the Anubis squadron cut too deeply into the Nubian lines without seeing the approach of enemy chariots, they would find themselves trapped between two Nubian forces.

'Send the second wave of infantry!' Amenhotep yelled to his commander. The troops began to move at once but Amenhotep knew they were too far away from the battle. 'Foot-soldiers aren't fast enough. They won't get there in time.'

Antranak was already signalling to the second squadron of chariots to begin their attack. 'They'll bring the numbers back in our favour.'

Amenhotep nodded fervently. The second chariot squadron – who had dubbed themselves the Wings of Seth – had a reputation for callous brutality and he knew they would show no mercy during this battle.

'Your Majesty,' Antranak said with a frustrated edge to his voice. 'May I...'

'Not yet, old friend,' Amenhotep interrupted. 'I still need you by my side. We'll both be in the heart of it soon enough.'

Antranak hid his disappointment. 'I hope Prince Mentu leaves some glory for us.'

Amenhotep fought off the temptation to send Antranak to pull Mentu from the battle. The boy would have to learn in battle, just as Thutmose had, and so far, the Anubis squadron were keeping him clear of the worst danger. 'You already have enough glory for five lifetimes,' Amenhotep called. 'Let the boy have his first taste.' He prayed that it wouldn't be Mentu's last taste of battle.

Mentu thrust his spear sharply out to the side of his chariot, skewering two Nubians. He bellowed in triumph at the kill before the weight of the two dead men ripped the spear from his hand.

At that moment, the chariot charged over a Nubian soldier whose injured leg stopped him from moving aside. The horses didn't slow as they trampled over him. If anything, his death scream spurred them on. His broken body fell under the wheel of the chariot, kicking it up in the air and tipping Mentu from its back.

He grabbed desperately at the chariot and managed to grasp the rail but his feet had already slipped from the back of the platform and he was being dragged along. The driver of his chariot slowed and reached out a hand to grab Mentu but the young prince's grip on the rail slipped.

'Mentu!' The word choked from Miral as she saw Mentu spilled from his chariot and dragged along behind, it, clinging desperately to the edge of the chariot.

She grabbed at the reins trying to pull them from her charioteer's grip but he refused to let go, remembering Antranak's warning of dire punishment should he let anything happen to his charge. Abruptly Miral let go. In the heart of the battle, Mentu's driver had slowed to let him climb back aboard but the Nubians were taking advantage of the chariot coming to a near stop to swarm around it. Mentu had climbed back alongside his driver and both were hacking and slicing with swords but the charioteer was struggling to get his horses moving at pace again.

'Mentu!'

All Mentu could see was an ocean of Nubians surrounding his chariot. He had a sword in either hand and swung both with brutal ferocity. One Nubian fell, his head almost spliced in two and another screamed as Mentu's sword hacked through bone and gristle, severing his arm just below the elbow. Mentu had known from the moment he had lost his footing on the chariot that he was going to die but he was determined to kill as many of his enemies as he could so that he could face Thutmose with pride when they met in the next life. His sword swung again, burying itself in the neck of a Nubian soldier. He heaved the sword free and the Nubian's head lolled at a sickening angle with blood pouring from the gaping wound. But for every Nubian that he slew, Mentu could see ten more moving forward. He knew it was only a matter of time before they overran him. But then he felt the ground shake and the Nubians staggered backwards, fighting their own men for the chance to retreat. An instant later a chariot thundered past Mentu, close enough for him to reach out and touch. Painted on the side were wings.

'The Wings of Seth,' he breathed. The second chariot squadron had erupted through the Nubians from the opposing side of the battlefield and it took Mentu a moment to realise that he had a chance to survive his fall. 'Go!' he yelled. 'Move!'

The charioteer snapped his reins and his horses reacted instantly, moving through a gap caused by the intrusion of the Wings of Seth. Within moments the chariot had picked up speed and Mentu allowed himself a moment to praise the gods and thank them for his continued existence before returning his full concentration to the battle. He swung his sword again with all of his might and neatly sliced off the top of a Nubian's head as if it was an egg.

'It's all right,' Erimem called to Miral. 'He's moving again.' She saw her friend's shoulders slump and the girl almost sink to her knees with relief. Even though Mentu was still in the heart of the battle, his chances of survival increased a hundredfold if his chariot was moving.

'I thought I had lost him,' Miral pushed tears away with the heel of her hand. 'I will not weep. I will not disgrace him with tears.'

Erimem turned away to give Miral a moment to compose herself and as she did so, she caught sight of a slight movement in the huge rocky outcropping to their right. A thin column of dust was rising apparently from within the rock itself. She looked at the dust in confusion, following its trail back as it ran parallel to the battlefield, leading back towards the Nubian side of the plain and a terrible chill ran down her spine. She nudged her chariot's driver and pointed to the rising dust. 'Take us over there.' He looked uncertain, unwilling to disobey Antranak's orders, but Erimem had no time to waste.

She pulled her favourite fighting dagger and held it to the charioteer's chest. 'Do as I say or I will cut your heart out.'

The charioteer instantly set the horse moving.

At the rock face, Erimem leapt from the chariot before it had stopped and began to climb. Not knowing what else to do, her charioteer followed, struggling to pull his bulky frame up the steep rocks while Erimem moved nimbly from foothold to foothold. She was relieved that the face wasn't as sheer at this point as it was further along and she managed to move with some pace once they reached a small plateau, though she had to take care with the loose stones and boulders that littered the entire rock face. Another short climb led to another ledge. She moved forward and found that the ledge dropped steeply away below her into a winding gully in the rock as deep as six or eight men standing one on top of the other. Inside the gully, moving slowly to avoid disturbing the dust, was a long column of Nubian soldiers. They were, by Erimem's reckoning, halfway along the channel. She ducked back out of sight and hurried back the way she had come. She met her charioteer as he clambered onto the ledge, hurrying past him and leaving him to scrabble his way after her. At the foot of the rock face he only just arrived in time to leap onto the chariot as Erimem snapped the reins, taking the chariot back to the Egyptian lines.

Searching for her father or Antranak, Erimem saw that they had moved to the furthest side of the rise to gauge how the battle was faring on that side. If she went to them, the Nubians would be through the channel and attacking from the rear before they could mount a defence. She looked quickly at the forces that were still waiting to be introduced into the fight. The third chariot squadron would be useless to her but there was the third wave of the infantry and the archers as well. They would be used to mop up stragglers who tried to escape. Erimem's mind raced, working through her options. She urged the horses to pick up their speed and reined them in sharply beside the infantry's commander.

'Come with me. All of you.' The commander didn't move, startled by her appearance. 'The Nubians are behind us! There are passages through the rocks.' She turned her chariot. 'And bring the archers. Hurry!'

She snapped the reins, heading back towards the rock face. A few moments later she was aware of another chariot alongside.

'What's happening?' Miral called.

Erimem pointed at the dust. 'The Nubians have a way through the rocks.' She turned and was relieved to see the archers and infantry sprinting after them. By now she guessed that the Nubians were three quarters of the way along the passage. They couldn't have long before the enemy charged through wherever the path emerged. She pulled the chariot to a halt at the rocks and grabbed her bow and quiver of arrows. The infantry's commander arrived, breathing heavily.

'Leave half of your men here, Erimem instructed. 'The other half will follow me. So will the archers.'

'My lady, I don't…' his voice trailed off. Erimem had already begun to climb again.

'Do as she commands,' Miral snapped imperiously. 'Remember that she is Pharaoh's daughter. Obey her.'

The commander nodded and barked an order to his men. Moments later they were climbing.

On the far side of the field, Antranak's call pulled Amenhotep's attention from Mentu, who had safely retaken his place at the heart of the Anubis squadron for their next pass. The soldier pointed to the rocks on the opposite side of the plain. Hundreds of tiny figures could be seen swarming up the stone face and in their lead was a small, boyish figure in a white kilt and tunic.

'Erimem? What is she doing?' Amenhotep demanded.

'I don't know, Majesty,' Antranak replied. 'Should I go and find out?'

'No,' Amenhotep said, returning his concentration to the battle. 'We are winning through here, old friend. We will break their lines before long and then it will be over.'

Antranak nodded his agreement. The battle on the plain was going well but Erimem's actions worried him and he glanced nervously across at the rock face. He had no way of knowing that his Pharaoh had just cast an equally worried eye in the same direction.

Erimem reached the top of the rocks far more quickly the second time. Behind her, the soldiers and archers were following more gingerly, searching grips while trying keep hold of their weapons. Peering over the edge into the gully, Erimem saw the Nubians were even further along than she had feared. The first of their number had almost reached a cave-like opening in the rock ahead, obviously leading to their exit. The infantry commander reached the top of his climb and pulled himself alongside her. His face fell in horror as he saw the Nubian army below.

'Arrange your archers along the edge,' Erimem said quietly.

The commander nodded. 'What of the infantry? Why make them climb?'

Erimem pointed at the loose rocks and boulders.

In the trench that led through the great rocks, Bezir, leader of his section of the Nubians, was struggling to control his impatience. The trek through the passage took an eternity and the gully was only wide enough to take two or three men abreast at a time. This demanded more patience than any hunt he had been on, and while he skulked through caves, the battle was being fought out on the plain. But it would be worth the frustration when he swept through the rear on the Egyptian army. His father's death at the hands of Pharaoh's soldiers would be avenged.

A trickle of dust spilling down the side of the gully caught his attention. He followed its path up, just in time to see a stone dropping towards him. He leaped backwards and the stone bounced off his shoulder. He looked up and saw an Egyptian boy standing on the lip of the gully. No, it was a girl, though she was dressed like a boy and covered with dust. She was tossing a stone easily in her hand and looked little more than a child. Abruptly, she pulled her hand back and let fly with the stone. It cracked Bezir on the arm and he swore. He would gut her for that. But then she made a small gesture and a row of archers, stepped forward stretching almost halfway back along the gully.

Bezir shouted an order for his men to run for the cave at the end of the gully but even as he shouted his order he heard the girl's voice and the hiss of arrows singing through the air followed instantly by the shrill screams of his men. The closest men ran for the cave but from above there was another sound, the scraping of stone on stone, and then the rumble as Egyptian soldiers pushed the biggest boulders over the side into the gully. The first thirty men managed to make the safety of the cave and the protection of an overhanging lip but immediately behind them a boulder at least as tall as a man crashed into the gully crushing a handful of men and Bezir saw his brother's skull split open like a ripe fruit as the rock smashed him to pulp.

The boulders were being pushed into the gully at regular spaces along its length cutting off any hope of escape and the Egyptian archers were merciless, letting fly volley after volley into the trench, cutting down countless Nubian soldiers. Among the archers, Erimem was unleashing arrow after arrow, oblivious to the screams of the dying. Each death was a small piece of retribution for Thutmose and would set his soul at peace. When the final Nubian in her view fell, Erimem fought a wave of disappointment. She pulled away from the edge of the gully. Further along, archers were still firing into the crevasse, but her moment of bloodlust had passed. She would leave the archers to finish their work.

She made her way down the face of the rocks and dropped nimbly to the ground. The troops waited, unsure of what they should do. They had expected to be in the heat of battle by now and instead they were waiting staring at rocks. Miral, who had been passing back and forth in front of the troops in lieu of their commander swung her chariot in an arc towards Erimem when she saw her friend climbing down.

As the chariot curved towards Erimem it came within a dozen paces of the side of the rocks and as it passed one of the thick bushes that tenaciously clung to the side of the rocks, the bush was suddenly thrown aside and the Nubians who had escaped into the caves poured out of a small opening behind it. Their leader, spying the chariot just ahead ran for that. Miral shrank behind the side of the chariot as a spear hurtled towards her. It slammed into the back of her charioteer instead and he toppled backwards onto the ground.

She reached for the reins but turned abruptly as she heard a roar. Sprinting towards her chariot was an enraged Nubian. In his hand he carried what looked like a wooden club with a vicious, hooked blade embedded in the end. She scrabbled frantically for the sword that hung in a scabbard on the side of the chariot but she couldn't find the handle. The Nubian was almost on her when he was rocked backwards off his feet by an arrow thudding into his neck. Incredibly he managed to lurch to his knees. Erimem already had another arrow in place and she fired again, this time slamming an arrow into the Nubian's chest.

Instantly she nocked another arrow and fired again. The third arrow took the Nubian in the eye and ripped his head backwards as the arrow head splintered the back of his skull. Spurred on by the sight of the Nubian chief being so mercilessly destroyed, the Egyptian soldiers descended on the Nubians hacking at them wildly. Erimem didn't join the attack. She turned to see whether Miral had managed to control her horses and saw that one Nubian had somehow managed to escape the carnage. He had almost reached the chariot and Erimem grabbed for an arrow. Her last arrow. She nocked the arrow quickly and took aim quickly before letting fly.

She missed the Nubian by a whisker but ripped the club from his hand. Undeterred he leaped into the chariot beside Miral – and then stopped, frozen like a statue. Embedded in his chest, pushing up between his ribs was a long fighting dagger, similar to the ones Erimem favoured. Miral pulled the dagger free and plunged it into the Nubian again, pushing him backwards until he fell from the chariot and lay twitching on the ground. A soldier reached the chariot just before Erimem. He pulled the dagger from the Nubian's chest and slashed it across his throat. Erimem helped Miral down from the chariot. She felt the other girl's hands shake under the thick, slippery coating of the Nubian's blood that covered her arms and the front of her dress.

Erimem took the dagger from the soldier and wiped the side of the blade on the ground, cleaning it of most of the blood, before handing it back to Miral. 'No more than he deserved.'

'Princess?' The commander of the soldiers she had commandeered had climbed down from the rocks. 'The Nubians in the gully are dead, so are the few who escaped. What should we do now?'

The question took Erimem by surprise. She hadn't thought past stopping the Nubians from outflanking them and she had never expected an experienced soldier to ask for her orders. 'I… I…' she stammered. What would her father have said here? Or Antranak? 'Resume your previous position,' she said firmly, hoping that she sounded confident.

'The commander bowed. 'As you command, Princess.' He turned to his troops. 'Back to position! Move. Back to positions!'

Erimem turned back to Miral. She seemed to have regained her composure. 'We should go with them.'

Miral nodded. 'I want to see that Mentu is all right.' Her voice sounded brittle and Erimem squeezed her arm reassuringly before picking up the reins and urging the horses forward.

\* \* \*

'Majesty!'

'I see them, Antranak.' There was relief in Amenhotep's voice as Erimem and Miral's chariot galloped back into view with the archers and third wave of infantry following close behind. The reappearance of the Egyptian soldiers had an immediate effect on the Nubians, who began to fall back. Amenhotep briefly considered whether this could be a trap but his instincts said that the panic was real. He signalled for the final wave of soldiers and the last squadron of chariots to enter the battle. 'Time to finish this,' he called to Antranak. Taking the reins in one hand and gripping a spear in the other, Amenhtep charged towards the battle. Antranak's chariot thundered after him a few moments later.

When the final Egyptian troops entered the fray the battle became a rout and then turned into a massacre. Outnumbered and ultimately surrounded, Nubians were slaughtered by the hundred. Seeing his men die in such numbers, the Nubian chief threw himself in front of Pharaoh Amenhotep and begged for the lives of his people. Amenhotep agreed to let the remaining soldiers live before crushing the Nubian chief's skull with an Egyptian war club. The chief had known it would happen and Amenhotep couldn't help respecting the man's courage in sacrificing himself for his men.

Seeing their chief dead, the fight died in the Nubians and they were gathered together, waiting for the inevitable execution. Instead, on Pharaoh's orders, they were tied to posts and castrated. The youngest and strongest would be taken back to Thebes as slaves. The rest would be sent back to their homes as a reminder of how brutally Pharaoh dealt with anyone who opposed him.

Erimem found Mentu at the centre of the Anubis squadron, letting the horses take advantage of the shadow thrown by the cliff face. They were raising skins of wine in toasts and were already embellishing the truth to turn their battle into a story worth retelling. Mentu had a good number of kills to his name and by the time the squadron had finished elaborating on the battle, he would have a good number more.

Mentu knew that his immediate acceptance among these hardened fighting men was entirely down to his position as a prince and to the prestige it would bring the squadron to have the heir to the throne among them, but he had fought hard and late in the battle and he had saved the lives of the men in one of the chariots by hacking across the backs of two Nubians who had managed to clamber onto the other chariot.

Any reservations the men of the Anubis squadron had held about Mentu had disappeared and, for the first time, Mentu understood why Thutmose had loved the army so much. It wasn't the thrill or the excitement of battle but the comradeship, the sense of belonging among men who had shared a common experience. They shared the glory and the celebration and they would share the mourning for any of their number who died in battle.

Mentu raised his wine-skin in triumph as he saw the chariot approach with his wife and sister both aboard but the smile on his lips died as he saw the blood stains on their clothes. He threw the wine aside and ran to them. 'Are you hurt? What happened?'

'We're fine,' Erimem assured him, but Mentu wasn't listening. He had lifted Miral from the chariot and was inspecting the front of her dress.

'There's so much blood.'

'But none of it is mine,' Miral promised. 'I'm not hurt.'

'But the blood...' He pulled his wife to him.

'Is from a Nubian soldier she slew,' Erimem said proudly, dropping nimbly to the ground beside Mentu.

'And you?' Mentu asked. 'How did you get so dirty?'

'By making sure that an army of Nubians didn't attack us from the rear,' Miral informed him. 'She led half the army to stop them.'

'It wasn't half the army,' Erimem said, uncomfortable at the scrutiny the Anubis squadron were giving her. She knew they were weighing up Miral's story and working out how much it had been exaggerated. 'Only enough men to stop them attacking our flank.' She explained about the gully and the Nubians using it as part of planned ambush.

'So you climbed that?' Mentu asked, pointing at the cliff. 'I knew I called you *Little Monkey* for a reason.'

'She was incredible,' Miral said, looking proudly at Erimem from the comfort of Mentu's arms. 'A warrior.'

'I think I should find Antranak,' Erimem said, eager to find some respite from the praise.

'He'll be with our father,' Mentu said easily. 'Just follow the sound of two loudest voices on the field and you'll find them.'

Erimem forced a smile and leaped back up onto her chariot. She was feeling strangely distanced from the triumph all around her, as though she didn't belong among it. It wasn't the screams of the Nubian prisoners being castrated or the corpses or the metal tang of blood that filled the air. Something was gnawing at the edge of her mind, something she couldn't quite bring to the fore and examine. She wondered if perhaps it was Thutmose's spirit watching over the battle. If he was watching over her perhaps it was he who had made her look towards the cliffs and see the rising dust when she had. If her brother had visited her, she hoped that his ka would find eternal peace now that his murder had been avenged.

She forced herself to ignore the feeling of discomfort and cantered across to Antranak. He was at the heart of the battlefield beside her father, who was offering a prayer. Erimem was surprised to see that her father had chosen a spot where the grass was glistening red with blood for his prayer.

Amenhotep finished praying and raised his sword high overhead before swinging it down, gouging a deep furrow. From a leather purse tied to the belt at the waist of his lather armour, Amenhotep pulled a ring with an oval stone of a brighter blue than any lapis lazuli Erimem had ever seen. She recognised the ring instantly as having been one Thutmose had worn on the most ceremonial occasions. Amenhotep dropped the ring into the gouge he had cut and then pushed the two sides of the ground back together. He offered another short benediction before standing. He seemed surprised to see Erimem watching.

'Thutmose was with us,' he said.

'I know.'

Amenhotep pulled himself up onto Erimem's chariot and inspected her. She was dusty, her hands and knees were scraped and patches of her clothing and arms were turning brown with drying blood. 'Does this look like a princess of Egypt to you, Antranak?' he asked.

'No, your Majesty,' Antranak replied. 'More like a boy beggar from the market.'

'My very thoughts,' Amenhotep agreed. 'Perhaps the market beggar would explain why she stole a third of Pharaoh's army?'

Antranak's head tilted with interest. 'I would like to hear that as well,' he agreed.

Erimem sighed. She had a feeling that she was going to be telling that story many, many more times before the day was done. Oddly, she didn't mind. Her strange mood had passed and she felt the same comfortable sensation she had felt as a child when Antranak and her father had teased her. 'I was trying to stay out of the way,' she began...

# Chapter Thirteen
## Apotheosis

haraoh's armies marched into the two towns recently held by the Nubians and were disappointed to find no resistance. They swept further south and east but the Nubians had abandoned towns on the edge of their own lands, retreating into the heart of their own territory. The towns were taken as a trophy of war and garrisons established.

Amenhotep always spent time in a newly conquered land. This land was Egyptian now and history would remember the man who had taken it. He would make sure of that by building monuments and temples to the glory of this victory. He would see to it that Thutmose and Mentu were honoured in these great feats of building – even Erimem would be remembered – but the victory would be remembered as his, as was his right as Pharaoh.

He watched with satisfaction as Mentu and Miral settled into a comfortable marriage. It would change in time, when Mentu became Pharaoh and found himself taking more wives to appease political needs but, for now, Miral was the rock Mentu would need as he grew into his role as heir. And Miral herself had a pleasant way of dealing with people that had ingratiated her both to the travelling court and to the troops. She had even forced herself to make peace with her father, and as a gift for his assistance, Amenhotep had awarded Gadamare trading rights in this new part of his empire as well as custody of the smallest of the towns on the Red Sea so that he could trade more freely.

As for Erimem, she had almost been adopted by the soldiers she had led. He had expected her to be treated as little more than a mascot but instead they showed her the same respect they gave to all of their commanders and were brutal in putting down anyone who doubted her right to that respect. Erimem seemed slightly bemused by it all but she took the cheers of the men with good grace.

After two months in his new territory, Amenhotep had demanded a hippopotamus hunt. It was a sign to Antranak that he was ready to leave and begin the trek home. And so, after a happy and successful day spent hunting the river giant in its river and swamp-lands, Pharaoh announced that they would be breaking camp and returning to Thebes.

The trek back was slower and less frantic than the march south to war had been. Pharaoh ordered a less direct route back to Thebes, meandering through the largest towns in the south lands and accepting the praises of his people. After a battle he liked the people to see the army. They felt safe seeing the victorious troops and the soldiers had their hearts lifted by the acclaim of the public. And, as the slow march home continued, Amenhotep was pleased to see the Mitannite forces becoming more integrated with his own soldiers. When Miral eventually became queen of the Mitanni, it would be easier to assimilate her people into Egypt if the army was already used to fighting as part of Pharaoh's forces.

Thebes was half a morning's ride away by Erimem's estimation. She found the thought of returning to the palace left both a sweet and sour taste in her mouth. She was relieved that the war and the long, dusty journey were both over and she would be pleased to see Fayum and old Shemek again.

And she had such stories to tell her handmaidens that they wouldn't believe. The sadness was that she knew she would slide back into her old life and become the dutiful princess again, living quietly and staying out of the way until she was needed. In the past few months she had felt like a young bird stretching its wings and now she was going to be forced back into the nest.

She spent less time with Miral and she was glad of it, because Miral and Mentu were spending as much time alone together as they could, which was as it should be. She noticed that Miral had become a kind of go-between in discussions between Pharaoh and the Mitanni and felt guilty at the momentary pang of jealousy in her belly. She had spent years held at arm's length from her father and it had taken the tragedy of Thutmose's death for them to regain the warmth they had once shared. Miral, on the other hand, had found herself embraced as a daughter almost immediately. Erimem knew it was unfair of her to feel any resentment and she put it down to her mixed emotions regarding the return to her mundane life at the palace.

Cresting a rise, Erimem looked across at Mentu's chariot. Miral was nestled against his shoulder. Their lips moved as they talked quietly and Erimem felt the last of her resentment fade away. Miral looked across and caught Erimem watching them but she showed no sign of anger at her moment with Mentu being observed. Instead she offered a friendly smile and settled back against her husband. He shifted the reins across to one hand

and slipped his free arm around Miral's waist, resting his hand on her stomach. They were happy and in love and Erimem's dark mood evaporated in their glow.

She flicked her reins and hurried after Antranak. She wanted to know what to expect in the victory procession through Thebes.

Teti lay in his bedchamber, sweat dripping from his brow even though he was shivering. The room smelled of old sweat with hints of vomit, and urine and human waste hovered in the air as well. It was the smell of sickness.

Teti coughed and struggled to sit up but two small hands pushed him back. Mari, the servant girl who had flirted with him early in his illness had stayed with him. As the priests and physicians had found themselves unable to cure the Prince, Mari had, by default, been left as Teti's main carer. She had attacked the role with determined vigour, remaining cheerful in spite of the Prince's failing health, staying with him, talking to him even though he was both weak and still shy in female company. She had even lain alongside him on his worst nights.

'My father is coming home,' Teti said hoarsely, struggling against the gentle pressure of Mari's grip. 'I have to be there to meet him. He'll be disappointed if I'm not there. He'll be angry.' Teti sounded ready to cry.

Mari firmly pushed Teti back onto the bed. 'Your father is a wise Pharaoh. He will understand that you are ill and he will love you anyway.' Teti nodded, too tired to fight any more. 'Now rest so that you have some strength when he does get here.'

Teti's eyes closed and he drifted into a restless sleep. After a short while, Mari slipped out into the gardens and settled into a small shaded courtyard. Everyone in the palace was busy preparing for Pharaoh's return so she knew that she wouldn't be disturbed. A small stone bottle was waiting exactly where she had been told it would be, and she slipped it into the folds of her dress before returning to her duties. She never even paused to wonder why her employer had chosen this as the day she was to finally kill Teti.

It seemed as if the entire city had turned out to greet Pharaoh's procession and, in all probability, not many of the city's inhabitants would have missed the event. Pharaoh's triumphant return always led to an enormous celebration.

As was his right, Pharaoh led the cavalcade, proudly taking the cheers. He thought briefly of Thutmose, who had accompanied him the last time he had returned in triumph but he knew that he couldn't wallow in the past. Mentu was the future of Egypt now and he had acquitted himself well in his first battle. Amenhotep noted that some of the women in the crowds lining the streets had taken to wearing wigs in the hairstyle favoured by Miral. He didn't care for the idea of Mitannite culture seeping into Egypt – Miral would have to be moulded into something more Egyptian. Amenhotep held his sword aloft and the cheers grew even louder.

Immediately behind Amenhotep, Miral was nestled close in to Mentu's shoulder. Protocol dictated that Mentu should have ridden in his chariot alone and not have elevated a mere wife to as honoured a position as this, but no one had ever assumed that Miral would be anywhere other than by Mentu's side when the procession reached Thebes. Erimem's chariot followed behind Mentu's with Antranak following her and King Gadamare behind him. If the Mitannite king was put out by his lowly place in the procession it didn't show. In fact, he seemed to be enjoying the parade more than anyone. Behind him, the chariots and foot soldiers of the Egyptian and Mitannite armies forced a spring into their step and ignored the complaints from their weary bodies. They eyed the taverns and the young women lining the streets, already prepared for the long, wild night ahead. Shackled and exhausted, the Nubian slaves, now reduced to eunuchs, looked at the people of Thebes with dead eyes and hadn't even the strength to react when they were spat on by the Thebans. Most of them wished they had died in the battle at Khesh.

The parade continued, winding through the streets of Thebes before finally reaching the familiar huge sandstone walls of the palace and even Amenhotep was relieved to be home after a long, tiring campaign.

But the reception inside the palace was more muted. Nesmut, the vizier, led a small party along with Horemshep. They greeted Pharaoh with the news that Prince Teti's health had worsened considerably in the past few days. Nesmut had broken off and left Horemshep to deliver the news that the physicians and priests tending Teti doubted that he would live through the night. Amenhotep had leaped back onto his chariot and hurried to Teti's quarters with Mentu, Erimem and Antranak following behind him.

They found Teti in his bedchamber, attended by the serving girl Erimem had seen with him months before, while priests milled back and forth in Teti's outer rooms. Teti was both sweating and shivering and his eyes were unable to focus properly but his spirits raised and a smile ghosted weakly across his lips as he heard his father's voice.

'Teti?'

Teti tried to reply but only managed a choked, gurgling noise.

'He hasn't spoken for some time, Mighty Pharaoh,' the servant girl explained quietly. She wiped sweat from Teti's face before moving quickly aside to let Pharaoh move closer to his son. Amenhotep looked at his son's sweating form and the glassy, unfocused look in his eyes. He beckoned Mentu and Erimem forward before turning back to Teti.

'You looked after Egypt well while we were away,' he said gently. 'I knew I could trust the land to your care.' He took the cloth from Mari and mopped Teti's brow gently. His hand brushed Teti's skin and he almost winced at the scorching heat that burned his son. 'I'm very proud of you, Teti.'

Teti's eyes flickered and closed. He knew that he was dying but he wasn't saddened or afraid. His mother would be waiting for him in the next life and he left his current life surrounded by the people he loved, with his father's words in his ears and for the first time in years he was sure of his father's love. He felt the world slip away. He was sure he could hear his mother's voice and he began to smile.

The time between Teti closing his eyes for the last time and his death was thankfully short. He felt no pain and passed from this world with a peaceful smile on his lips. A priest examined Teti briefly before confirming to Pharaoh that the boy was indeed dead. The Pharaoh's shoulders bowed. Miral put an arm around Mentu, who had slumped in a similar fashion to his father. Erimem wanted to go to her father and to hold him but everyone remembered how the Pharaoh had erupted with rage at the death of Thutmose and of his retreat into solitude. So she waited alone, and desolate tears began to run down her cheeks. She felt a slight pressure on her arm and found Antranak standing by her. She buried her head in his shoulder and wept for her gentle, kind brother.

'Enough now.' Amenhotep's voice didn't carry any sign of a rebuke, only a tired resignation. 'We shouldn't mourn Teti but offer thanks that he has moved into his next life.' The Pharaoh settled Teti's hand on his still chest and rose from the bed. 'He struggled with this life. He will have more peace in the next. We will bury him alongside Thutmose so that he is never alone.'

Erimem forced her tears away. She would cry again when she was alone. Her father set a hand on her arm and she squeezed his hand before he moved on and patted Antranak's shoulder. 'Thank you for taking care of her, my brother.' Erimem thought that he suddenly looked very old. The joy of victory against the Nubians and the great parade through Thebes had disappeared to be replaced by a misery that looked set to crush him.

Erimem saw that Miral was whispering something to Mentu. He seemed unsure but allowed himself to be persuaded and gave in.

'Father,' Mentu said uncertainly.

Amenhotep stopped by the door. 'What is it?'

Mentu seemed uncomfortable but carried on. 'This sad time is not ideal for this news, but if we tell you this now, perhaps Teti's ka will hear us.' He slipped an arm around Miral. 'My wife is carrying my child. In a little more than six months, she will make you a grandfather.'

A wry, humourless smile drifted across Amenhotep's face. 'You were wrong, Mentu. This is a good time to tell me this news. I will pray to my brothers for Teti's spirit tonight and tomorrow we will talk about your son.' He glanced at Miral. 'You are bringing life into my palace again. Thank you.'

They followed Amenhotep from the bedchamber, all of them eager to let the priests begin their blessings of Teti's body. Amenhotep walked straight out of Teti's quarters without saying another word but Erimem stopped with Mentu and Miral.

'I should have known when I saw you put your hand on Miral's stomach when you were on your chariot,' Erimem said to Mentu before turning to Miral. 'And you will have to stop riding in chariots.'

'I know,' Miral nodded. 'But I have a few months left when I can be active. I will attend Teti's burial ceremony.'

'And then you will rest until the baby is born,' Mentu said firmly.

He will be a good father, Erimem thought and then she remembered Hanek, who also claimed to be carrying Mentu's baby. Would he have been a good father to Hanek's child as well, she wondered?

'You have my love and hopes,' she said, squeezing both of their hands before beginning the trek back to her apartments. She turned as she heard footsteps running behind her. She had expected to see Antranak lumbering towards her. Instead it was Fayum. 'I'm all right, Fayum,' she said wearily. 'I don't need an escort back to my rooms.'

'I think you do,' Fayum said darkly.

'What do you mean?' Erimem asked.

Fayum looked around nervously. 'I'll tell you later.' He paused for a moment. 'I am sorry about Teti. I know the physicians and priests did everything they could for him.' Fayum took Erimem's elbow and hurried her forward. 'We should hurry. I will be happier when we have your bodyguards nearby.'

'I should add my congratulations as well,' Antranak said, bowing stiffly to Mentu and to Miral. 'I'm pleased your father could hear some good news today.' They began walking from Teti's quarters back towards Mentu's new, larger apartments, which were closer to the heart of the palace and to Pharaoh's chambers than his old rooms.

'We hadn't planned to tell him until tomorrow,' Mentu answered. 'It seemed the best thing to do.'

'It was,' Antranak agreed. 'And now I should issue orders for the troops to stop their celebrations. They shouldn't be drinking and carrying on with women at a time like this.'

'Wait,' Miral said, putting a hand on Antranak's arm. She indicated the sun, which had just touched the horizon. 'It's almost dark. It would be difficult to find all your soldiers once night has fallen. Let them celebrate tonight and tomorrow they will mourn Teti.'

'I don't know,' Mentu said. 'My brother should be mourned properly.'

'Not by drunk soldiers angry at being taken away from their women,' Miral offered reasonably.

'You're right,' Mentu said thoughtfully. 'They haven't seen women for a long time and many of them will already be drunk.' He mulled the problem for a long moment. 'Let them have tonight to celebrate, Antranak,' he said finally. 'And tomorrow they will give respect to Teti.'

Mari slipped into the courtyard where she had collected the poison. The sun had almost set and the courtyard was shrouded in shadows. She was eager to be paid and on her way from Thebes. She heard the trailing ivy behind her rustle and thought it was the breeze but then a hand clamped across her mouth and a muscular arm pinned her arms to her side. A second man slipped from behind the curtain of ivy where they had been waiting and pulled at her jaw. Mari struggled to keep her mouth tightly shut.

This second attacker had a bottle similar to the one she had been given. Abruptly, the man holding her dropped his grip to her stomach and jerked backwards, driving the air from her body. Instinctively, Mari's mouth gasped open and the second man pushed the bottle in, tipping the contents into her mouth. He caught her nose and jerked her head back. The more Mari struggled, the more she needed air and eventually she gasped, letting both air and poison down her throat.

Horemshep emerged from the shadows behind a pillar as Mari's body jerked in her death throes. He nodded to the priest holding the poison who set the bottle on the ground by the bench. 'Poor child. Distraught at Prince Teti's death, she chose to take her own life to stay with him. Tragic.' He smirked. 'Simply tragic.'

'Sit and tell me what has you so worried,' Erimem said to Fayum. She was concerned but fought to keep a weariness from her voice. She wanted to be alone, to cry and mourn Teti but Fayum had been insistent, almost desperate. She sat and pulled off her wig, letting it drop to the floor.

Fayum sat, looking around nervously. Other than Erimem's personal bodyguard of four palace guards and a couple of handmaidens, there was no one in the room with Erimem and Fayum.

'I have something to tell you,' Fayum said in a low whisper.

'Then tell me,' Erimem said, making no effort to hide her impatience.

'It's Hanek. I haven't heard a message from her or seen her since she left. But I began wondering about the things she said. The things she said about not remembering anything about the Mitannite soldier who had seemed to be her lover. I began to wonder if perhaps she was telling the truth, so I asked Linsis and the other handmaidens to find the food that had been delivered to Hanek. The food had been thrown to the beggars but they did find the wine jars that she had drunk from.'

'And?' Erimem demanded. 'Is it important?'

'The wine was drugged,' Fayum said. His hands fidgeted nervously in the air as he told the story. 'I took the wine to the priests who have knowledge and learning of these things. They told me that the wine was laced with a drug that brought on a deep and sudden sleep.'

'Does it also leave a headache and a difficulty in concentrating?' Erimem asked quickly.

'Yes,' Fayum nodded, surprised. 'How did you know that?'

'Because Hanek complained of having difficulty in focusing her thoughts when she woke and she also mentioned a headache. But why would the Mitannite soldier drug Hanek?' she wondered.

'She is a very attractive girl,' Fayum offered. 'Perhaps she refused him, so he drugged her and had his use of her.'

Erimem shook her head thoughtfully. 'It looked as though they had... been intimate.' She cursed herself for still being so prudish with sexual matters. 'But Hanek assured me that nothing of that sort had happened. And a woman would know,' she added.

'So why would he drug her and arrange her as if they had just spent a passionate afternoon together and then do nothing but leave her to be found?'

Erimem's lips pursed and a little crease appeared between her eyes as it always did when she was thinking. 'Unless he wanted her to be found.'

'Why would he want her to be found like that?'

'I'm not sure. He would have to have known someone was visiting her or it would have been a waste of his time. But the building was usually abandoned at that time.'

'He can't have expected to be seen.'

'Or perhaps he always intended to be seen,' Erimem countered. 'What better way to discredit Hanek than to have her seen having an affair with a Mitannite guard? He was loyal to Miral,' she mused. 'He was angry that Mentu had insulted Miral by choosing Hanek over her.'

'And so he did this to her?'

'But how could he have known I would be going to visit Hanek?' Erimem pondered.

'He must have overheard you with Miral,' Fayum said.

'No,' Erimem said firmly. 'He was removed from duty when Miral said he was becoming aggressive towards Egyptians.'

'She was right,' Fayum snorted a mirthless laugh. 'He murdered the guard, Khofrek, and plotted with the Nubians. He would have killed Mentu and you if she hadn't stopped him.'

Erimem sucked on her bottom lip thoughtfully. A thousand facts and ideas were running around in her head, jumbled together so that she couldn't draw any meaning from them. Her thoughts kept going back to Khofrek and the single blow to the heart that had killed him but she couldn't explain why. But then a memory came to her and a connection instantly snapped into place. The vague worry that had burrowed into her head a few months before suddenly took shape and made sense. There was barely enough of a link for it to be called tenuous, and the thought of someone so prominent at court betraying Egypt made her stomach lurch but she knew that it made a sudden, terrible sense. 'We need to find Antranak.'

Miral looked at the tangled bedclothes, all twisted and rucked, that lay across her bed, as evidence of her recent love-making with Mentu. There had been desperation in his passion, as there had been on the night before the battle, but this was different. This time he was desperate for the love of his wife and she had been happy to give him the comfort he needed. Once he was spent he had fallen asleep in her arms, his head held against her bosom. He had looked so peaceful sleeping that she had almost been reluctant to wake him when word came requesting his presence in the throne room, but she had roused him and he had set off, preferring to face whatever duty was required himself than have anyone disturb his father.

Miral stood by the doors leading to the broad terrace and pulled a cloak around herself against the cold night air. It wouldn't do for her to be struck with a chill now that she had the baby growing in her belly to think of. The baby who would one day be Pharaoh. She closed her arms around her stomach protectively and then a movement caught her eye. A light flashing in an arc across the sky before falling to ground. A flaming arrow. It looked like a falling star, a portent of doom or a sure symbol of good fortune, depending on which god you worshipped.

Miral turned away from the doorway and crossed from the bedchamber into a small side-room. She opened a wooden chest and carefully removed a box as long as her forearm and half that in both depth and width. She made sure the lid was secure before carefully lifting the box. She carried it through to the largest of the living rooms as though it contained something precious and delicate, and was setting it down on a table when she heard footsteps behind her. 'Your Majesty honours me by visiting us tonight,' she said sweetly but the smile became fixed on her lips as she turned and saw Mentu standing in the doorway. 'I assumed it was our divine father,' Miral flustered. 'Who else in this part of the palace would enter our rooms?'

Mentu nodded. 'Pharaoh can go anywhere.'

'Why are you back so soon, husband?' Miral asked. 'I thought you had been summoned to the council chamber.'

'I was,' Mentu replied. 'But on the way I was intercepted with a message from my friend, Fayum. He told me I shouldn't trust any Mitannite. Not even you.'

'Priests!' Miral snorted. 'No one trusts a word they say.'

'I trust Fayum,' Mentu said softly. 'But I trust you more.' He moved into the room, confusion clear on his face. 'He has to be wrong.'

Miral held out a hand to her husband. 'Come with me, my lord. Lie with me and I will calm your thoughts. In the morning when Ra is in his sky, this will make sense to you.'

Mentu shook his head in frustration. 'I don't understand why...'

'Hush, my love.' Miral set a finger on his lips and silenced him. 'Fayum knew Teti all his days and is as upset as you are at his passing.' She drew him close and pressed a kiss against his chest. 'Whatever Fayum said, you can deal with in the morning.' She lifted his hand in her own and slipped it under the soft material of her dress until he cupped her breast. 'Tonight, I will love you and watch over you.'

He could smell the fresh fragrance of her hair and the gentle scent of her perfume and the feel of her soft skin was intoxicating. He remembered their passion from earlier in the night and from all the other nights she had spent with him, writhing beneath him, her legs wrapped around him until he had felt as though they had become one being. He wanted to feel that contentment again. He needed to feel that love in the way he imagined some men needed poppy juice. He let Miral take his hand and lead him back into their bedchamber.

Word of Prince Teti's death hadn't reached Thebes and the great city was brightly lit as it celebrated the return of their victorious soldiers. The prostitutes did brisk business and every tavern was overflowing with soldiers and revellers, doing their best to drink the city dry. They were joined by their new Mitannite allies who joined in the celebrations but seemed overawed by the scale of it all.

As the night wore on and the Egyptians got steadily drunker, they didn't notice the steady trickle of soldiers leaving the parties and taverns to return to their camp. Any Mitanni who were spotted leaving were usually sent on their way with good-natured insults about not being able to hold their drink. The Mitanni soldiers staggered and lurched their way out to their camp on the edge of the city and it was only when they were sure that no one from Thebes could see them that they straightened and walked with a purpose, far more sober than they had appeared a few moments earlier. While the Egyptians had been drinking, the Mitanni had been surreptitiously tipping their wine and beer onto floors and out of windows, slowly watching their allies drink themselves into a stupor.

At their camp, the Mitannite army prepared quietly and efficiently, arming and organising itself into small battalions ready to move into position. As the crescent moon disappeared from view behind some high, fast-moving cloud, word was passed through the ranks and the army began its move.

Miral peered down at her husband's face, calm and relaxed in sleep. His chest rose and fell with a steady, slow rhythm. He was a handsome man, she thought. By most standards a good man, too. Once he had accepted her as his wife, he had been a kind and honest husband to her, ensuring that she was happy and had everything she could want. She had no doubts that he would be a good father too. The love he had shown for Teti, who could never have grown to be more than a child showed her that. But how would he be as Pharaoh? She would find that out soon enough.

Slowly, making sure that she didn't wake Mentu, she slipped from the bed and quietly made her way through to their large reception room where she slipped into a comfortable short dress that stopped just above the knee. She hurriedly pulled a cloak over the top of her dress and made her way to the table where she had left the box she had retrieved earlier. To her relief it was untouched and the lid was still in place. She had been lucky so far but she knew that it was deep into the night and she was short of time. She carefully lifted the box and headed for the doorway.

Mentu's voice stopped Miral dead in her tracks. 'Where are you going?' He was barefoot and dressed only in his kilt, standing in the doorway to the bedchamber watching her. Even in the low light, Miral could see the suspicion in his eyes as surely as she had heard it in his voice. 'Where are you going?' he repeated, walking slowly towards her. 'Were you running away from me? Or is there truth in what Fayum told me?'

'Go back to bed,' Miral said with a firm edge underlying her soft voice. 'Go back to sleep. I will be back soon.'

'You didn't answer me,' Mentu stated. 'Can I trust you?'

'Go back to bed,' Miral repeated firmly. She had no time to continue the deception, especially when he saw the evidence in her hands.

His voice lowered. 'Tell me, Miral. Tell me the truth.'

Miral didn't reply but she could see that her silence was all the answer Mentu needed. She could see the disappointment, the surprise and the betrayal in his eyes. 'Go back to bed,' she repeated slowly. 'You won't be hurt, I promise you that. And you will be Pharaoh. That won't change.'

'What are you planning to do?' Mentu asked slowly.

Miral's arms were beginning to ache from carrying the wooden box. 'What will happen will happen no matter what you or I do now. My father's soldiers are already moving on the palace. Go back to bed and tomorrow it will be over. You will be Pharaoh and I swear on our baby's life that you will not be harmed. You will have a long and peaceful reign, guided by your queen.'

'A puppet!' Mentu spat. 'How is my father to be killed?' he demanded.

Miral didn't answer but her eyes flickered towards the box she was carrying.

'Put the box down!' Mentu demanded, striding towards her. 'Put it down now and I may spare your life at least until the baby is born.'

'Spare my life?' Miral snorted. 'The arrogance of the Egyptians is beyond belief. Your palace – your nation – will belong to us before the night is out and your life is in my hands – but you talk about sparing my life?'

'How is my father to be killed?' Mentu repeated.

'Why do you care?' Miral screamed. 'Until Thutmose died you were nothing to him. Neither were Teti or Erimem. He ignored you all except when he wanted you to perform some task his precious Thutmose couldn't face. Don't deny it! Don't! You have spent too many nights in my arms telling me how rejected and unwanted you felt. You will be a better Pharaoh than he ever was.' She was almost pleading. 'When I lay with you and felt you inside me and I told you that I loved you, it wasn't lies. You are a good man and you will be a great Pharaoh and a loving father. You won't favour one of our children over another. You won't ignore a child and you won't attack your neighbours. I know you. This world will be safer with you as Pharaoh. You can't stop this, Mentu. If you try hundreds of people will die and the result will be the same. Stay here,' she begged. 'Please.'

'And no one else will be hurt?'

'No one,' Miral promised. 'I swear to you.'

'And tomorrow I will be Pharaoh?' Mentu's voice drifted thoughtfully.

'Yes,' Miral whispered urgently. 'Tomorrow you will sit on the throne of a country at peace with itself and its neighbours.'

'Did you kill my brothers?'

The question took Miral by surprise. 'I...'

'Were you responsible for their deaths?' Mentu asked in a brittle voice. 'Did my loving wife kill my brothers?' He strode towards her. 'Did you?'

The rage in Mentu forced Miral to take a step back. She had seen him angry, depressed, passionate... but never in a murderous rage like this. As he came closer he pulled back his hand. Instinctively, she threw the box she held at him. It fell short, thudding into the floor and splintering half a pace from his feet. He sneered at Miral and opened his mouth to deliver an angry response when the smashed wood at his feet moved. He peered at the splinters in surprise and then his blood chilled as two deadly glistening black heads pushed their way through the broken wood. A third followed and Mentu recognised them as black-necked cobras.

In the time it took him to register the snakes, the serpents had freed themselves from their wooden prison along with a fourth snake of the same species. Agitated by being so violently disturbed the snakes writhed and hissed, baring their fangs at the nearest target. Mentu tried to back away but the nearest of the cobras reared up. Mentu knew what it was doing and brought his hand up to protect himself but the snake was faster. It spat a stream of venom up into his face. His eyes instantly felt as if burning coals had been plunged into them and he choked trying to spit out the venom that had sprayed into his mouth. He staggered back, blinded, desperately trying to get away from the snakes but his foot caught on a low stool and he tripped. As he tried to scramble to his feet, Mentu felt the razor sting of fangs burying themselves into his leg. Before he could move he felt another snake bite into his leg and he screamed.

Miral stifled a scream of her own as she watched the third cobra strike at Mentu. She made a move to help him but stopped as she saw the fourth cobra glide across the stone floor towards her. Mentu twitched and spasmed as the venom coursed through his body and Miral felt a lurch in her stomach. There was nothing she could do for her husband and she was suddenly very afraid. Everything had gone wrong. She ran towards the open door to the terrace and disappeared into the darkness.

Outside the palace, Mitannite soldiers moved in small groups of six, sticking to the shadows and moving patiently and quietly until they reached the edge of the clearing outside the palace's gates. They waited, searching for any sign of movement on the ramparts of the palace's high walls but there was none. They waited until past the time for the guards to change but there was still no hint of movement inside the palace. The sleeping draught their ally had promised to feed to the palace guards had evidently done its job. Eventually, the giant gates slowly began to swing open and two figures quickly waved flaming torches before disappearing back inside the gates. Gadamare gave the signal and his soldiers began to sprint across the open ground towards the gates. With every step that took them closer, Gadamare waited for the arrows to flash down from the battlements and cut his men down but the arrows didn't come and after what seemed like an eternity, the Mitanni spilled through the palace's gates onto the broad square in front of the palace's front steps. Gadamare allowed himself a brief moment of exultation before sending hushed orders for the troops to form into ranks. Even though they were inside the palace, they still had the task of securing it and Gadamare knew it wouldn't be as easy or as bloodless as he had told Miral, but he was confident. He was just about to give the order to move when he heard the echoing creak of the palace's great gates closing. He turned just in time to see the gates thud shut and on the battlements dozens – hundreds – of torches caught light, illuminating the courtyard as Egyptian soldiers leaped to their feet from the lying positions they had held as they watched the Mitanni charge into the palace. And then, from inside and all around the palace there was an ominous, regular thudding. Gadamare recognised the sound only too well. It was the march of an Egyptian army. The Egyptian forces emerged in three ranks. One from either side of the palace and one through the palace's main doors with Antranak at their head.

Gadamare looked desperately for an escape, for some kind of explanation as to how this could have happened, how the Egyptians could have known... but it was too late for them to worry about that now. Now they had to fight. He bellowed for his men to charge and the ground shook as the Mitanni began to run.

At the head of the palace steps, Antranak and his troops waited. He swept an arm down and on the battlements, the archers took their cue. Arrows, many of them covered with oil and set alight flashed through the night sky and the air was instantly filled with the screams of injured Mitannite soldiers.

Antranak held his men in position, letting the archers go about their deadly work. He waited until the archers on the battlements couldn't fire without the risk of hitting their own men and then he violently cut downwards with his sword. At the signal, the Egyptian troops charged at their Mitannite adversaries and within moments the sound of clashing swords filled the air.

Amenhotep strode into Mentu's apartments with a foul temper welling in him. Miral's message had been obscure and vague. She had asked to see him but she hadn't arrived at Pharaoh's suite, and Amenhotep was sure that by now she would have known better than to assume that she could summon Pharaoh in his own palace. He had been praying to the gods, begging his brothers to look after his sons in the afterlife and to give protection to his only remaining son, Mentu, and to his unborn grandson. He was exhausted. The emotions of the day had drained him and he wanted to sleep, though he knew that it would be difficult to find any rest that night. Mentu's rooms were in near total darkness with only two small lanterns burning when Amenhotep entered. He assumed that Mentu and his bride had retired and was ready to leave without disturbing them when he heard a rasping movement in the room. Looking around he saw no one else in the room and he called for his personal guards. As they entered, one saw the dark shape of a serpent slithering across the floor and another guard sliced it cleanly in two with a single blow of his sword.

'Mentu? Mentu?'

He was answered with the sound of a piece of furniture scraping slightly on the stone floor. Mentu was lying on the floor behind a long couch with his foot resting against a low stool. Coiled near his bloodied legs were three almost pitch black shapes. The flick of their tongues betrayed them as snakes and Amenhotep's guards attacked with fury, slicing the serpents into pieces. Before the guards were finished, Amenhotep had dropped to his knees by Mentu's side. His son was still breathing but his chest rose and fell slowly, each breath agonised and laboured.

'Mentu?'

The prince's eyes flickered but his eyes showed no sign of recognising his father.

Amenhotep slid his arms under his son and lifted him. 'Leave him!' he snapped as one of his guards moved to help. 'Bring physicians and priests – and the experts in the ways of snakes. Go!' he yelled. 'Or die where you stand!' The guard ran out of the room and Amenhotep carried his son with ease through to the bedchamber and set Mentu on the bed, smoothing the tangled bedclothes under him. Amenhotep knew that cobra bites were nearly always fatal but he clung to the hope that Mentu would survive. Most men would have already been dead from the bites of the reptiles. Mentu was strong. He had a Pharaoh's blood running through him and Amenhotep refused to accept that Mentu could die. He couldn't lose his only remaining son. He began to pray desperately to his brother gods. 'My life for his,' he said desperately. 'I give this life up to you if you will spare my son. I will do it willingly.' He continued to pray until two terrified priests scuttled into the room with one of his personal guards close behind. 'Tend to him,' Amenhotep demanded. 'And if he dies, so do you.'

'Majesty,' the bodyguard said, 'we are under attack. The Mitanni. The battle is being fought in the courtyard in front of the palace.'

Amenhotep looked at Mentu's deathly figure lying on the bed and his desperation boiled into an uncontrollable anger. He snatched a sword from one of his escort. 'Two of you will stay here. The others attend me.' He ran from the room, heading for the battle.

The battle was finely balanced. The Egyptians had the better tactical positions but the Mitanni had greater numbers and they fought tenaciously. Erimem watched the battle unfolding from a parapet where she had been one of the archers who had rained down so much death into the Mitanni. But now she watched the fighting with growing frustration. She didn't dare use her bow and arrow with the armies locked together as they were but she was desperate to help her people win the day and she knew that they would need every blade they could find.

'Forget your bows!' she yelled to the archers. 'Use your swords. Fight!' The archers hesitated momentarily, uncertain about leaving their assigned posts. Erimem grabbed the hem of her dress and yanked hard, tearing the material up past her knees. Using a dagger she made a quick horizontal incision in the material and tore it so that the dress now stopped above her knees and gave her far greater freedom of movement. She scooped up a spear and ran for the nearest stone stairs leading down to the square. Even though their orders had been to stand firm on the ramparts, the archers snatched up their swords and followed Erimem into battle.

Antranak's sword scraped against bone as he slashed his blade hard across a Mitannite's chest. His opponent dropped to the sandy ground. Antranak recognised the thrill of battle and embraced it. He parried a Mitannite soldier's attack and slammed the hilt of his sword into the attacker's face, feeling the nose crack under the impact. His sword slashed down, cutting off the Mitannite's cry.

A scream from behind made Antranak turn. A Mitannite soldier was bringing his sword down towards him and Antranak knew in that split second that he didn't have time to defend himself but them the Mitannite's head jerked back and his chest pushed forward violently. He dropped to his knees revealing Erimem standing behind him, holding the spear that she had plunged into the Mitannite's back.

'I told you to stay safe!' he yelled at Erimem.

She shrugged. 'Someone has to look after you. And you have saved my life more than once.'

'Be careful!' Antranak bellowed, but Erimem had already picked up the sword dropped by the Mitannite she had killed. She spun away and drove the sword through the nearest Mitannite but not in time to save the archer he had slain, an archer who had followed her instructions. Whatever responsibility Erimem felt for the archer's death she pushed aside and concentrated on the battle. Even though they had seen her fight at Khesh, the Mitannite soldiers seemed surprised to see Erimem confronting them, and each one was eager to have the glory of killing the Pharaoh's royal brat. Erimem couldn't match any of the soldiers for strength but she had never been able to match strength with the soldiers who had taught her to fight either and she knew how to best them. She deflected Mitannite blows rather than meeting them head on and let her opponents' momentum take them off balance. Her quick, nimble footwork allowed her to move aside and cut them down before they had a chance to recover. She spun away from a Mitannite spear and chopped downwards with her sword cutting away half of the Mitannite's hand before shearing the spear into two. Without mercy she drove the sword forward, deep into the Mitannite's groin. As she twisted the blade free, blood spurted from the gaping wound, spraying the bottom of her torn dress. But Erimem didn't notice it. Through the battle, she had seen a gleaming wave of shining black hair move through the mêlée. Erimem sidestepped a flailing sword and lashed out low with her own, cutting into a Mitannite soldier's knee. She moved on, leaving the Mitannite for one of her men to finish. It took her precious, dangerous moments of scanning the mass of clashing metal and flesh to pick out the hair again but she did spot it, around thirty paces away, moving towards Gadamare.

'Miral,' she hissed. Any futile hope Erimem still harboured of Miral not being part of this disappeared as Miral slashed a fighting dagger across the back of an Egyptian soldier's neck, cutting through the muscle so deeply that the white of his spine showed. 'Miral!'

It was a primal, animal scream and, even through the clashing of swords and roaring of battle, Miral heard it. She turned, searching for the source of the voice and soon saw Erimem, cutting through the battle towards her. A Mitannite soldier raised his club and moved to intercept Erimem. His reward was for Erimem to slam her sword deep into his chest. She didn't try to rip it free but pulled her fighting dagger instead. Miral looked frantically between Erimem and the Mitannite soldiers surrounding her father. Realising that she couldn't reach the safety of her father's guard before Erimem caught her, Miral turned and fled back into the palace.

Erimem burst from the fray and sprinted up the stone steps after her. She kept Miral in sight as they ran through one of the great halls leading through towards the throne room. Miral hurried through the giant doors into the throne room. From there she would get outside into the darkness and try to reach the breach in the wall Erimem had spents nights observing and then she would get to the river and a boat. She had only made it halfway across the throne room when she heard Erimem scream her name again. She turned.

Erimem was at the doors, covered with blood and sweat, her face a mix of rage and betrayed hurt. Miral knew that she had no hope of reaching the doors without Erimem catching her. She drew her fighting dagger.

'Let me go and you don't have to die tonight, Erimem.'

Erimem hefted her own dagger and began to slowly walk across the broad throne room towards Miral. 'One of us has to die tonight and you are responsible for enough death in this country.'

'You?' Miral sounded surprised. 'It was you who alerted your army?'

'Yes.' Erimem continued to move closer.

'How did you know?' Miral asked, keping her eyes firmly on Erimem, weighing her as an opponent.

'Because Hanek was drugged,' Erimem said, slowing as she closed on Miral. She began to circle, gauging the other girl and wondering with a part of her mind why Miral wasn't afraid of her. The Mitannite bitch had to know that Erimem was skilled with most weapons, so why wasn't she showing any fear? 'She was drugged and left to look as though she was having a relationship with your bodyguard. But Hanek hadn't been touched by any man since Mentu,' Erimem continued. 'Your guard didn't touch her in that way. Perhaps he was supposed to but didn't have time. You sent him there

170

so that I could see him coming from her room. It could only have been you – you were the only person who knew that I was to be visiting Hanek.'

'Why would I want to do any of this?' Miral asked. 'I already had Mentu.'

Erimem's brow crinkled with concentration. 'At first I thought it was spite because Hanek had been Mentu's favourite or perhaps fear that he would go back to her, but it was something more devious than that. You wanted to make my father trust you so you arranged for your bodyguard to be seen with Hanek, for him to lead me into a trap and then for him to be with you when he was uncovered as a spy so that you could kill him. Did he know that his death was part of your plan, Miral?'

Miral didn't answer, concentrating on Erimem, making sure the Egyptian girl didn't manoeuvre herself into a position from which she could strike.

Erimem's anger grew, fuelled by Miral's silence. 'You sent your bodyguard through that entrance because you knew I would be watching. You wanted me to kill him.'

'Instead I had to do it myself.' Miral shrugged. 'It worked out better that way.'

A memory flashed through Erimem's mind. 'He was with you when you when you met with Thutmose in the stables. Did you have him kill Thutmose? Did he damage Thutmose's chariot so that it would crash?' Still no answer came. The lack of a denial could only be a confession. 'You killed my brother,' she hissed.

'I had Betu, my guard, follow Thutmose and cut through his chariot's axle,' Miral said, taking a half step forward. 'He even arranged a line of boulders on the path to be sure that the axle did break – and to make sure Thutmose didn't survive.'

The cold, matter-of-fact manner in which Miral told the story forced Erimem to take a step backwards. 'Why?' she asked softly. 'Thutmose had never hurt you.'

'Four of my brothers have died in battle with Egypt,' Miral yelled. 'Battles that your father caused because his arrogance makes him think he has the right to rule everyone in his country or in any other.'

'You killed Thutmose as revenge.'

'No,' Miral snapped. 'As self-defence. We knew that we couldn't defeat Egypt in war, so we chose a different path. I was sent to marry into Pharaoh's house. We thought I would be married to Thutmose but he refused me.'

'He refused you twice,' Erimem said rerunning the scene of Miral and Thutmose in the stables. 'The day he died, you offered yourself to him again. That was why you were promising to be a good wife to Mentu. That was why you killed him, wasn't it? So that he wouldn't tell Mentu or my father that you had gone to him like a whore.'

Miral bristled at the insult but continued. 'If Thutmose had accepted me, then he would have been allowed to live, but I had to marry the heir to your throne. I thought for a time that Mentu would never accept me – but you were so helpful. I would never have snared him without your help.'

Erimem's stomach tightened. 'I thought I was helping a friend, a sister.'

'And you were.' Miral's words came with absolute sincerity. 'The love I have for you is real, Erimem. You have shown me nothing but kindness and I am grateful to you for that. I swear to you that you were never in any danger from my people. Only your father and brothers interested us.'

'Then why did you arrange for crocodiles to attack me as I crossed the Nile?'

'I didn't. Betu made a mistake. He wanted to kill Hanek, not you.'

'You lie easily, Miral.' Erimem picked on a word Miral had said. 'Brothers? Did you have plans for all my brothers?' Her mind raced. The scale of Miral's betrayal threatened to swamp her but she forced herself to think clearly. 'Did Teti die of fever?' she demanded.

'He was weak,' Miral replied. 'Even if we hadn't poisoned him he wouldn't have lived long. You know that.'

'You murdered him.'

'He was weak and a simpleton but he could have been used as a figure for the army to rally round after we had taken the palace.'

Erimem digested the information, marrying it to what she already knew. 'You would have to have killed my father.'

Miral nodded. 'It was supposed to be so clean, Erimem. Your father would die in a tragic accident, bitten by cobras in his rooms. Mentu would take the throne and I would be behind him. My father's army would be at his disposal and take over the running of the palace. We would have moulded Mentu into a real leader, into a man worthy of being Pharaoh. He would have been Pharaoh and I would have been a loyal wife and subject to him.'

'If he had let you murder our father! Is a man who would do that really worthy of being Pharaoh?'

Miral said sadly. 'You won't believe me – and that doesn't matter now – but I did genuinely come to love Mentu. I would have been happy to spend my life with him raising our children but he wouldn't listen to me. He only had to do nothing. If he had done nothing it would all have worked.'

'*Did* love him? *Would* have been Pharaoh?' Erimem tasted the bile in her throat. She choked it down. She waited, desperately hoping Miral would tell her that she was wrong, that Mentu was alive and unhurt but the look in Miral's face told a different story. The regret and sadness in the Mitannite girl's eyes said that she had been telling the truth about her feelings for Mentu. She *had* loved him.

Erimem didn't care. Miral – her friend, her sister – had murdered her brothers. She had cut down all three of them and planned to take their father's life. It didn't matter if Miral *had* ever loved Mentu or if she had genuinely felt warmth for Erimem. All Erimem could think of was the pain that this so-called friend had caused. The hatred she now felt for Miral erupted in a scream torn from the heart of Erimem's being and she leaped at Miral, swinging her dagger at the Mitannite's face.

\* \* \*

The battle was going badly. From his position halfway up a set of stone steps leading to the ramparts, Horemshep could see that the Mitanni were losing. They were surrounded and most of their remaining number had formed into a circle protecting their king. They were outnumbered and being mercilessly cut down.

With no hope of reinforcements, the Mitanni would be slaughtered and, if Gadamare was taken alive, he would certainly tell of Horemshep's involvement in this plan when Antranak tortured him. Horemshep could barely imagine the tortures Pharaoh would inflict on him if his part in the death of the princes was uncovered. A bellow from the palace made Horemshep turn and his blood chilled.

Amenhotep, surrounded by his elite personal escort was charging from the palace, sprinting down the steps and into the battle. The soldiers formed a point in front of their Pharaoh and cut through the Mitanni, hacking a path through the faltering Mitannite lines. Roused by the sight of their Pharaoh fighting in their midst, the Egyptian troops became even more intense and brutal until the final protective line around King Gadamare crumbled and Pharaoh's guard broke through. Two of Gadamare's generals threw their swords aside and fell to their knees in surrender. They were cut down without mercy. At Amenhotep's command, his guard moved aside to let him see Gadamare.

The Mitannite king was terrified, looking round for some vestige of his forces to protect him but his soldiers were involved in their own desperate skirmishes. There was nowhere for him to run, no one to protect him and nowhere for him to hide. He was alone. Gripping his great curved sword, Gadamare charged at Amenhotep, swinging his sword at the Pharaoh's head. Amenhotep parried the blow, and stepped to the side. His sword cut through the air and slashed a deep wound across Gadamare's back. The Mitannite king tried to turn but Amenhotep's sword was already flashing down, cutting across Gadamare's arm. Gadamare dropped his sword, his fingers suddenly dead and unresponsive. He flailed for the weapon with his other hand but already he could see Amenhotep raising his sword again.

Amenhotep swung the sword with all of the rage, loss and hate that he possessed, shearing through Gadamare's neck with a single stroke. The Mitannite king's head toppled to the ground and landed with a wet smacking sound in the paste formed by the blood and dust.

From his vantage point, Horemshep saw the Mitannite king beheaded and felt hope grow inside of him. There would be no prisoners taken here and only a few of the highest Mitanni knew of his involvement. There was a good chance that he would escape unscathed. A movement below caught Horemshep's eye. Two Mitannite soldiers were running along the side of the wall, pursued by three Egyptian soldiers. Drawing a dagger, Horemshep dropped onto the Mitanni. All three of them spilled to the ground. He was on his feet before either of the soldiers and stabbed his knife deep into the first Mitanni's heart. The second Mitannite pulled himself erect in time for Horemshep's dagger to slash across his face. He screamed in pain but his screams were cut short as the Egyptian soldiers fell on him.

The battle was more or less over. A final few Mitannite stragglers were being finished off by the Egyptian soldiers or begging for mercy. They would all be dead before long and Antranak made his way towards Amenhotep, limping slightly from a flesh-wound on his leg. 'It's finished, Majesty,' he called.

Amenhotep's blade chopped down another of Gadamare's generals and he roared with frustration that there were no more Mitanni left to kill.

'Majesty?' Antranak repeated.

Amenhotep spun and pulled his sword arm back, desperate for Antranak to be another enemy. He caught his swing and let his hand fall. 'Antranak.'

'We have them beaten,' Antranak said. He suddenly realised that he was out of breath and exhausted.

'No prisoners,' Amenhotep stated. 'They all die.'

Antranak nodded and relayed the order. 'Majesty, have you seen Erimem?'

'Why should I?'

'Because she was in the heart of the battle,' Antranak answered. 'I told her to stay safe. She had done enough by coming to me with her warning. I think I saw her running towards the palace but I can't be certain.'

Amenhotep was already running towards the palace.

The clash of blades echoed around the throne room. Miral parried Erimem's blow and swung with her own dagger but Erimem had already spun out of range. The fighting daggers were as long as a man's forearm with shorter prongs projecting on either side of the main blade, and were closer to swords than to knives but in combat they were used in close quarters with short stabbing and slashing blows. Normally each combatant had two of the daggers and a duel was fought with a constant flow of blows, parries and counterattacks.

Miral and Erimem each carried only one of these daggers but their fight was as swift and ferocious. Each blow was aimed to kill or maim, slashing at a face or stabbing at a heart and each attack was met with a desperate defence and countered with an equally vicious counter. In playing her role as dutiful wife and princess, Miral had never shown her skill with a knife or sword but she was at least Erimem's equal with the daggers and was matching the younger girl attack for attack. She lunged and was blocked and instantly pulled the dagger back to deflect Erimem's response.

As Erimem's blade touched her own, Miral twisted the weapon in her hand and slid the dagger along Erimem's blade until the smaller side tines of their daggers locked. Miral jerked her head forward, slamming her forehead into Erimem's cheek and the Egyptian girl staggered backwards, stunned. She felt the dagger being wrenched from her hand and heard it skid along the stone floor. She forced the momentary fuzziness from her mind and saw Miral approaching. The Mitannite stabbed forwards once, twice, forcing Erimem to back away. Miral thrust forward again, and Erimem tried to grip the older girl's wrist but she was too slow and Miral flicked out with the dagger, nicking Erimem's forearm.

'You should have let me go,' Miral hissed. She lunged again and Erimem felt her shoulder brush against something solid. She thought she had reached the stone wall, and that she had run out of space to back into but there was give in this object and she risked a quick glance at it. It was an oil burner, a tall pole with a shallow bowl of oil. Twenty or more of them burned, illuminating the throne room. She spun behind the pole and heaved at it, tilting it towards Miral.

The Mitannite girl leaped back as burning oil splashed onto the floor and up at her legs. She screamed in outraged pain as the scalding oil blistered her shins and calves. Through the pool of flames she saw Erimem hurrying running along close to the wall.

Miral ran around the edge of the blazing pool of oil in pursuit. She reached the end of the pool and turned in towards Erimem – and barely had time to register an object hurtling towards her before it slammed into her chest. It was a shield from the far south, made of wood and animal skin. Although it was light, the force Erimem had put behind the throw forced Miral back a step. She could see now that Erimem was pulling at the weapons that adorned the wall, trophies of previous campaigns. She realised that if Erimem could loosen the spear she was pulling at, the Egyptian girl could run her through without coming within range of her dagger.

She charged at Erimem, who wrenched violently at the spear, breaking the bottom section away and managed to use the broken shaft to block Miral's attack.

The impact stung Erimem's hands but she refused to let go. She backed away, throwing desperate glances around the throne room for a weapon but all she could see was Miral closing on her with a dagger aimed at her throat.

Amenhotep arrived at the throne room half a step ahead of Antranak. They both took in the scene instantly. Erimem was armed only with what looked like a short club and was backing away from Miral who held a fighting dagger. They watched Miral close for the kill but Erimem gripped a lion skin that was pinned outstretched on the wall and pulled the pelt down on Miral. The skin didn't harm Miral but it gave Erimem the chance to run past the Mitannite back across the throne room to scoop up her dagger. As she picked it up her foot slipped in a patch of oil and she barely regained her balance in time to fend off and attack from Miral.

The Mitannite girl attacked at a frenzied pace. It was clear that she had seen Pharaoh standing in the doorway and that her chances of escape were fading. She cut and slashed at Erimem forcing the younger girl backwards, desperately defending herself against the onslaught. Blow after blow rained in and each parry became more frantic until Erimem yelped and her foot skidded up from under her.

'Oil,' Antranak hissed.

Miral seized the opportunity and lunged forward, dagger raised to strike but Erimem pushed up on the foot that had apparently skidded. At that moment Miral registered that there was no oil near her. Erimem's knife hand lashed out and Miral realised that she had been tricked before she felt the searing pain of Erimem's dagger ripping across her throat. She stood still for a moment, blood gurgling from her open neck and then she toppled to the floor

Erimem dropped to the floor beside Miral. She was exhausted but she wasn't finished with the Mitannite. 'I kill you in the name of my brothers. For Thutmose, for Teti and for Mentu. I give your life and that of the bastard in your belly as an offering to the gods that my brothers find peace. I curse you and the day you came here. I loved you as a sister and you betrayed everything.' Miral's mouth opened and closed, like a fish on the shore gasping for breath. 'But you were never the one really in my brother's heart,' Erimem hissed. 'He loved Hanek before you and he gave her a child before he took you into his bed. Mentu will live in the son Hanek is carrying.'

Bloody froth spilled from Miral's throat and a jet of blood spurted from a severed vein and splashed across Erimem's face. She tasted the metallic tang of Miral's blood and spat it out. 'I should let you lie here and bleed to death, let you drown in your own blood.' She lifted her dagger and pressed it against Miral's side. The Mitannite girl tried to stop Erimem but her hands didn't seem able to do as she told them. Erimem pressed the dagger against Miral's ribs. 'This is how you liked to kill and it's how you will die.' She pushed the dagger with all her might, feeling the blade scrape against Miral ribs and she kept pushing until she felt Miral's struggles stop.

By some miracle, Mentu was still alive when Amenhotep led Erimem and Antranak into Mentu's quarters. The miracle quickly turned into a curse as they watched Mentu fight the venom for four days before finally succumbing to the poison.

His resilience to the cobra's bite amazed the physicians and for a brief time on the third afternoon there was a stirring of hope that the Prince might recover but the chill night brought a fever that cruelly swept away those hopes and as the fourth night came to an end and the sun began to show itself on the horizon, Mentu's rasping breath finally stopped.

Erimem had thought that she had wept so much that she would have no tears left to cry. She was wrong.

Word of the Mitannite attack and the Prince's murder spread across the land like an uncontrolled fire. Any Mitannite found on Egyptian soil was attacked without mercy and the nation fell into a mixture of outrage and mourning, weeping along with their Pharaoh.

Erimem didn't see her father in the days following Mentu's death. She heard from his bodyguards that Amenhotep had locked himself away in his private temple, alternating between begging his brother gods to return his sons and railing against the gods, hurling insults and curses at them for their hard-hearted cruelty and she knew that mixing with his grief was a frustration borne of impotence. He was the most powerful man alive and yet he hadn't been able to protect his sons. Six days after Mentu began his journey to the next life, Amenhotep entered the Palace of Concubines and remained there for over a full month, desperately trying to impregnate one of his wives. Erimem heard from her mother that Amenhotep had become obsessed with fathering another son, even to the point of taking Techvis to his bed, despite promising the memory of Thutmose that he would never touch her. When his wives failed to show signs of bearing him another son, he declared them too old or barren and took six new teenage brides. None of them showed any signs of pregnancy and Amenhotep sank further into despair. In his heart he knew that he was the one who was too old and it was his seed that was too weak to impregnate his wives. His failure was complete.

Erimem found herself in limbo for much of the time following Mentu's death. While her father was locked away, decisions had to be made and she took them in his stead. She gave orders for extra chambers to be cut into the final tomb already being prepared for Thutmose so that her three brothers could spent the afterlife together, and she ordered craftsmen to begin work on the sarcophagi and death masks for her brothers. They would rest adorned with gold and precious jewels. Their tomb would, in time, be painted with images of their victorious battles or in Teti's case, representations of his mother and of their father, so that they could protect him always.

As preparations were made for Mentu and Teti to be interred alongside Thutmose in his mausoleum while the tomb was built, Erimem found herself being drawn into taking her father's place in accepting salutes from soldiers preparing to march with the dead princes' bodies and at ceremonies at which precious oils were blessed so that they could anoint the bodies during mummification. It was only a short step from there for her to take his place at vast ceremonies to offer prayers and sacrifices to the gods and then to putting the royal seal onto minor laws and proclamations. Both Antranak and Horemshep had agreed that the country still had to be governed while Pharaoh was absent but it was only when Antranak took her aside and mentioned the fact that Erimem realised that she was now Amenhotep's only heir. The thought terrified her.

Erimem felt a distance grow between herself and her father. It wasn't the same as had happened when he had concentrated his affections on Thutmose. Then he had only ignored her. Now she felt that he actively avoided her as if he resented a daughter being alive while his sons were dead. She also wondered if he despised her for murdering his grandchild when she had killed Miral. Erimem had a discreet search for Hanek begun. By now Hanek would have given birth to Mentu's child and that baby was the true heir. Erimem resisted the temptation to tell her father of Hanek and the baby. She couldn't bear to raise his hopes and then see them torn away if Hanek couldn't be found or if the infant had died.

In public, Erimem wore a dignified regal mask but in private, when no one could see her, she wept at the futile waste of her brothers' lives and at Miral's deception. She asked the gods how they could allow it all to happen without intervening. She demanded to know why her brothers had had to die, why Miral couldn't have accepted a peace between their lands bought with a marriage, why her father had to suffer so... and ultimately she stopped asking. The gods she had been taught to worship would never have allowed this to happen. There were gods for justice, gods of truth... if they existed they couldn't have let this happen. It was heresy she knew but she didn't care. She turned her back on all of the beliefs she had once had. The gods had abandoned her and now she abandoned them.

On the seventieth day after Teti's death, a procession led through the Necropolis towards Thutmose's mausoleum. Hundreds of soldiers lined the route and stood guard over the princes' temporary resting place. Priests led by Horemshep were at the head of the procession with Amenhotep and then Erimem following behind in her place as heir to the throne. In their wake came Pharaoh's wives and then the remainder of the court led by Antranak, who had foregone his usual place with his troops to march in the grim procession. Behind them were the official mourners and the public who had chosen to join the mourning. There were thousands of them, stretching back from the wealthy and noble at the front to the most common bringing up the rear. Each of the mourners at the head of the procession carried a gift for one of the princes to take to their eternal life. The procession began at dawn with the first rays of sunlight and the ceremonies and rituals of interment finished as the sun's journey across the sky to the far horizon brought dusk.

Erimem watched the mourners return to their homes and in the days and months that followed, she caught sight of their lives resuming their normal routines. For their Pharaoh, there was no routine to go back to. His adult life had been spent preparing a son to one day assume the mantle of Pharaoh and rule the country. He had spent years tutoring first Thutmose and then Mentu for the task that would face them. Now they were gone and he had no male heir. For a time he threw himself into the politics of Egypt, resuming his arguments with Horemshep, but he had no heart for the fight and took to taking a chariot deep into the barren red lands, often visiting the place where Thutmose had died. As usual he drove his own chariot and, if the Isis squadron were to be believed, Pharaoh always drove too fast. But who could tell him to slow down?

Horemshep stood hidden in the shade of a large boulder on a hill looking down at a desert plain. There was carnage below him. His alliance with the Mitanni had failed and the Hyksos mercenaries led by Yanis were proving equally incapable. The mercenary chariots had attacked Pharaoh's chariot escort and killed most of them but Amenhotep himself had a long headstart on the mercenary chariots and would make it back to Thebes long before they caught him.

Amenhotep looked back over his shoulder. He knew that he could outrun his pursuers and make the safety of his city. But why should he run? He was a god. Since the day he was born he had been taught that he was a living god, that he could do anything he chose and that no man could ever match him. Yet in the past year he had failed to protect his family, his country and had failed to father more sons. Doubts had crept into his mind. Was he really a living god? He pulled back on the reins, slowing his chariot and he drew his favourite sword. A god would never run from bandits.

Horemshep watched with amazement as Amenhotep's chariot stopped and the Pharaoh leaped onto the sand. Within moments, he was surrounded by mercenary chariots. Even though he was a good way distant, Horemshep heard Amenhotep's voice thunder out.

'I am Pharaoh and I am a living god! No mortal will harm me!'

Amenhotep's sword slashed through the air cutting down the first five mercenaries to attack him but five more attacked and more followed them. Amenhotep disappeared under the assault of more than a dozen swords.

Horemshep shrugged. The Pharaoh and his sons had brought it on themselves by insulting Horemshep and the priests. Pharaoh had tried to curb the power of the Council of Priests and alter tradition. The next Pharaoh would be more agreeable, he was sure. All he had to do now was remove that brat, Erimem, and he could put his own choice of Pharaoh in place.

Erimem recognised the heavy footsteps and looked up at Antranak. The warm smile died on her lips when she saw the expression on his face. His cheeks were wet with tears and he looked as if his soul had been broken apart. She knew that only one thing could have affected him so badly. She felt as if a weight had slammed into the pit of her stomach.

'My father?' she whispered.

Antranak nodded miserably. 'Yes, my Pharaoh.'

# Epilogue

ome now, Carra,' Dr Zahi Haliwas handed a glass of champagne to Carra Wilton. 'You must admit that this is impressive.'

Carra took the glass and drained half of the champagne in one gulp. 'Bollocks.'

Zahi smiled indulgently at his young friend. 'I'm glad your speech was more eloquent than that,' she said mildly. 'This find of yours has made my country's history newsworthy for the first time since Carter found Tut-Ankh-Amun's tomb. My children even think I'm "cool".' He chuckled at the thought. 'I think I would lose that very quickly if my esteemed colleague had said "Bollocks!" in her speech.'

'I could have, you know,' Carra grumbled. 'It was live on news channels all over the world. I could have said exactly what I think of this...' she wafted her hand around them. 'This!'

The National Museum of Egyptian Antiquities in Cairo was playing host to a black tie reception to mark the opening of their latest exhibition. Royalty, heads of state and some of Hollywood's elite had gathered among the academics and politicians to see the unveiling of *The King's Lost Sons*. The tragic story Carra had uncovered as she, her team and Zahi, Egypt's most prominent scholar on her own ancient history, had explored the tomb had captivated the world's press for months. The riches in the tombs were beyond comparison, putting even Tutankamun's tomb to shame.

'We should be examining these artefacts, not exploiting them,' she said sourly.

Zahi gave a wry smile. 'I know,' he agreed. 'But it's politically wise to do this. It will help with our funding, help maintain interest in our history...'

'I know,' Carra replied. She pushed a stray lock of red hair back into place. 'But I still don't like it.'

She wandered into the crowd, nodding politely at various dignitaries and making small talk when she couldn't avoid doing so. After a time, she began to move to the periphery of the room and saw a small, slim, strikingly pretty girl peering intently at the exhibits. The girl's hair was short and she had a delicate, expressive face and intelligent brown eyes. The backless dress she was wearing was of a midnight blue silk with thin strands of silver threaded through it and perfectly complemented the soft coffee-brown colour of her skin. On one wrist she wore a gold bracelet in the style of the Middle Period of Egypt's history, and even from a distance Carra could see that it was a beautifully crafted facsimile. The two rings the girl wore were just as expertly made. Initially, Carra assumed that the girl would be looking at the precious jewels but instead she was staring at a large photograph of the hieroglyphs in the tomb.

'It's the entrance passage to the tomb,' Carra said.

'Yes, I know,' the girl nodded without taking her eyes from the picture.

Carra pointed at the hieroglyphs. 'They say...'

'Pharaoh's beloved sons, taken from the world and their father's embrace before their time was right.' The girl cut off, a catch in her voice and her eyes scanned the image until she found a section near the end. 'Brothers together for all eternity.' A sad smile pulled at the corners of her mouth. 'I hope they found peace.'

'They did,' Carra assured her. 'For 3,500 years anyway.'

'Their tomb was not robbed?' the girl asked.

'We don't think so,' Carra said. 'But the fourth chamber is a mystery.'

'Fourth chamber?'

The girl's surprise caught Carra off guard. 'I thought everyone knew the story. Three brothers buried alongside their sister. Only, when you open their sister's coffins... she's not there. No mummy, no canopic jars. No body at all. And the hieroglyphs in her tomb are unusual.'

'Show me.'

'Over here.' Carra led the girl to another image of hieroglyphs. 'We're wondering if it's some kind of code...'

The girl's delicate fingers traced the symbols through the glass. 'Taken to the heavens by the gods in a magic box, Erimemushinteperem, Pharaoh, warrior and bringer of peace is remembered with those she held in her heart. She is remembered by her successor and father of her brother's son.'

'That's a line we didn't understand,' Carra interrupted. 'Father of her brother's son would surely be her brother?'

'Or perhaps the new Pharaoh took in one of her brother's sons?' the girl said softly. 'They were friends.' She ignored Carra's puzzled expression and continued reading. 'Her beauty is eternal as the moon...' she laughed lightly. 'Flatterer, Fayum.'

Carra looked at the girl with interest. 'You read hieroglyphs remarkably well.'

'I learned a long time ago.' Her eyes flicked past Carra and she nodded a brief greeting to a very pretty young woman perhaps a few years older than herself with bobbed, shoulder length dark hair who was wearing a backless shimmering black evening dress. Beside her was a tall fair haired man of around thirty in an evening suit. They were both looking at the girl with obvious affection. 'I should return to my friends,' she said. She began to walk towards the waiting couple then stopped and turned back. 'You will tell people that these princes were loved. They were real people, not just exhibits. They were loved and they mustn't be forgotten.'

'I'll make sure they're remembered,' Carra promised. 'And the messages their sister left in their tombs let everyone know that they were loved. By the way, who are you? Are you in one of the classes at the university?'

The girl simply smiled. 'Goodbye,' she said and rejoined her friends. She linked arms with them and they disappeared into the crowd.

Carra peered at the artefacts from the tomb and found herself staring at Mentuhotep's death mask, an exquisitely crafted single piece of gold, but after talking with the girl she found that the mask now looked cold to her. 'I wonder,' she whispered. 'I wonder what happened to your sister.'

## ABOUT THE AUTHORS

**IAIN McLAUGHLIN** and **CLAIRE BARTLETT** have written two *UNIT* audio dramas together for Big Finish Productions, *Time Heals* and *The Wasting*, as well as *Doctor Who* short stories.

The character of Erimem debuted in McLaughlin's first work for Big Finish, the *Doctor Who* audio play *The Eye of the Scorpion*, and also appears in his novella, *Blood and Hope*.

# Also available...

# N E W
## WORLDS

*A series of novels and short-story collections,
each featuring different new stories
with exciting and popular characters...*

## Wildthyme on Top
ISBN 1-84435-155-6

*An Iris Wildthyme short-story collection edited by Iris's creator, Paul Magrs.
Featuring stories by Jonathan Blum, Stephen Cole, Jake Elliot,
Philip Purser-Hallard, Craig Hinton, Kate Orman, Lance Parkin,
Jacqueline Rayner, Justin Richards and Stewart Sheargold*

## The Coming of the Queen
ISBN 1-84435-156-4

*An Erimem novel written by Iain McLaughlin,
Erimem's creator, and Claire Bartlett*

## Project: Valhalla
ISBN 1-84435-157-2

*A Forge novel written by the Forge's creators,
Cavan Scott and Mark Wright*

# Also available from...

# BIG
## FINISH

# Doctor Who: Short Trips

*A series of short-story anthologies featuring contributions from many of* Doctor Who's *most popular authors from the worlds of television, print and audio, as well as new talent and fresh voices – including Robert Shearman, Eric Saward, Marc Platt, Kate Orman, Lance Parkin, Paul Magrs, Jacqueline Rayner, Steve Lyons, Justin Richards, Gareth Roberts, Rebecca Levene, Nicholas Briggs, Nev Fountain, Jonathan Morris, Juliet E. McKenna, Gary Russell, Simon Guerrier, Joseph Lidster, Jim Mortimore, Tara Samms, Cavan Scott, Mark Wright, Dave Stone, Mark Michalowski and many, many more...*

# Other books available from

## BIG FINISH

### Doctor Who

*The New Audio Adventures – The Inside Story*
by Benjamin Cook (ISBN 1-84435-034-7)

### Star Quest

*The Star Quest Trilogy* by Terrance Dicks
(ISBN 1-84435-066-5)

### Professor Bernice Summerfield

#### Anthologies

*Short-story and novella collections featuring stories by popular authors*

*Professor Bernice Summerfield and The Dead Men Diaries* edited by Paul Cornell
(ISBN 1-903654-00-9)

*Professor Bernice Summerfield: A Life of Surprises* edited by Paul Cornell
(ISBN 1-903654-44-0)

*Professor Bernice Summerfield: Life During Wartime* edited by Paul Cornell (ISBN 1-84435-062-2)

*Professor Bernice Summerfield: A Life Worth Living* edited by Simon Guerrier (ISBN 1-84435-109-2)

*Professor Bernice Summerfield: A Life in Pieces* by Dave Stone, Paul Sutton and Joseph Lidster
(ISBN 1-84435-108-4)

#### Novels

*Professor Bernice Summerfield and The Doomsday Manuscript* by Justin Richards (ISBN 1-903654-04-1)

*Professor Bernice Summerfield and The Gods of the Underworld* by Stephen Cole
(ISBN 1-903654-23-8)

*Professor Bernice Summerfield and The Squire's Crystal* by Jacqueline Rayner (ISBN 1-903654-13-0)

*Professor Bernice Summerfield and The Infernal Nexus* by Dave Stone
(ISBN 1-903654-16-5)

*Professor Bernice Summerfield and The Glass Prison* by Jacqueline Rayner (ISBN 1-903654-41-6)

*Professor Bernice Summerfield: The Big Hunt* by Lance Parkin
(ISBN 1-84435-107-6)